I0525091

SYN

E.A. RODRIGUEZ

DEDICATION

For my daughter Willow.

ACKNOWLEDGMENTS

This journey of putting the fantastic dreams in my head onto paper could never have been possible without the help and support of my family and instructors. Thank you for poking and prodding me to do this. Thank you France Belleville Van Stone and Bill Cifuni for keeping the awesome flame of art alive. Thank you, Uncle Alex for being so damn cool. Thank you for all of your help.

Copyright © 2014
E.A. Rodriguez
All rights reserved.

ISBN-13:978-0692356678
ISBN-10:
0692356673
Published by Enrique A. Rodriguez

Cover Art and Design by Marcie Miller-Rodriguez

Coveted Images © by Marcie

Alleyway Photo by Adin Jenks

All rights reserved. No part of this publication may be reproduced, stored in a retrieval system, or transmitted in any form or by any means, electronic, mechanical, photocopying, recording or otherwise, without the prior permission of the copyright owner.

This is a work of fiction. All of the characters, organizations, and events portrayed in this novel is either products of the authors imagination or used fictitiously. Any actual references to person(s) of historical significance are also used fictitiously.

PROLOGUE

In the dusk of the twenty first century, after the great economic collapse, the scientists of man had unveiled their most crowning achievement to date. They were able to create life. In the form of true artificial intelligence, humanity found a way to rise from the ruin of their past conflicts. Soon after, humankind began to manufacture synthetic humans most commonly known as syn. In the beginning, they used the machines to rebuild a broken society and re-civilize shattered nations.

After humanity had reclaimed most of their former glory, the synthetics were repurposed for use as aides for the disabled, servants for the wealthy and laborers for corporations. Many androids were used as soldiers in foreign wars and sent out to restore order to de-civilized regions of the world. As the popularity of these robots grew, so did their capacity for learning new tasks. The syn began designing themselves. The production of new, more advanced synthetics took the markets by storm. These new droids were capable of performing delicate procedures. They were being manufactured to meet the demand of new and growing industries. They became the doctors and architects of a new blossoming world.

The synthetics were not just popular with growing corporations; soon the machines became the tools and vices of the public. Demand for more human-looking syn grew. Their heavy metal exoskeletons vanished, replaced by new and cheap skin alternatives that served its purpose for a time. Owners of small shops and brothels began to fill their staff with eye pleasing machines. This caused resentment in their human counterparts, who were now out of a job with no way to pay their mounting debt. Still, the public supported the advanced machines.

The more "realistic" synthetics could imbibe water, eat food for energy; they slept and even dream, flooded the markets. It was then, that the syn became more than just complicated advanced machines. They became nearly human. It was not long after that the humanists, who thought the droids too closely resembled divinely created human beings, began to protest in anger.

When the more human than droid individuals, along with their flesh and blood sympathizers began marching for equality and civil liberties, the fascist group, Chosen emerged. The suave business tycoon and old war survivor, David Jennings led a bloody campaign against the machines.

The Chosen believed that the synthetics were a disease that had to die to prevent all humans from becoming an endangered species. To the Chosen, the machines had their place and it was not by the side of human beings. They believed that the synthetics should remain programmable servants.

The once semi-peaceful protests held by the Chosen, turned into public executions of the newer model synthetics, who believed they possessed the spark of life. The syn believed they had a soul.

Violent demonstrations organized by people who shared similar beliefs to the Chosen, fueled outrage on a wide scale. Soon the machines, alongside their sympathizers took to the steps of the Lincoln Memorial in Washington D.C. for what was supposed to be a peaceful demonstration. Many human and artificial lives were lost that day. Armed with simple picket signs, the droids and their human supporters were mercilessly slaughtered by mobs of humanist groups. Trials were held, but judgment was passed only for the human beings who had murdered other humans. In the eyes of the courts the synthetics were only polymer and carbon fiber machines. Their deaths meant nothing to the governments of man. The peaceful Syn, who only wanted to live and love, were not safe under the law as a human man or woman may be. To the people pulling the strings, they were only the property of their owners.

After the court's ruling to ban the advanced human synthetics (A.H.S.), a recall was issued. Many of the machines, who had once held on to dreams of being more than just a serial number, fell into a depression and self-terminated. Some willingly presented themselves to their manufactures for a system wipe, while others took up arms and tried to fight for their freedom. A small few took to hiding in plain sight.

Those who chose to blend in with the masses were unwilling to give up on the world in which they were "born." With the help of their human companions, the hopeful synthetics were able to obtain birth certificates and social security cards. For a lucky minority, love found them in the midst of all the turmoil. Marriage to human mates became a way for A.H.S. to camouflage themselves from the eyes of those who would see them reduced to mindless husks, doomed to a life of hard manual labor and servitude.

A decade has passed since the last and bloodiest war between machines and man had been fought. Many of the Seeker Soldiers, who were modified to search for syn had dwindled. Most signed on with the Chosen.

The media no longer presented the topic as a hot button issue. In fact, it had seemed that humanity felt sympathy for the manufactured beings. The Chosen still employed modified humans to find hidden synthetics. Although the methods of hiding used by the Syn had greatly improved, they were not fool proof. Often, Syn would be detained and taken away to have their light extinguished or worse.

CHAPTER 1

Present Day

The orange glow of the street lamps above reflect off the steel and glass buildings that soar high into the dusky sky. The warm, amber, tones melt into the chilly, violet, hues of the darkening atmosphere. The exhaust of older vehicles that burn fossil fuels now blackens the once white snow that blankets the city. The grimy sidewalk is peppered with the random trash from the pedestrians milling through the streets looking for an open shop. The frenzied consumers waited three days before the eve of a holiday to purchase some last minute Christmas gifts for those they didn't think enough about until now. Smart, driverless, automobiles, whiz almost silently through the streets, shuttling their merrily drunk passengers to pre-programmed destinations to sleep off their buzz or to find the next party.

Imogen Harper sits on the cold aluminum bench of an enclosed bus stop. The holographic advertising screen to her right plays on, telling anyone who is listening what size his or her waist should be. A few other folks sit next to her shivering just as she was, but she's not really cold. Her snug, charcoal grey, woolen, pea coat, along with the white thermals under her ripped up blue jeans keep her petite body quite toasty. Her nose, on the other hand is practically frozen and glows bright red against her milky white skin. The light freckles along her nose and cheeks rest like caramel sprinkles against rosy flesh. Her curly, scarlet hair swings loosely in the frigid breeze around her face and occasionally tickles her cheeks, but she cannot be bothered with that. Not now. She focuses on her shoes to take her mind off what she is here to do. Her old-fashioned Chuck Taylor sneakers look worn almost to the point of falling apart, but she loves their look.

Imogen tries to think of anything to pass the time until the people around her in the bus shelter leave. So, she makes as little eye contact as possible. She doesn't want anyone to be able to describe her to the authorities. The young woman with her child, steals glances every so often. It's almost like she wants to say something, but doesn't have the nerve to or is just socially awkward. Or maybe, Imogen just looks guilty already. Whatever it is, she does not want to look at the woman. When Imogen does look up, she eyes the squat building across the street. She looks past the neon lights crowding the large front windows, past the heavy metal posters and glares at a man she despises. Maybe that was the reason for all the stolen glances?

Imogen tries to work up the nerve to walk into the tattoo and modification parlor across the street called, *The Frog Palace*, after the nickname of the owner. Francis Ogmayer, is a man with heavily modified eyes. He owns the small shop and spends damn near all of his time there. Francis, also known as *Frog* in some circles, was the whole reason her life turned upside down. He was why she had lost everything. He was the reason why she was just a ghost of her former self.

During the wars, Francis was a seeker, but no war means no work. It would seem that whenever he was running low on cash, he would go find himself a Syn, kill it and collect the hundred thousand dollar bounty. He has not been out hunting the past few months and it was getting to be about that time when he was running low on his poison of choice. At the moment, he's violently yelling at his young, eccentric employee. Frog always got irritable when he had to ration his stash.

Imogen shifts from side to side on the metal bench. She's not really uncomfortable. She's trying to hide that she's readjusting the chilled metal of the gun grip in her belt strap. The thing is digging into her back, but it's only a minor discomfort.

"Boy, this winter is the worst yet," the young woman standing with her six or seven year old daughter chimes.

"Yeah. The weather guy said we're due for another couple of inches," Imogen brushes her thick, curly, vermillion, locks from her ice blue eyes and lightly freckled nose.

An automated salt truck putters away, spilling its chemically enhanced anti-freezing agents all over the slightly, upward curved street. The old trucks have been in operation for the better part of a century and they are still going strong. Don't try to fix it if it isn't broken.

The double-decker bus pulls to a slow, squealing, stop in front of the enclosed waiting area. The graffiti along the side is so stylized that it's illegible, but Imogen really wasn't trying to read it anyway.

"Well, this is us," the woman says, then takes her daughter's hand and steps inside the bus. The aged driver looks at Imogen with probing eyes and for a long moment she's unsure of what to say or do. She nods and smiles. Apparently, the gesture was enough, because the driver pulls the lever to shut the doors and pulls away from the curb to continue his route.

For a long while, Imogen sits on the bench. Her hands are buried in her thick coat, busily picking away at her finger nails. Her chin is pressed against her chest as she watches her breath drift through the air as a steamy vapor. Her eyes water and she uses her shoulder to wipe away the rapidly cooling tears. She knows who is in that parlor and what she must do, but fear grips her mind.

<*What if something goes wrong?*> Imogen squashes that thought just as quickly as it had arrived. She didn't need doubts ugly, egg-shaped head screwing with her mind. Not now. She wasn't sure how this was going to go down and she knew that failing now would be detrimental to her cause. The man was a fucking jackal and if she displayed any sign of weakness, he would gain the upper hand or even kill her. She has to exude total control and confidence.

"You can do this," Imogen whispers to herself while taking deep, measured breaths. The streets are practically empty now. She slowly stands. The cold metal of the gun in her back isn't a frozen discomfort anymore. It's an icy reminder of the best way to give someone what they deserve. From where she stands, she can't see anyone. She can see almost the entire parlor through the large windows and it looks empty. Panicked, Imogen checks to see that the neon lights are still flickering and advertising that the place is open. Being mindful of the traffic, Imogen makes her way across the street.

Once in front of the small, dirty building, she can see that there isn't a soul manning the front desk. She knows from her little stakeouts in the past that there is usually a young twenty something girl with orange hair sitting at the counter. Imogen scans the layout of the shop, being sure not to overlook some important detail. Tattoo guns and modification tools lay sprawled at the work stations. Even the old retrofitted television was still on and playing some god awful fetish video.

Imogen takes another calming breath, places her hand on the metal door handle and pulls. The lock clangs against the frame. It's locked. Caught completely off guard by the unexpected obstacle, Imogen tugs again and again at the metal and glass door, making a loud clanking sound with every tug. She was hoping that the noise would at least draw the attention of someone inside. After a minute or two, it was obvious that they did not hear the racket she was making.

Stepping back a couple of paces, she re-evaluates the situation. Imogen notices that the gate attached to the parlor and the adjacent apartment building is ajar. She pushes on the iron bar but the gate only moves slightly. The snow and ice are locking up the hinges. She pushes the gate a little harder, adding a few inches to the opening and squeezes her small frame through the gap. The alley is narrow and dark. Some old trash, that had probably been there for months lie in scattered piles along the passage. A dead cat lay frozen at her feet but she easily steps over the poor thing. As silently as she can, Imogen heads toward the back of the building.

The snow in the small, gated, employee parking lot rests undisturbed, save for the solitary set of footprints made by someone, who must have come in earlier in the day. She examines the heavy backdoor exit. At first it seems that the door is shut tight, but upon closer examination, she can see that someone had left a piece of cardboard between the latch and its home in the frame. Slowly and carefully, Imogen slides the door open. She steps inside and is immediately bombarded by loud heavy metal music. She eases the door shut, making little to no noise, but she did not honestly think anyone would hear her over the ear-bursting music playing over the loud speakers.

Imogen reaches behind her back and pulls the frosty gun from its resting place. The lights in the hall are dim and barely illuminate the pathway to the front of the shop. There are three black doors in the small space, one to the left and two on the right. They break up the poorly crafted graffiti artwork on the walls. The door closest to her is marked *Restroom*, but there doesn't seem to be anyone in there, however the two on the right both show bright lights seeping through the gap at the bottom of the door.

She steps toward them and the task of deciding which one to open becomes null when she hears muffled grunts coming from the door labeled *Office*. Imogen checks her gun to ensure that it is indeed loaded and ready to go, then gently wraps her thin fingers around the doorknob and twists. The door slides open without a sound and what she finds on the other side sends her system into overdrive.

The orange haired woman lies on the desk face down, tied to it like some sort of freshly killed doe from a hunt. Her face is swollen and purple from being beaten. The girl peers up at the redheaded woman who has just walked into the room. The young woman must've seen something tender in the eyes of the newcomer, because she silently pleaded with her pitiful, non-puffy eye. The clutter on the floor must have come from the desk because there was a broken table lamp laying in several pieces. Surprisingly the thing was still lit. Oddly distorted shadows dance along the wall like a strange puppet show.

<*The girl must've put up a fight.*> Imogen smiles inwardly. Francis is so focused on getting his pants off, that he doesn't realize that someone has entered the room. Imogen slams the door into the dry wall with such force that the doorknob crashes through it.

Francis whirls around. His boney frame heaving from the exertion. His dirty underwear screams for someone to get the brown stains washed from it.

"Fuck off bitch!" he exclaimed. Before he can make a move, Imogen raises the barrel of the gun so he can see that this is a serious moment and he might want to pay attention.

"Who are you?" The lanky man says, raising his hands slowly. Imogen completely ignores his query and gestures to the girl.

"Untie her," Imogen demands. Francis slowly moves around the worktable and begins to untie the knots that bind the battered woman to the cheap desk. When he is done, he raises his hands again. Imogen can tell the boney man is seething for having his fun time ruined by a woman. That makes her happy.

The punk rocker woman slides off the desk, sniffling, then gathers her things and begins to head toward the exit. She then has an afterthought. She whirls around and delivers a swift kick to Francis's grapes, then runs for the door. Lying in the fetal position on the floor, Francis screams in pain and frustration. He makes a quick move for something behind his desk, but stops short when he feels the cold steel of a gun barrel pressed against his temple.

"Ah ah ah," Imogen warns as she grabs the small tuft of hair atop his head and drags the small man screaming to the middle of the room. "Do you remember me, Frog?" Imogen questions as she slowly stands. The big gun is still leveled at his face. The quivering man cocks his head. The small, metal, photoreceptors in his eyes focus in and out. For a long moment they both say nothing, then realization crashes over the frog faced man.

"You're a Syn," he says with a wilting voice. Imogen nods slowly, allowing his slow mental faculties to work through it. "You're dead. We killed you," he said after another long moment.

Imogen crouches down and places the gun directly between his shiny eyes.

"You tried, but one has to be alive to be killed. Right?" she says evenly. The man gulps as she continues, "You are going to tell me where I can find all your friends or, I will most definitely kill you."

Frog begins to shake as if the chill from outside had reached his small bones in his warm office. He takes his "eyes" off the gun and rests them on the ghost of a machine that stands before him.

"If I tell you, will you let me live?" he asks. Imogen purses her lips considering the question.

"I might. Now talk."

It surprises Imogen how easily the man spills everything he knows. Of course she knew that he was a self-serving, spineless, snake, but she couldn't have known that he would be so quick to snitch. She figured that the small, desperate man would do anything if it meant saving his own skin. For a moment she pitied the wretched thing. She patiently listens, making mental notes about all the haunts they like to frequent. What Imogen relishes most of all, is that she now has names for the bastards who ruined her life.

Once Frog spills his guts out in a blabbering mix of sobs and somewhat intelligible speech, Imogen stands. She turns and begins to walk out of the small office. The thought of killing this man turned her insides in knots. Frog began to mumble under his breath, and at first, Imogen paid him no mind. Truth be told, she doesn't know if she has it in her to murder this poor bastard and that nagging feeling of doubt lasts right up until he opens his mouth to curse her.

"They gonna kill your sorry ass bi..." is all he gets out before she paints the wall with his brains. As the chunks of tissue mixed with skull slide down the wall, leaving a bloody, streaky, mess, Imogen counts the grey matter. She couldn't find much. She stares unblinking at what was left of Frog. The nearly naked man looks so frail and small as he lay there.

Flashes of Imogen's former life streak through her mind as beacons of light during this dark visceral moment. Echoes of laughter painfully push their way through to the surface of her consciousness, trying to make her not see the dark, bloody, substances, clinging to the wall. She is trying not to let her consciousness burn this image in her mind.

"It wasn't always this way," Imogen softly whispers to herself. Her wide eyes are fixated on the blood splattered on the wall.

CHAPTER 2

18 Months Earlier

The smells of various disinfectant products, rubbing alcohol, along with the distinct scents of medical wraps, hang stiffly in the sterile, baby blue, and tan physical therapy room. Paper cutouts of colorful cartoon animals adorn the walls alongside posters of inspiring images emblazoned with positive messages. Soft, delicate, music flows from the overhead speakers to bathe the room in an aura of total relaxation.

Kyle rests on his back. Palms flat on the soft, rubber, matted floor. He holds his right leg up, while, Imogen holds his ankle in the crook of her neck and uses her hands to keep his knee straight. Her dark hair falls around her right shoulder. She uses her hand to brush it back.

"That's it, Kyle. You're doing great," she says, brushing back more of her dark hair.

The young child grunts at the pain of having his hamstrings stretched, but smiles at the achievement of keeping his leg straight.

"Can you hold your leg up there all by yourself?" Imogen releases her hold on the boy. Kyle, knowing a challenge when he hears one, smiles and holds his leg above him. Imogen applauds his new found dexterity. Kyle smiles confidently.

After the hour long session, Imogen helps Kyle into his exo-suit and snaps the locks around his legs.

"Thank you, Mrs. Hoppa," Kyle says with a toothy grin.

"Don't mention it Mr. Lee," Imogen smiles back. Kyle takes rhythmic steps to the door that leads to the waiting room where his parents sit patiently four days a week. The old servos make a whining noise with every step. Acting as if she had almost forgotten, Imogen turns and reaches into a cabinet above the sink and pulls out a small box with a lush, hand painted, green landscape all around it.

"What's that?" Kyle asks.

"Why, it's a surprise for my favorite little strong guy," Imogen answers as she swoops down playfully and holds the small box out for the little boy to grab.

Kyle takes the box, opens it carefully as not to damage the carefully painted scene around the outside of the tin.

"Cookies!" The boy smiles and asks with barely controlled excitement, "Can I eat one now?"

"Just one for now. Save the rest for after you eat supper," she nods playfully.

The boy devours one of the soft homemade cookies and with messy hands he charges in and hugs his therapist.

"Thank you, Mrs. Hoppa!" Kyle mumbles with a mouth full of mushy cookie. Imogen smiles and pulls chunks of chocolate chip out of her hair. After a few heartbeats, she walks him out to his parents.

◊

An hour later, Imogen, along with two co-workers eat snacks at their desks, while waiting for the clock to hit that magic hour that tells them it's time to punch out. Beth, the youngest of the three, leans back in her padded, mauve, swivel chair, stretching like a cat. Her blonde ponytail snakes its way down the backside of her chair.

"Ahg," she groans, "This day seems like it has gone on forever," her arms tingle with the exertion.

The graying Japanese mother of two chuckles at the thoughtless remark, "It could be worse. You could be working a double," she smiles at the younger lady to show that there are no hard feelings. Imogen scrunches her face in disgust at the thought of having to head over to the main hospital to cover for another med tech.

"Sorry Eve." Beth says, trying to sound sincere.

On the television screen, flashy gold lettering scrolls across over a blue background. A woman with short auburn hair and lightly tanned skin stands in front of a clear desk. "Good afternoon. If you are just tuning in, I'm Tanya Hurst. Tonight my guest is the President of Pharma Corp and founder of the Humanist group, *Chosen,* David Jennings. Thank you for being with us this afternoon."

The screen splits and to the right of the woman is the ageless man. His salt and pepper hair over his tanned skin makes him stand out against the white backdrop of the room in which he sits. The eggshell silk suit is barely visible on the screen.

"Good afternoon Tanya. Thanks for having me on the show." the slick man replies with a southern drawl.

Eve and Imogen cringe at the sight of the man on the screen, while Beth's eyes glaze over with fascination.

The news anchor continues, "Recently your organization, Chosen has come under a lot fire due to their, as some would say," she pauses, searching for a neutral way to organize her thoughts. Failing to find a polite way to describe their methods, she settles on generalizing, "barbaric handling of outlawed Syn." The newscaster shuffles some papers on her desk.

"Some folks seem to think that the methods used in apprehending these banned robots could use some finesse. While others think that your organization is staffed with criminals. What do you have to say about such allegations?"

The sleazy smile doesn't waver as he shifts in his seat to get a little more comfortable. He chuckles as he speaks, "First off, I'd like to say that the public has every right to question some of the actions taken by our associates," he says officiously, "But keep in mind that we are a government funded agency. Every action we take is in the best interest of the people. Our job is to locate and detain these dangerous machines for reprogramming. Sometimes a nonviolent outcome isn't always possible. Due to the violent actions taken by these robots, our team of specialists are forced to destroy them."

"I see," Tanya cocks her head slightly as she prepares to ask her next question, "I'd like to know your thoughts about the ongoing speculations that these 'robots', as you put it, have reached some higher cognitive thought processes and possess what some would equate to a soul? Some would say that what your 'specialists' are doing is tantamount to murder."

Mr. Jennings shifts in his seat again, only this time a barely perceptible squint of disapproval penetrates his collected demeanor. Tanya continues with her inquiry, "Some would say that these 'living' mechanical beings are equivalent to a biological human being. Some think they deserve equal rights and protection under the law. What are your thoughts when it comes to this interesting string of theories?"

David Jennings chuckles as if he had just heard an awful joke. He scratches lightly at his eyebrow pretending to consider that the syn may actually be living beings. He collects himself before he replies, "I'm not sure who started this rumor or why, but those ideas are based on absolutely nothing. Would you say your personal computer had a soul because it found an easier way to locate your files? No. Of course not. It's a tool that uses ones and zeros to process information."

Imogen slumps back into her seat. Hearing this man, who means nothing to her, compare her kind to a simple computer is like a punch to the gut. His harsh comparison makes her feel about as big as a gnat. Her emotions flare and she was about to respond to the outrageous remarks, but Eve grunts in disgust. "Can you believe this asshole?" Clearly she's not buying what he's selling. Eve grabs the remote and fingers the power button, turning off the TV.

Beth shrieks in outrage as the screen goes black. "I was watching that!"

Eve shakes her head, "Honey, that man is about as useful as a fart in a space suit," she says laughing. "Besides, it's closing time." Eve flicks the remote on the desk and yawns. She tucks her tablet in her bag and sets it on the floor next to her feet.

Chagrined, Beth pouts as she gathers her things. Imogen couldn't see how a young woman could alter her world views just because she has a crush on a man.

Imogen *pops* up from her seat in excitement and grabs her purse. She has patiently waited for this day for what seemed like forever.

Eve calmly collects her personal items and with a sly smile she asks, "Today the day eh?"

Imogen lets loose a squee, "Yup! Today we fill out the last of the paperwork and then Darioux and I will have our beautiful baby boy."

The statement must have eased the tension in the small room because both women visibly relaxed with a smile that could have melted what was left of the ice caps.

"Congratulations! You guys must be so excited," Beth says as she moved in for a hug.

Imogen scrunches her shoulders with delight before Eve embraces her and plants a small kiss on her cheek. "I'm so happy for you," Eve says. "Go. We'll lock up."

Imogen smiles, elatedly at them both then prances out of the office and to the glass double doors that lead out to the parking lot. She reaches into her brightly colored hand bag and pulls out a small black cylinder, presses a tiny silver button and speaks into it, "Start." The short command causes her small, metallic, black, hatchback to power on. The almost silent whir of the electric engine starting fills her with nervous anticipation of what the future holds for her and her soon to be complete family. Another command unlocks the doors and she slides into the leather seat. She adjusts the rearview mirror so she can see the blue and grey infant car seat nestled in the backseat. She takes a deep breath, then engages the manual driver mode, rather than use the auto-drive. She felt it would be better to know what to do if the vehicle's CPU ever stopped working and she had to take control. It was rare that a vehicles CPU had a catastrophic failure, but rare wasn't the same as never. She wanted to know how to keep her new son safe. Besides, she likes the control it gives her. It makes her feel free and somewhat powerful to control a four thousand pound car. She grips the steering wheel, puts the car in gear and drives off to meet her husband, Darioux, at the adoption agency.

CHAPTER 3

Present Day

Blake Sparx sits in a low backed office chair in the main room of his one bedroom apartment, furiously punching away at one of his two holographic keyboards. The overhead light in the connected kitchen does little to brighten the large server filled room. The bluish white glow of the four holographic computer monitors reflects off his thick prescription glasses. He could pay to have corrective surgery or have implants, but then that would mean less credits to spend on the latest gizmos. His short red hair also glows in the dim light of the computer screen. His short but stocky build makes him look like a giant in his little padded chair.

Mounted on his desk are ceramic busts of super heroes and plastic action figures of most, if not all of the latest comic book heroes available on the market.

He slaps his hands together in exaltation of his successful hack of the city's monitoring systems. He reaches down to take a few massive gulps of his energy drink and gets right back to work. He searches for the main security log that is responsible for storing the recordings made of Washington and Third Street. Then he locates the files that hold similar information for a three block radius and replaces them with a video of a cat, leg outstretched and furiously cleaning itself. He laughs out loud and slaps his palm against the desk causing one of his figurines to topple over. His mirth is cut short as he replaces the toy to its original upright position, then giggles to himself.

He turns around in anticipation when he hears a key enter the deadbolt on his door and waits with his fingers interlaced behind his head. A petite redheaded woman walks in, then quickly shuts and locks the door behind her. She begins to unbutton her frosted coat and heads for the nearest window. She peeks through the dark green blinds to ensure that she had not been followed.

"Oh don't worry. You're good on that front. Why? Because I'm the man." Blake says as he does a very unflattering victory dance in his seat.
Imogen turns her head in his direction then moves to examine the monitor. The video of the cat with its leg stretched high above its head vigorously

digging at something in its crotch, still plays on one of the monitors.

"Wow. Really?" she says with a small yet, humored smile that reaches her eyes.

"Oh come on! You know it's funny. I just wish I could see their faces when they find it." Sparx's eyes grow mischievous with the thought of hacking into the cameras of the Public Surveillance office building.

"As funny as that would be, we need to stay focused," Imogen places her hand between him and his keyboard. Blake's jaw gapes open. She might as well have slapped him in the face.

"But it would be priceless." he says in protest.

"What we are doing can get us killed at any moment," Imogen reminds him, "We need to be on our A game." The deadpan look, Imogen gives him turns his tongue to lead.

Blake grabs an animal cracker from a dish on his desk and leans back in his seat defeated. Sulking, he bites off the head of the cookie.

Imogen glances at the far right screen and notices that there are several tabs pulled up. The active page displays the personal information of one of the people who had invaded her home on that fateful day nearly two years ago. The portrait style mugshot of one, Pete Roberts stares back at her with those dead, ice blue eyes. His short crew cut accentuates the block-like head that sits atop two massive shoulders.

"What's this?" Imogen asks.

The short techno geek mumbles as a scolded child would after his parents had found him with his hands in the cookie jar before dinner.

"What?" Imogen asks. She wasn't paying attention to what her friend was saying. She was lost in memory.

"Those are complete bios on the assholes who broke into your house," he says as he shoves the last of the elephant cookie into his mouth.

Imogen flips through the floating windows, scanning the collection of data on, Desirae Deponet, a sultry brunette, who had helped the murderers gain access to her home. The next tab displays an image of Dominic Vespucci, a chubby, harry thing that enjoys many forms of debauchery and is just a downright creep. Desirae is listed as working at a gentleman's club named, *The Cave* while Dominic is listed as unemployed, but his home address is listed. She entertains the idea of tossing an electrical device in his bathtub and watching him fry.

"Oh. This is good," Imogen says, committing every bit of information to memory, then she reaches over to snag a cookie from the plate.

"It's old." Blake responds. Imogen looks at the young man not understanding. Blake leans forward and highlights the dates on the files. "It's old information. These files haven't been updated for at least two years. It's almost like they don't exist anymore."

Disheartened, Imogen sits on the floor and lies back against the couch, feeling suddenly tired. She removes the pistol jammed in the back of her pants, alleviating the cause of the sharp pain setting off her sensors and sets it on the floor next to her.

"What's wrong? Blake asks.

Imogen slides the heavy hunk of metal off to the side then rubs her eyes in frustration. The information she got from Francis about the other three individuals was practically the same as the files Blake had pulled up on his screen. "Francis told me the same thing."

Blake looks down at her, "Well that doesn't make it meaningless." Blake takes a drink from the highly caffeinated can of liquid and chucks the empty container into the waste bin, "Even if they no longer live at the documented residences, you know where they like to hang out." Blake reassures her. He stands and stretches his cramped legs. The popping and cracking of his bones ease the tension in his back and neck. He slowly pads away to his bedroom, and calls out, "Get some sleep girly. You've earned it."

Imogen leans to the side to lie on the floor. She rests her forearm on her head and breathes deeply. With her eyes closed, she begins to recall the last few moments of Frogs life, right before she blew a massive hole in his head. The experience of killing another being had left her feeling powerful but also a little empty. Even though Frog was an awful human being, he deserved to rot in some prison somewhere. He should be some big guy's girlfriend for protection. She rolled the cocktail of emotions around in her mind like an oddly colored pebble. The dark thoughts made her head spin. She would have to analyze these feelings later. She's too tired to think of Francis Ogmyer as anything, but a vicious animal. She pulls her pillow from the sofa, places it under her head and closes her eyes. The image of blood and brain matter splattered on the wall is still fresh in her mind. She doesn't know how long she stood there counting every grey chunk she saw, but she knows now, that it was too long. Slowly, Imogen pulls her thoughts away from the gore of earlier events and moves on to more pleasing memories of Darioux.

She takes herself back to a time when life was much simpler. To a time when she wasn't so worried about someone finding her or trying to kill her. When she wasn't consumed with the pain of loss.

Tears roll down her cheeks. She tucks her thumbs into the sleeves of her black sweater and wipes the tears away. Imogen rolls onto her side so that the pillow can catch some of the flow of her sorrow and rests her covered hand at the bridge of her nose, so that the cloth can catch the rest. She allows herself to weep.

After the sobbing that racked her body subsides, she imagines herself back in her home, laying in Darioux's arms. His strong hands gently caressing her hair. She imagines that she can feel the warmth of his chest on her cheek. Gradually, the bunched fibers that are her muscles begin to relax and she drifts into a much needed sleep.

CHAPTER 4

18 Months Earlier

Just outside the old brick building of Angel's Hands Adoption Agency, the adolescent trees sprouting from their plots of dirt, which were carved out of the sidewalk, sway in the cool lazy summer's breeze. The sun's rays softly kiss all that it touches. Children enjoying the long break, ride their bicycles through the city, laughing and shouting meaningless insults towards each other. Automated passenger buses and cars glide almost noiselessly up and down the street. A siren wails in the distance but quickly fades into the ambiance of the large metropolis. The sounds of distant horns, the busy highway, and the many pedestrians of the city, blend with the gentle gusts blowing the trees.

On the bleached stone steps of the building sits Darioux, with his finely tanned leather messenger bag resting at his feet. His dark blue buttoned down shirt rests comfortably on his broad shoulders. The sleeves are rolled up neatly under his elbows. His neatly pressed grey slacks rise above his black leather shoes, exposing his black socks. The thin, well-kept, micro braids, dangle around his lightly bronzed face.

He scrolls through the contents of the news article he is reading on the thin glass-like computer he holds in his hands. The report tells of the tragic end of the latest synthetic to be destroyed in a clash with Chosen operatives. He scowls at the poorly chosen words that the reporter had used to describe the fate of the poor being.

He glances up from the device when he hears tires rolling over asphalt and come to a slow stop just beyond the curb of the sidewalk in front of him. Smiling, he powers down the small tablet. Grabbing the lip of his bag, he stows the square computer in its folds and stands to meet his wife. Imogen steps out of the car, still wearing the dark green hospital scrubs and white tennis shoes from work. Her thick, dark, curly, pony tail, bounces behind, as she skips around the car to hop onto the sidewalk and embrace Darioux. He bends over slightly to wrap his arms around her waist, while she has to stand on the tips of her toes to plant a playful kiss on his lips.

"We're almost at the finish line baby," he says looking into her brown eyes.

"I know. I thought this day would never come," she nods with excitement. Hand and hand they walk up the steps and enter the agency.

◊

A small bespectacled woman sits on the other side of the overly large oak desk, with an engraved brass plaque that reads, *Mrs. Honecker.* She sits at the edge of her seat, with her face scrunched in concentration. It was almost as if someone had assigned this desk to her as a joke, but she decided to keep the massive thing to show that she was that much bigger than they were. The aged woman glances over a fairly thick stack of documents.

The fake plant behind her looks like it hadn't been cleaned in ages. A thin layer of dirt coated every plastic leaf, making the plant look coffee stained, rather than true green. The certificates that hung on the grey walls were in similar disarray. The once white paper seemed to be a sun bleached yellow, though there wasn't a window anywhere near the small office.

The small woman's shoulder length, black dyed hair frames her thin face like an old war helmet. The small crinkles around her mouth seem to deepen a bit as she purses her lips in deep thought. She peers up at the couple and smiles with genuine warmth as she slides the stack of papers over to them to sign.

"I know it looks like a lot, but I can assure you that it won't take as long as you think," she softly smiles. Darioux looks over the small printed documents.

"Now you'll both need to sign where needed," she says, then the tiny woman hands them each a pen.

Taking the pen in his right hand, Darioux signs his name then slides the first page over to Imogen, who signs with her left. The woman explains the purpose of each legal document as they make their way through the pages.

"This one just states that, for the first few months, we will be making regular visits to ensure that everyone is adjusting well, needs are being met and so forth," the older woman says with the tone of someone who has spoken those words many times before.

After about a half hour of signing their names or initialing small spaces on just about every page, the couple move on to setting a date for placement of the adopted infant. After only a couple of minutes they reach a date and all three of them sign and date one final page. The social worker takes the documents, scoots off her seat and leaves the small cubical to make copies. The happy couple exchange anxious but truly happy glances. Ten minutes pass and the tiny woman returns with two separate maroon folders. She hands one to Darioux.

"These are your copies, Mr. and Mrs. Harper." The small woman looks at them both. She is truly happy to see them smiling, "Two weeks from Friday, someone will be over with little Markus and we can see how everyone gets along, but, I suspect that there will be no problems here."

Mrs. Honecker, holds out her small hand for a shake with a large toothy smile stretching her face, "Congratulations to you both." The couple alternate shaking hands with the middle aged lady. She nods and smiles with true delight.

"Thank you so much for walking us through this process. You helped make our dreams come true. Thank you." Imogen says wiping misty eyes.

The cool air being pushed through the small vents in the dashboard mixes with the warm heat trapped inside the car. Darioux's hand slides off the steering wheel to turn the dial on the radio, lowering the volume of the music playing through the speakers. He then laces his fingers in-between the small delicate fingers of Imogen.

"We've come a long way. Haven't we?" he says, glancing over at his wife who sits buckled in the passenger seat.

She looks over at him, smiling and says, "I never thought this would happen. We're going to be a family honey."

He gives her hand a gentle squeeze. "You're happy now-just wait until the baby cries all night and we can't get any sleep," he says jokingly.

"I'm not worried about it. I'm looking forward to it actually," she says confidently.

The thin dreads bob back and forth as he nods, "Good. Then you got nightshift," he says laughing.

Imogen realizes that he's trying to shirk some responsibility. She turns to Darioux, smiles then punches his bicep. "Oh? Then you're on diaper duty mister," she miles.

"Fair enough," Darioux smiles and programs the car to drive them home.

As they pull in to the underground parking garage of their apartment building, Imogen looks at their intertwined hands. Her fine eyebrows furrow, causing a worried crease between them. She knows that they have talked about horrible scenarios before and what steps they could take to prepare, but the fear of losing their happiness never leaves her mind.

"Honey," she says. Darioux turns his head as he switches off the ignition. "Do you ever worry about what will happen if anyone ever found out that I was..." worry creeps into her fine features.

"No," Darioux says clearly and definitively. She looks down. Her eyes glisten with a fine layer of tears.

"But what if someone does find out? What if I get wiped? What if?" she counters with a fine layer of glistening tears forming in her eyes. The fear present in her voice melts her hope by small degrees. She had hoped that with so much time separating the past wars it would have allowed people to see her, to see the synthetics for what they truly are and not as some threat to humanity as a whole. Sometimes wishful thinking is just that and the reality of the world seems to always disappoint.

Darioux places a curled finger under her chin to gently lift her head, "They will have to go through me to get to you. Even if saving you means I have to die, so be it." The certainty in his voice soothes her, but only a little. She has seen what the seekers do to synthetics and those who protect them. She couldn't imagine that ever happening to her or Darioux. A tear rolls down her cheek when she sniffles.

"I love you. The word '*love*' doesn't even come close to what I feel for you." Darioux says and wipes away the stray tear with a gentle touch.

"I love you too," she nods. Imogen shakes her head from side to side and continues, "I don't know what I'd do if I ever lost you." Imogen realizes how lucky she truly is for having a man in her life that can look past the propaganda to find the truth.

He smiles then softly kisses her full pink lips, "Well it's a good thing I'm not going anywhere then. You're stuck sweetheart." They smile and try to shake the reality of their unique circumstances.

Darioux looks at his watch in feigned surprise, "Oh! We gotta hurry," he quickly spouts, trying hard to sound surprised and worried.

"Hurry for what?" she asks. The expression on her face conveys her bemusement.

Darioux opens the door, steps out, then leans back into the car to face his wife, "We gotta hurry up and shower if we are going to make it in time." His sly grin shows that he's got a plan. He winks at her and continues, "So we don't lose our reservation at that restaurant you've been wanting to try out."

Imogen smiles and scrambles to unbuckle the seatbelt. Darioux slams the driver's side door shut, thumbs the button on the wireless key and says, "Lock," as he runs for the elevator.

Just as Imogen pulls for the handle to her door and opens it, the small notches to the left of the handles flick to the side, locking all four of the doors.

"Ha!" Imogen shouts with a big smile, then gives chase. They run through the private parking garage of their building like children playing an innocent game of tag. Weaving in and out of parked cars they hoot and holler, all the while the smiles on their faces express their overwhelming joy of just being in each other's company. When Imogen finally catches up to Darioux, she jumps on his back, wrapping her arms and legs around him like a four armed cephalopod latching on to her prey.

"Ah! You got me," Darioux pants from the chase. "Okay get down," he breathes heavily, resting his palms on his knees.

"Uh uh. You've got to carry me. It's your punishment for trying to be slick." Imogen teases. Her lips are pressed gently against his earlobe.

Darioux laughs heartily then tucks his hands under her soft but toned thighs and begins marching toward the lift.

Once they reach the elevator, Darioux leans forward and tilts his body so that Imogen can press the call button. Imogen plants a kiss on his bronzed cheek while they wait. Imogen swings her dangling feet while she rests her head on one of his rounded shoulders. She couldn't imagine herself anywhere else, but right here and with this man who views her as an equal. She sometimes forgets that there are more and more people flocking to the banners of the synthetic plight every day. The misguided fear that had been placed in the hearts of man would soon fade. Soon she would be free to pursue her goals and passions without fear. As long as Darioux was by her side, she knows that anything is possible.

"You know it's a good thing you're light, because if you weren't, I would have to trade you in on a newer model," a mischievous smile creeps across Darioux's lips as the words leave his mouth.

Imogen's mouth gapes with amused shock, "Oh yeah mister? Good luck with that. But be warned. The newer models aren't made as well as I am."

She knows that he's joking of course. That is one of the main things she loves about Darioux. He always knows how to make her smile and forget the outside world.

The newer model syn didn't look half as good as the first model infantry bots that were deployed in place of the human soldiers over ten years ago. They were more of a bulky robot than a syn. She was one of the last to be developed and Darioux knows that. She wasn't shipped to a store or bought. The manufacturers saw the heated climate of society and released her from the collective to be free. There were less than twenty advanced human synthetics out of one hundred and fifty, roaming the planet now. Not many were lucky enough to find love.

The bell to the elevator chimes upon arrival, the double doors open and they enter.

CHAPTER 5

Present Day

Dominic Vespucci pushes his way through the growing crowd outside of Francis's modification shop. His small but thick frame carves a wide path through the rubber neckers on the other side of the street. The sun, high in the sky, beats down on the scene, but offers little warmth against the cold that nips at his nose and chin. His thick, dark brown hair hangs loosely around his shoulders, serving as a buffer between his ears and the cold. A short redheaded man wearing thick glasses jostles Dominic as he pushes through the mass of people. The younger man moves on without apologizing. Dominic pays the little punk no mind and readjusts the collar of his coat. He pulls the collar above his neck to keep the freezing wind from blowing down his chest.

Several police vehicles block the view of the main entrance to the small shop. Their flashing lights still pulse within their clear plastic casing like the tiny strobes of a nightclub. The small black coroners van parked in front of the building, still has its engine running and the back doors are wide open. Yellow holographic projection police tape stretches from one light post to another on either end of the shop, cordoning off the front door.

Men in uniform stand outside, while others can be seen moving about within the shop, most likely collecting evidence. A light blue car pulls up to the curb. An older man with salt and pepper hair wearing a fine navy blue tailored suit under a black overcoat, steps out. Accompanying him is a young brunette woman, wearing a black pants suit with a brown coat. She steps out of the car, produces a glass tablet and begins tapping away. They begin talking with the officer in charge of the scene.

Dominic finally notices the male reporter in the middle of the street giving live commentary. He nudges his way closer to get an idea of what had happened inside the shop. He bumps several people out of the way and nearly knocks an older woman to the ground. The woman almost screams an insult, but one look from Dominic and the words stall in her throat.

"As we have stated before, officials are combing through possible evidence, as well as public surveillance footage, but no leads yet as to who committed this grizzly murder," reports the small Latino man.

Dominic can't help but notice and chuckle at the man's lower half that is shaking like a leaf in a strong breeze, while his top half remains strictly business. He reaches up to a small device implanted behind his ear, but he pauses when he spots the medical personnel wheeling out a corpse. Dominic squints and somewhat regrets that he hadn't gotten ocular implants. He wants to get a closer look, but stepping out from the crowd would only bring unwanted attention.

The thick, black, plastic bag shakes with every bump the med team rolls over and the two men struggle to keep the table with wheels steady on the lumpy snow covered ground. It seemed that the lifeless body is going to topple over, but the men stabilize it and are able to get the silver cart loaded into the van. They shut the double doors and one of the men moves to the drivers' seat.

"The body has been identified as forty one year old Francis Ogmyer, who owned the body modification shop you see behind me," the reporter gestures to the building beyond him. The reporter continues, "According to police, he has been deceased for at least fifty three hours."

The news was like a kick to the solar plexus. Dominic had thought that Frog had once again done something to get himself arrested. Hearing that Francis is the one in that bag had completely taken him by surprise. He reaches up to his ear and presses a small protrusion just behind his earlobe and barely whispers, "Call David." The small bones in his ear vibrate, as the nano-phone pulses with each ring.

"Thank you for calling Chosen public relations. How may I direct your call?" the female secretary says with a silky flowing voice after a few rings.

The mortician hands some paperwork to the brunette, female, detective and climbs into the van. The old black van sputters and drives away. Dominic moves to find an easy path to exit the tightly packed mass of onlookers.

"I need to speak with David." Dominic whispers, but to the delicate microphones beneath the skin of his lips, it sounds as if he is talking plainly.

The woman on the other end of the line replies with a well-practiced tone to hide her apathy, "I'm sorry but, Mr. Jennings is in a very important meeting right now. Would you like me to take a message?"

◊

Congressman Kenneth McDowell sits in a black leather couch patiently listening to his host. His grey, off the rack suit, bulges around his swollen belly. His red nose and cheeks speak of a life spent chasing failed dreams at the bottom of a bottle. The cool glass of sixty four year old

Macallan whiskey rests in his hands, half full. The single ball of ice is still perfectly smooth and only beginning to melt, watering down the fine beverage.

This little meeting was supposed to be all business. Civil, quick and easy, but when it comes to organizations who are used to getting their way, quick and easy is always thrown out the window.

"The President is looking for a reason to cut your funding. Frankly, I can't say that I blame him. The nano-machines are raising concerns on the hill. There are," the chubby man searches for delicate words, "dangerous implications of population slavery with the adjustments your scientists have made." McDowell slightly twitches to take a drink, but decides any gesture of enjoying his host's hospitality would be seen as an opening for negotiation. "As for your little *'policing'* force of seekers, the House has noticed the shift of public opinion and views them as more a nuisance than a lawful arm of society. With all of the violent allegations, black listed employees and unfiled paperwork, it's a miracle this little circus of yours gets any government funding at all," the Congressman says dryly.

Congressman McDowell watches his host, David Jennings calmly pour himself another glass of the richly smooth, four hundred and sixty thousand dollar whiskey over a spherical chunk of ice. The clean cut man takes a sip of the golden liquid and smiles with pleasure.

"You see Ken. Can I call you Ken?" David starts in a melodic tone while stepping over to the thick, high backed, leather seat across from McDowell, "Our organization is truly for the betterment of society as a whole. We can go through and file paperwork on every little thing that we do, just to keep the folks on the hill satisfied. That's not the problem." David takes another sip, then holds the glass out for his servant, a lobotomized syn to hold like a slave. The human looking machine stands by his side waiting for commands. "The issue is that we are doing the government's dirty work for them. The loyal men and woman of this, 'circus' put their lives in harm's way every time they go out to get one of those murderous robots," David pauses to taste the golden liquid. He hands the glass back to the synthetic servant, "Isn't that right Mr. Roberts?" David gestures to the hulking mass of muscle standing by the door.

The chubby Congressman peers over his shoulder. He didn't notice the man standing there before. It was hard to imagine that huge frame sneaking into the room, but apparently he had.

"Why, Pete over there has taken out, well I don't know, a couple hundred of these 'sophisticated' can openers in the past two years." The unpleasant tone in David's voice, unnerves McDowell.

David leans back in his leather chair, folds one leg over the other, taking care not to cause any permanent wrinkles in his two hundred thousand dollar suit and smiles malevolently. The Congressman shifts uncomfortably in the heavily cushioned couch. Clearly feeling the hostility, McDowell concludes that this would be a good time to stop playing the tough guy and try to smooth things over with this cold man. The plump man peers over his shoulder then back at David.

"I'm only saying that..." McDowell stumbles over his words.

Mr. Jennings holds up a single finger, forestalling the next few words the overweight Congressman was about to let fly out of his chubby jowls. Pete Roberts steps behind the uneasy man.

"I know. You're only the messenger," David starts coldly, "The thing is that there are people out there, including myself who don't like the idea that these," he searches for the right words but settles on speaking plainly so that the fat man sitting across from him can clearly understand, "Things are running about, pretending to be one of Gods creations. As for the nano-machines." David continues, "They will help keep the idiotic sheep in line." David glances up at Pete, giving him a silent signal. Before the thick little man can blink, two massive arms lock around his neck in a choke hold. The Congressman's hands fly up to try and wrench the heavily muscled arms free from his throat.

The glass of ridiculously expensive whiskey shatters on the white and grey marble floor. The pressure is tight enough to partially cut off the flow of blood to the brain, yet weak enough to allow the man to remain conscious.

David lifts his hand and the server droid places the glass of expensive drink in his palm. He takes a slow sip and he stares, unblinking at the old man struggling to breathe, "The public, along with these machines, need to know their place. I will do anything I have to do to make sure that those things are put in their place. If that means telling your wife about your secret excursions to de-civilized Thailand and those little boys you enjoy so much, I will." David leans forward in his seat, uncrossing his leg, "If that means killing the President of the United States, I will."

The Politician stops flailing so he can concentrate on staying conscious. His face turns a shade of rosy red. David nods toward Pete and the large man releases his hold on the Congressman's neck. The fat man falls to his knees, sucking in air as he sobs. He looks up to meet the cold dead eyes of David Jennings and see's that the well-dressed man is lazily holding out a red silk handkerchief. McDowell climbs to his feet taking the small cloth and begins wiping his eyes.

David, still looking at the spilled scotch on his floor, ignores the defeated politician. David gestures toward the door, excusing the fat little man. The shaky Congressman staggers toward the door still sniffling and using the red material to catch his tears.

"Don't forget to convince your buddies on the hill to extend my funding!" David calls out to

McDowell. The suave businessman smiles victorious as he takes another sip of his whiskey. He lifts his head toward the melancholy synthetic and waves at the mess on his floor, "Oh Silvia, do clean this up." The single minded, brunette droid bows, then immediately moves to get the cleaning supplies.

A buzzing sound from the arm of the chair yanks David's attention away from the droid on its hands and knees cleaning the floor.

"Mr. Jennings. You have a call from a Mr. Vespucci. He says that it's important," the secretary says.

David presses a button on the arm of the chair then one behind his ear, "To what do I owe the pleasure," he says in a cheerful tone.

"Have you seen the news? Frog is dead," the frazzled voice on the other end says.

David cocks his head in surprise. He calmly gets out of his chair and speaks a command to the room, "T.V. on." A large image flickers to life on the far wall. He moves his hands in short waving motions to flip through the channels.

"No greetings from you after all this time. No invitations to parties anymore. I was starting to think you didn't like me anymore," David says to break the silence while also feigning heartache. He can imagine Dominic rolling his eyes at the statement which causes him to faintly smile.

"Cut the shit David," Dominic replies, taking labored breaths. He can't believe that David would take a nonchalant attitude toward the death of one of his employees, but then again, the man always knew how to keep his cool.

Jennings stops flicking his hands when he spots the live news cast being shot right in front of the trashy parlor that Francis owned.

"Police are treating this as a homicide and ask that anyone who may have any information relating to the case, to contact their offices."

David chuckles as if he had just heard a lame joke.

"Do you see it?" Dominic asks impatiently.

"I see it, friend. The question is, why should I care?" David says, folding his arms in front of his chest.

Dominic sighs tiredly at David's lack of technical knowledge.

"You should care, because Frog's ocular implants were connected to a hard drive that saves visual data." Dominic pauses for a moment while he waits to see if Jennings will connect the dots and realize the immense gravity of the situation. After a few short moments, Dominic opens his mouth to politely explain.

"I'll make a few calls to some buddies of mine. That *data* could be very damaging if the wrong people got a hold of it," David says before Dominic can utter a word. His clipped tone suggests that he understands how bad things could get if a fraction of that data comes into public view.

David Jennings terminates the call and stands there silently fixated on the large screen. He examines the live broadcast and curses the day that he paid for Francis' operation. Pete's hulking mass stands by the conference room door awaiting instructions. The suave business man folds one arm under the other while tapping his lips with his forefinger.

"Pete," David addresses the big man with a calm confident voice, "I want you to personally take care of this debacle. Leave nothing to chance. I want to know who did this and then I want you to take care of them."

Pete swings his head to one side, popping the bones in his neck and replies, "Consider it already done, Mr. Jennings."

The big man turns and exits the room. David stands in front of the large broadcast for a few more seconds, silently planning his next move. In his younger days, David had to learn to make excellent snap judgments. In those days, during the great collapse, it was too easy for orphaned youngsters to trust the wrong adult. Many of the children he had known made that mistake and were killed or worse yet, sold on the black market to *"Houses of pleasure."*

"Investigators suspect that Mr. Ogmayer's murder may be related to his activities with the humanist organization *Chosen*," the obviously cold reporter says. The man's quivering has finally made it to his upper body, causing him to sound as if he sits atop of a large vibrating platform.

Silvia hears the words from the broadcast and stumbles. A small can of cleaner tumbles from the small bucket in her hands. David turns when he hears the small clatter. He steps toward the droid, who is just watching the metallic can roll away. Annoyed, David jogs over and places his foot atop the cylinder to stop its journey. The expressionless machine looks up at her master. David looks at her expectantly. She says nothing and bends over to pick up the small can. David watches as she shuffles back to the storage closet to put up the cleaning products.

David sighs in annoyance and reaches for his glass on the bar. He watches the live coverage until a new segment starts then tells the room to power down the television. He walks over to the large bay windows and peers down at the city below, "Damned fools," he mutters under his breath.

CHAPTER 6

18 Months Earlier

The setting sun sets the sky ablaze with hues of hot pinks and golden oranges mixed with fiery reds. The light breeze kisses Imogen's skin like a soft goose feather running along the length of her exposed calf. Her navy blue evening gown, that she had purchased nearly a year ago, but never had an occasion to wear, was finally being put to good use. She takes the hand of her husband as he helps her out of the car. She smiles up at him and he smiles back. Both are lost in the visage of each other's faces. Sadly, the beautiful moment is cut short when a rowdy trio of men begin hooting and hollering at a young woman walking alone down the street. It's plain to see that she is uncomfortable and is trying very hard to ignore their cat calls.

"Some people," Darioux says as he shakes his head from side to side.

Husband and wife make their way across the busy street to the onyx jewel-like structure which has a young doorman patiently waiting to welcome guests to partake of the restaurant's fine cuisine inside. The black reflective face of the stylishly sleek building shines as though it exuded its own luminescence from the glass that covers its façade. The young man, no older than eighteen, holds the door open to the lavishly extravagant restaurant and the couple walk inside. This was their date night and they weren't about to let an obnoxious group of Neanderthals ruin it.

Inside the richly decorated restaurant, soft music plays from a live band on a circular stage in the middle of the large room. The mood lighting inset in the dome ceiling casts a warm relaxing glow for the guests who dine at mirror smooth tables. Each guest is promptly serviced by their own waiter, who stands by the table to wait on their every whim. The establishment oozed opulence.

Darioux and Imogen follow the hostess to their reserved table and sit down.

After only a moment of looking at the menu, Imogen leans forward, eyes wide and says in a small voice, "Holy crap! Dude, can we afford this?"

"We can tonight baby." Darioux says with a smile and lifts his eyes to peer at his wife from over the menu.

Imogen's eyes snap back down at the descriptions of the delicious and highly detailed menu.

"There are no prices next to anything." She says in a hushed tone as not to disturb the other patrons. She looks up and notices a man standing at the table wearing a tailored suit, who was not there a moment ago. A white cloth hangs neatly from his forearm folded just under his chest. She didn't even hear the guy walk up to the table. She smiles awkwardly at him.

"Is everything alright madam?" Their server says, peering down at his guests.

Imogen glances up at the man standing as still as a statue by the table. She can't help but notice how large his nostrils are and how much styling product it must've taken to slick his hair back the way it was. The man looks like a caricature out of a Monty Python cartoon. Imogen giggles a little bit before she composes herself and answers, "Yes. Everything is fine."

Darioux smiles at his wife again and sets down his menu. His eyes radiate a smile as he looks at his wife, "Do you know what you want Gen?"

Imogen skims over the menu trying desperately to find something that sounds like it would be reasonably priced. "I will have the…" After searching and finding nothing that she could really justify spending an exorbitant amount of money on, she orders a salad and a glass lemonade. The server nods as if they were casually discussing the weather and he turns, poised and ready to memorize Darioux's order.

With much more confidence than his wife, he orders a surf and turf dish with a bottle of wine. The oddly featured server nods his head then strolls back to the kitchens to communicate the order to the chefs.

"Are you insane?" Imogen silently mouths. Darioux looks at his wife quizzically. "You just ordered the equivalent of a down payment on a house!" she continues in a hushed and increasingly stressed tone.

Darioux smiles again and places his hand over hers and rubs his thumb along the top, feeling her fine bones.

"Honey," Darioux smiles, "You are looking at the head systems engineer of Micro Corp. I think we can handle this expense at least this one time." He says with a wide smile.

Imogen's jaw goes slack and for a second it seemed as if she were going to have a meltdown, but then she jumped out of her chair, ran around the table and hugged him. The guests nearest them watched her with haughty disapproval, but she didn't care. As far as she was concerned, those ritzy squares can go get bent.

"Oh my God! Baby I am so proud of you." She chirps into his ear and plants a kiss on his cheek.

The farthest patrons looked and probably thought that she had accepted his marriage proposal, so there wasn't too many of them upset at the outburst. Imogen notices that she has just disturbed everyone and slowly makes her way back to her seat, apologizing with every step.

"When did this happen?" she asks with barely contained joy.

Darioux takes her hand again, smiling broadly, "The other day. I was kind of waiting for the right time to tell you."

Imogen congratulates him again and then realizes her blunder, "You just let me order a stinking salad?"

Darioux chuckles deeply and assures her that she will have a chance to order something with a little more substance than some leaves in a bowl.

The young married couple discuss the events leading up to Darioux's promotion. When their food is served they continue to engage in conversation with topics ranging from the state of current affairs to music. Like professional ballroom dancers they flow into one topic and through to another never missing a beat. When the time for dessert came around, they decided to split a large and heavily topped banana boat. It was the perfect treat for a perfect meal.

With night fully in bloom, the couple leave the restaurant. They notice that the same group of loud mouthed men were still at it. They were across the street, still hooting and hollering at every passersby. Imogen and Darioux try to ignore them as they make their way to their car, but one of the men steps out to block a small family. The lanky man with the mechanical eyes begins gesturing toward the couple's child who couldn't have been more than seven or eight years old. The father smacks the thug's hand away from his son. The father steps forward to place himself between the man with the ocular implants and his wife who is clutching their child. The other two thugs begin to circle the small family like wild jackals ready for the kill.

Darioux opens the door to the car and allows Imogen to enter, but his eyes never leave the wild scene unfolding only fifteen feet away. Imogen firmly places her hand on her husband's with unspoken concern.

"Baby don't," she says looking completely terrified. He looks down to see the worry that shadows her eyes. Just as he was about to shut the door so they could be on their way home, a horrified shriek rips at his ears and his attention is pulled away from his wife. He sets his eyes on to the family in distress. Darioux looks up in time to see the husband take a fist to the jaw from one of the bigger thugs that knocks him to the ground. The older gentleman never saw the blow coming. He doesn't move much after the blow. The shorter but thick man yanks the wife away from the child and the lanky man begins to stomp on the bleeding father.

"Hey!" Darioux calls as he begins to jog over to the confrontation. He looks over at the Doorman who is frozen in fear and yells, "Call the police!"

The child reaches for his mother, who is hysterical and reaching back calling his name, "Chris! Christopher!" The father lay barely conscious on the wet ground. Darioux can't make out what the three men are saying until he is right on top of them. A cold ache forms in the pit of his belly. They are seekers and the child is synthetic.

The biggest of the three men notices that Darioux is getting close to their operation, he charges like a bull and crashes into Darioux. They go sprawling and the big man knocks him to the ground. Seeing her husband assaulted, Imogen exits the car and rushes over to him not realizing that she was now putting, not only herself in immediate danger but her husband as well.

The frightened child cries as the frog faced man pushes him and shreds the child's clothes.

"Please stop. I'm like you! I'm alive!" The small boy pleads. That's when the short stocky man strikes the dark haired kid with a ball peen hammer in the back of the head. The boy's mother screams as she helplessly watches the back of her son's head crack open. The boy stumbles and turns around in a daze, still repeating his words from earlier, "Please stop! I'm alive!" The short greasy haired man swings the hammer even harder and it connects with the boy's face shattering his left cheek. Tiny chunks of metal and plastic twirls through the air like confetti. The boy drops to his knees. The mother no longer has a voice. The silent screams are a testament to her complete horror. She howls noiselessly and grasps at her chest.

Imogen stops in her tracks when she realizes that these men will kill her without hesitation. Darioux backs away as not to draw attention to his retreat. The three men are occupied with the easy pickings they have in front of them, they hardly notice the people backing away around them. The married couple knows that they need to leave before the seekers notice that Imogen is not human. The repeated ping of hammer on dense plastics and light metals echo in the streets. So too does the haunting distorted voice of the child repeating the words, "I'm alive. Please. I'm alive."

Darioux and Imogen reach the relative safety of their car just as the blow that ends the boy's life stuck and sends metallic debris skipping across the pavement. Imogen reaches the door and pauses for a moment to take one last look at the grieving mother holding what was left of her son. As she moves to take her seat in the car, she locks eyes with the frog faced man. Absolute frigid fear rips at the hopes and dreams of her future when she peers into the expressionless eyes of the small man. He smiles ruefully and bends the knuckles of his fingers to wave her a dreaded goodbye as the car pulls off and speeds away.

The mother crawls over to the shell that housed her son. The tears flow like twin waterfalls down her face. When she reaches the small body she pulls it up to her chest and silently screams. Flashing lights from the slow to arrive police vehicles, pulsate through the night as the sirens wail like wild banshees. All the woman and her husband ever wanted was a family. She was infertile and they were unable to have a child of their own naturally. They didn't have the money to adopt a human child and having a surrogate was out of the question due to the expense. Now she and her husband were going to be arrested, fined up to two hundred and fifty thousand dollars and spend a minimum of five years in prison.

The boys just wanted to celebrate her birthday and do something special for the woman who does so much for them. Now they have lost their son all because they were in the wrong place at the wrong time.

The seekers high five each other, celebrating a job well done. They kick large chunks of what was the child's head into the street. Flakes of glittering metal sparkle in the tall lamps bright light.

CHAPTER 7

Present Day

Imogen sits hunched over the micro fiber couch, rolling her Tungsten Carbide wedding ring around her index finger. The pale morning light filters through the slats of the blinds on the window. The tight beams of light catch every particle of dust that dances through the air in its path. She leans back, letting herself sink into the thickly padded back cushions. She reaches down into her pants pocket for a sterling silver necklace then threads it through the loop of the metal ring then affixes the necklace around her neck.

The old fashioned tumblers of the deadbolt protruding out of the front door, slide into place with quick tiny clicks. A swift turn of the key unlocks the bolt. Blake enters the modest apartment. Imogen turns her head and notices that he's been out shopping. The rumpled woven bag in his hand sways as he turns to shut and lock the door.

"New toy?" Imogen asks. He had been spending insane amounts of money on upgrades and new gadgets for his many devices. Imogen only had minimal upgrades before. She was limited by what she could do on her own. Having Blake around allowed her systems to be completely overhauled. She wonders what new thing he had for her now.

"Oh yeah. I got your new cooling system." Blake smiles like a school boy who has just aced a pop quiz.

Imogen perks up at his reply, <*What else could he have now?*>

"Let those bastards try and identify you through heat now." Blake pulls the hardware out of the bag and holds up the box, showing his chocolate covered teeth with a huge smile, "Want to install it now?"

Imogen stretches before she moves from her comfortable seat on the couch, to the hard plastic chair near the dining table. She turns the chair around and sits facing its back. She lifts the back of her shirt to expose her well hidden access panel. Blake removes his large coat and throws it over to the couch missing it by a foot or two. He opens the unmarked box and pulls out the tiny cube along with all of its tubes.

He sets the device on the table and rolls his desk chair directly behind Imogen and turns on the overhead lights. He begins pressing pressure activated points on her back in the sequence required to unlock the panel, "So, how is your morning going?" he says in a mock parental voice. He adjusts his glasses then picks up a few delicate tools from his little pouch. He leans forward and begins working.

"Dull and uneventful, mother," Imogen rests her chin on the flat of the chair back support and huffs.

"Aw. What a shame my dear. Well, mine was a bit interesting," he replies without missing a beat. He peers down at the many components within Imogen, through the magnified portion of his glasses. Blake pulls out the old heat suppressing unit, sets it down on the floor then begins to install the new one. "While I was out obtaining this little jewel for you, I came across a homicide and there was all these people gathered about," he continues with the playful parenting voice.

Imogen winces at his words and the pinching sensation along her spine as he connects the distribution tubes.

"I thought that I recognized one of the looky-loos, so I went to have a closer look," he grunts with some effort as he connects another tube. "And as luck would have it, I did know the son of a bitch." Blake drops the motherly tone as he connects the last tube and begins to fill the main tank with a special liquid.

"Who was it?" Imogen asks impatiently. Blake closes the panel and helps her pull down her shirt and tries not to sneak a peek at her nude body. He pats her on the back, taking a deep breath. He pinches the instruments in his fingers then places them in their little holders in his tool pouch.

"One pudgy and greasy looking Dominic Vespucci," he answers plainly.

Imogen turns around in surprise. She meets Blake's eyes asking a silent question. When he doesn't answer right away, Imogen throws her hand up to punctuate the sense of urgency.

"Cool your engines doll face. I hit him up with a tracker," He pulls a tiny playing card size monitor out of his pocket and tosses it to her. "Now you'll know where that walking chode is, at all times."

Imogen looks at the slim device elated, but the joyful expression quickly fades to a grimace. Blake opens his mouth slightly to say something, but closes it when he hears a high pitched laugh emanating from the speakers hooked up to his computer. He turns clapping and giggling like a small child who just received a surprise.

"What is that?" Imogen asks. Blake dashes over to his PC and punches a few keys on the keyboard. A flicker of light and the main monitor shows a security room while the other displays the video of the cat deeply engrossed with whatever is irritating its junk. The screen overlooking the security center shows a man in uniform, who spends too much time chowing down on pastries, kicking over a small trash can and gesturing wildly. Blake laughs hysterically at the monitor.

"You just couldn't help yourself," Imogen says with a smile. She leans over to partake in the dismay of the city's security monitors. The team of techs work frantically at their stations.

<Blake's hack must've been solid for them not to find it,> Imogen thinks with a slight smile.

A large man in a thick military coat steps into view, thrusts the fat man against a wall and holds him there. They seem to be in a heated and one sided conversation. The rest of the employees jump and watch as their supervisor is manhandled by a beast of a man.

"Who is...?" Imogen says completely cutting off Blake's cackling. Her eyes narrow as she recognizes the intimidating mass of one of the men who had taken Darioux's life. She clenches her fist as a sudden heat warms her face.

Blake leans in and magnifies the high resolution image to show the small head sporting a circular scar on his cheek. The tiny head is attached at the shoulders of Pete Roberts. Blake glances up at Imogen with a deep worry in his eyes. She returns the look and then fixes her gaze back on the monitor, "I'm going to need some bigger guns." She says a bit worried. She thought that her pistol would be enough to handle anything that came her way, but this guy looks like he'd need to be blown away with a rocket propelled grenade.

"Guns?" Blake looks up at Imogen trying to smile. The sentiment didn't make it up to his eyes.

He was worried before about this path of vengeance they were on, but now he fears for her life. In an attempt to cope with the uneasy fear he feels, Blake falls back on a joke, "Try a whole combat suite upload. A small army couldn't hurt either." Blake adds, trying to lighten the mood, though they really didn't find it funny. Blake leans back in his chair and watches Imogen. He tries to read her body language, but doesn't like the uncertainty he can see in her posture.

The hulking mass of Pete Roberts has the squishy man pressed so hard against the wall that soon, either the man's clavicle or the wall was going to give out and break. The salt and peppered hair of the man vibrates as he struggles to keep his bones from snapping. "We'll find whoever breached the system! I swear!" the Head Security Monitor says with a whimper.

Roberts releases him from his crushing grip and shoves a thick finger inches from the flinching man's face, "You have forty eight hours. If you don't have what I want by then, not even your cat will be safe. Get me?" The man nods his head so fast his jowls make wet fleshy noises. Roberts eyes the overweight man for a couple of heartbeats, then turns and stomps out of the room. The middle aged man straightens his uniform.

"You heard the man. Get to work," his voice quivers with every word. He runs his hands through his sweat drenched hair in an attempt to get the disheveled mess looking somewhat neat. The fat man cries a bit as he waddles back to his office. The men and women of the security team begin typing furiously at the keys in front of their stations.

Roberts exits the tall building responsible for housing and monitoring all the security feeds throughout the large city. He pulls a cigarette out of his pocket and lights it. He coughs and spits the dislodged phlegm on to the steps of the center. He takes a pull from his smoke and begins to walk to his car to type out a message to David Jennings. He flips out a keyboard from the dashboard that looks like a toy next to his large hands. He knows that Mr. Jennings was not going to like the news, but keeping his boss up to date on his progress was just something Pete always did. After finishing his cigarette, Pete drives off in search of another angle to find clues.

Frogs former employee lay bound and gagged in the trunk of Pete's car. Her muffled yelps can't be heard over the bass of the hip hop music blaring through the speakers. Her bound hands pound against the metal underside of the trunk. She feels a warm trickle run down to her wrist. She is sure that she's bleeding. Her bare feet kick at the back of the seats. The last thing she remembers was laying in her bed to go to sleep. She had been waiting to be interviewed by the police and she would have told them that Frog got just what was coming to him, but waking up in the trunk of a car was the last thing she expected. Her garbled pleas go unnoticed by Pete. He'll get to her later.

As Pete speeds through the streets a message pops up on the windshield that reads: *"Hard drive?"* His level of authority and clearance gives him the power to practically kill someone if he thinks their giving him the stink eye. He wanted to end the fat man for being completely lax on the monitoring of their systems. Unfortunately, too many violent incidents can bring unwanted attention from government agencies that will only get in the way. He'll just have to stay as clean as he can on this one. For now.

CHAPTER 8

Present Day

Detective Eddie Mason pulls to the curb just outside the coroner's office. The old rundown building looks like it's in desperate need of a long and proper pressure washing. Mason wonders if a pressure washing would be enough to remove the green mold from its brick façade. The large, nearly square metal door was a burgundy color, once, but now it's just a rusted battered mess. Mason rubs his forehead then runs his hand along his neatly cropped black but graying hair as he sighs.

"I hear ya old man," Vivian says unenthusiastically. She punches something into her glass pad then tucks it away. She leans forward and pulls out the dashboard computer to log on to the network.

Ed looks over at his partner, Vivian Stern, who's practically fresh out of the academy, "Old man?

I'm only thirty-seven." The defensive tone in his voice is almost comical, but a little wounded. The grey hairs didn't sprout up until that terrorist bombing nearly two years ago. He had a hard time dealing with the fact that so many families had lost their lives and he kept hitting wall after wall when trying to solve the case. He had to learn to let that go, though he still kept old school files, just in case.

"Whatever Pops." She says with a playful smile. Vivian reviews the case info on the vehicles computer. She hands Ed one of the cables connected to the car's pc. He takes it in the tips of his fingers and inserts the end into a jack near the hairline behind his ear. Vivian does likewise. She presses the *Enter* key and downloads the data to their wet-drive.

Ed shakes his head after he has processed all of the background information on Francis "*Frog*" Ogmayer.

"What's up?" Vivian asks picking up on her partner's agitation.

"You know, this guy was a piece of shit and probably deserved every bit of what he got plus some." Ed gives her a tired look.

Vivian cocks an eyebrow. Mason knows that look and he hates it. It's that look that says, "*I know what you are about to say and I don't care.*" She gave it to him whenever he was on a rant about the wrongs of the world.

"Oh don't give me that look, Viv. You know as well as I do, that sooner or later that psycho would have killed an actual human being. You've seen what he's done to those synthetics."

Vivian scratches her forehead just under her hairline while she impatiently listens.

"All I'm saying is that, it would have only been a matter of time before we would have had to haul him in. I mean we can't even find his only employee for Christ's sake." The aggravation in his voice reaches critical levels. Mason knows it's time to calm down. It took him a long time to reach the point where he could recognize his point of no return. So when he feels the boiling in his chest he makes it a point to shut his mouth and breathe.

"Hey. I totally agree with you about that dead creep. But it doesn't change the fact that a murder has been committed." Vivian nods her head in agreement with her senior.

Ed raises his right hand to signify his understanding, "A spades a spade," he says then he opens the door and exits the car. Vivian follows close behind.

Inside the old building, the smell of different chemicals fill the air. Some used for cleaning and others for embalming. A thick bullet proof glass stretches from the top of the desk to the ceiling and separates the waiting area from the reception desk. No one seems to be manning the front. The detectives ruffle their noses.

"Can I help you?" says a nasally voice emanating from a square speaker mounted on the far wall. A small hatch in the ceiling slides open and a camera mounted on a slim pole descends to hang right in front of the duo.

Mason holds up his badge and I.D. to the camera, "Yeah. I'm Detective Mason and this is my partner Detective Stern. We are investigating a homicide and were wondering if we could ask you a few questions about the victim." The word victim leaves a grimy taste on Mason's tongue. He sneers a bit at the choice of words. Vivian looks at him, shakes her head and smiles with that smart ass smile she does so well. Vivian loves to give Mason crap every chance she can. She knows he hated using the word *victim* when discussing the homicidal seeker.

The camera retracts and for a moment there is silence. The detectives exchange a look, then the image of the empty office flickers and disappears to reveal a short man with angular features and thinning hair standing by the desk. The skinny man in the white coat points to the door to their left and presses a button to unlock it with a loud buzzing sound.

The tiny man grabs a thick sandwich from a foam plate and takes a bite, "Sorry for all the cloak and dagger stuff guys, but there are some crazies out there and one can't be too careful. Ya know?" The mortician snorts. "Dr. Westfield, but you can call me Spike," The man snorts again, "Artifacts of misspent youth," he adds with narrowed menacing eyes.

Vivian's lips part for a brief moment of humored disbelief.

The small doctor laughs, "I'm just joshin' ya. The names Phil. Follow me," he waves them on. He leads them to a narrow corridor and down the steps to where the corpses are kept on ice.

"Phil, we were wondering how the autopsy on Francis Ogmayer was coming along and if you had a chance to remove his ocular hard drive." Mason states while navigating the narrow passage that leads down to the storage freezers. He ducks under a low hanging ventilation duct that the others didn't seem to notice. If the autopsy was complete, it wouldn't be long until Frog's body was cremated.

The doctor opens the door to the storage room and leads the detectives to the mini fridge where Francis's body is kept.

Dr. Westfield opens the door and pulls out the cold metal sliding tray that holds Frog's body. The boney man sets his sandwich on the dead man's belly. Vivian winces.

"Oh yeah. I was going to finish up my report after I ate my lunch, but since you're here." The doc flips a panel on the tray to access his data pad and forward his findings to the officers. "I gotta say," Dr. Westfield says, "This guy took drugs like a fucking champion. Amphetamines, uppers, downers, you name it and was in this son of a bitch right here."

Detective Mason glances at what's left of Frog's head and notices that the implant has indeed been removed, "And what of the ocular implant and hard drive? Is it still functional?"

The old man shuffles over to a metal desk on the other side of the room, "Oh yeah. That thing's military grade hardware. He could have been blown to bits and that thing would still work." The doctor opens a drawer and pulls out a red plastic bag containing all the items that were on Francis's person when he died. Dr. Westfield moves to hand the bag over to Detective Mason, but is distracted when a chime echoes in the room. "Hmm. Someone's here," he says absently. "Excuse me," the doctor mumbles. The small man grabs his sandwich and takes another bite, which dislodges a large leaf of lettuce from the bread. It smacks wetly on the floor.

"Has all the info downloaded?" Detective Mason looks over to his partner.

Vivian checks the status on her data pad, "Almost," she answers plainly. "Looks like he transferred the visual data from the implant to include it in the file."

Mason nods his head appreciatively. Decrypting and converting all that data to actual video would have taken them weeks to complete. If they had taken it to one of their tech guys, possibly a few days, but that would have been time wasted.

"We should wrap this up." Mason says. Then, just as he takes a step toward the door leading to the stairwell they hear the loud crack of a high caliber gun.

The detectives draw their weapons and use extreme caution when exiting the room. When Mason enters the stairwell, he can hear Vivian on her nano-com reporting the gunshot, requesting back up and a possible ambulance on their location. Detective Mason takes each step as silently as he can while keeping his eyes and his gun trained on the entrance above. He can hear Vivian doing the same but he doesn't dare take his eyes off the cracked door above. He can hear the automated door that leads to the waiting area glide shut and lock. Then the faint hum of an engine start up. Mason half expected to hear the car's tires squeal as the perpetrator made his getaway, but nothing like that happened.

When Mason finally reached the top of the stairs and peeked through the opening in the door to ensure that there wasn't anyone waiting for him on the other side, he spots Dr. Phil Westfield. The old man lay flat on his back with a gunshot wound to the chest.

"Clear!" Mason yells back at Vivian. He kneels down by the doctor and notices that the red bag of evidence is gone. "Well shit." Mason says in frustration.

The old man died with his eyes open. Mason reaches down and gently uses his fingers to shut Phil's eyes.

Vivian walks up and begins a scan of the crime scene. "Look at the bright side pops," Vivian starts, "At least he included the data we needed as a D.L."

The flat, cold tone in her voice sounds too uncaring for Mason's liking. He stands, sighs deeply and holsters his side arm. The casual tone in which she had spoken of the old man's last moments of life turned Mason's stomach, "Yeah. I'm sure that'll be a comfort to his family." he says while gesturing to the family portrait motion graphic on the desk.

  Vivian focuses on the floor before her, almost ashamed for her thoughtless words, but it was a part of the job. People die every single day and there was nothing she or Mason could do to prevent it. Maybe when she'd been on the force as many years as he had, she would understand. Sirens and screeching tires of old patrol cars fill the silence within the tiny office.

CHAPTER 9

Present Day

Imogen doesn't feel much like leaving the relative security of Blake's apartment. In fact, all she wants to do is to sleep and forget about the world for a few hours. With the holidays coming and going, she didn't want the time to consciously think about the things she no longer has. She was getting heavy-hearted and Blake knew her well enough to notice. He along with his girlfriend, Amiya, convinces her that she could use the fresh air and human interaction.

Amiya thought that Blake and Imogen were siblings, so she didn't think it was that weird that they were living together. Amiya had never spent much time at the apartment, and Blake seems like he doesn't really mind either way. If he likes her, he has a funny way of showing it. Blake and his too young girlfriend had only been dating for a few months. She wanted things to get serious, but given the situation, Blake thought it best to keep their distance.

The tech convention is in town and Blake wants to see if they could find some new goodies to aid in the takedown of as he called it, *"the walking cock knuckle"* that is Pete Roberts. Amiya doesn't know the situation and Blake nor Imogen is going to let her in on their plans. She just thinks that they share a passion for technology and robotics.

The tech market is buzzing with patrons looking for the newest and flashiest toy to add to their *nerdgasm* collections. The many different booths are lined up like a mini strip mall. The line of tables form neat isles to funnel potential customers or clients neatly through the pathways to visit many, if not all sections. It's Saturday, so every geek with a vast comic book collection and their mother is out today.

Blake looked like a kid in a candy store that has to finger every little piece of shiny metal or spare part for vintage machines. Everything seems to be going well and Imogen is coming out of her shell. She found herself perusing items more casually, until she came to a stand that specializes in antique synthetics.

Some of the oldest and heaviest robots, were painted in vibrant day-glow colors, completely neutralizing their original war purposed ferocity. Other, later models sported a peach colored plastic that acted as skin. At first Imogen doesn't know how to react when she meets the dead eyes of some of these old models. There is a certain disconnect with these metal husks yet, she felt sorry for them. They couldn't think nor could they feel. They were either piloted by soldiers far away in some bunker or programmed to perform some mundane task. Imogen reaches out with a shaky hand and touches the cheek of an old pleasure bot.

<Did she ever love any of the people she served?> Imogen thinks to herself. The thought of this droids life saddens her. It must have been a lonely existence. Before she can fully focus on what life must have been like for synthetics in the early days, she moves on to other goods scattered on the four tables.

Blake manages to pull his attention away from a vintage video game console long enough to notice that, Amiya and Imogen were browsing the collectable droid and syn booth. He doesn't know how to read the expression on his synthetic friend's face, so he walks over to the stand and tests the waters.

"Find anything super cool?" he probes, once he reaches the table.

Imogen remains silent for the span of a few heartbeats and without taking her eyes off of a soldier class infiltrator unit, she answers, "Possibly."

Amiya is completely out of her depth when it comes to complex android systems, so she thought that she would leave the nerds to their toys, "Hey babe. This is all you and your sis. Imma go check out the newest PCs." She pecks him on the cheek and practically skips away. Blake barely notices her fading presence.

Blake looks over the tables that hold stacks upon stacks of spare parts and crystalline program shards.

"We don't serve your kind in here." Say's a gruff voice from a neighboring tent. Imogen and Blake stiffen for a moment, but their panic is soon snuffed out by the next words the man speaks. "Sparx, you sour bitch!" The tall man wearing the tee shirt that says, *I'm a pepper are you a pepper too?* embraces Blake in a massive hug and for a moment, Imogen wondered if she should run. When she saw the big man smiling, she knew everything was okay.

"Holy shit!" Blake exclaims in surprise, "Bigsby! God, I haven't seen you since the University." The two men hug again then shake hands. The joy of an old friendship re-ignited, lights up their eyes.

The big man aptly named Bigsby, made Blake look like a child. Bigsby is a little overweight but he carried it well and it even made him look muscular in places.

"It's been too long man. I see you are checking out my wares. What do ya think?" the big man throws his arms out wide.

Blake's jaw drops and then he throws his hands in the air and does a little happy dance that involves shaking his butt. He knows he looks ridiculous, but Imogen suspects that he doesn't care. That was something she enjoyed about him. He was silly and would risk embarrassment to make a friend feel better. That's just who he was.

Bigsby ignores Blake and turns his attention to Imogen, "Why 'ello me lady. What can I do for you?"

The man was obviously smitten, but Imogen hopes he is just trying to be kind.
Imogen looks around at all the old droid parts and says nonchalantly, "I'm just looking. My dork brother is one that you can do something for."

Bigsby shoots Blake a wounded look and pulls him aside, "Dude, you never told me you had a sisterus beautimus," he stage whispers. "Is she available?"

Blake chuckles as does Imogen, whose sensitive ears heard every hushed word, but she was a bit more conservative about it. She acts like she is clueless to Kevin's interest.

Blake turns around while simultaneously turning the huge man and says, "Gen I'd like you to meet Kevin Bigsby. Kevin my sister Gen."

Kevin extends his hand to greet the vivacious redhead. She smiles and takes his hand. "Hiya," the big man chirps. Imogen shakes his hand and returns the greeting. "So what can I get for you guys? I got just about everything needed to build your very own droid." He leans in closer to whisper to the *"siblings"*, "Even stuff you can't get in catalogs. BM"

Blake looks over, casually winks and smiles at Imogen as if to tell her, "*we can get a huge discount if you flirt with him.*"

The BM or Black Market stuff is why they were here in the first place. Finding a friend with the goods is just an added bonus. Imogen immediately understands the gesture, but doesn't feel too disposed to oblige, but it's not her cash they're spending.

Dominic hates the push of the crowds. So many pimply faced man-children scurrying about and drooling over last year's lame ass tech makes him physically ill. The bulimic wannabe super models who are dressed in skimpy costumes and paid to flirt with the unwashed, nerdcore masses is deplorable. These guys wouldn't stand a snowball's chance in hell with these women, but that didn't keep them from trying. Not to mention the insane price tag to get in was so ridiculous that attendants should be required to hand you a pair of clown shoes with your wristband. However, he thought it would be prudent to pick up some cheap mini cams to place around his apartment, just in case his paranoia was spot on and he needs to cover his ass.

It didn't take Dominic too long to find what he was looking for at a small booth with a giant eye bot standing watch on the side. The massive camera droid is wirelessly connected to half a dozen screens and displaying visuals it captured in multiple light spectrums. Dominic approaches the booth to browse. He fondles cams as old as he was and after a minute of not finding what he was looking for, he decides to move on. He is about to walk away and search another booth, when the owner of the table stand greeted him with a high pitched, prepubescent voice that did not match his age, "Looking for something in particular?"

The kid looks like he had yet to lose his virginity to the first thing with a hole. He is awkward in his posture and still combs his short blonde hair neatly to the side with some styling product. The kid looks like he crawled right out of the classic movie called *"Revenge of the Nerds"*. Dominic is a little disappointed when he didn't spot a pocket protector holding a wad of pens in the kid's breast shirt pocket. He figures the young twenty something to be a real code puncher and would at least know his stuff.

"Yeah. You got any of those M2-4HD nano cams?" Dominic asks in a gruff voice. He coughs to relieve the itching in his throat. The kid shakes his head in disappointment.

"Nah. Just sold the last one about thirty minutes ago. Sorry."

Dominic nods his head at the news, "Yeah. Thanks." Then the big man walks away.

Dominic visits every security cam booth at the convention and finds nothing even remotely close to what he is looking for. He decides it would probably be better to load his scatter gun once he got home, just in case. He is about to leave the outdated convention and thinks it would be a waste to leave without at least purchasing a trinket. He turns and heads back to some of the booths that caught his eye. He picks up a disruption coil and smiles, thinking of old memories. He set the copper thing down, then he notices a woman just staring at him. If her gaze was a lethal weapon, he'd be dead already. He quickly glances behind him to make sure that there wasn't something farther back that caught her eye.

The look in her eyes spoke of unseen depths of terror. He thinks he also sees a boiling rage behind the fear. He pretends not to notice the woman burning holes in his soul with her eyes and continues to peruse what could pass for vintage goods on the tables. Making sure to keep his senses trained on his surroundings, Dominic reaches down to grab an old set of plasma torches. A costumed hussy saunters his way, making sure that all the right parts jiggle.

"Hey sweetie," She starts to speak to him, but that was all she had time to say.

"Back the fuck up." Dominic snaps in a calm whisper, loud enough for the bubbly woman to hear. The booth babe cocks her head, huffs, then turns and walks away. She presses her *talents* against a more welcoming patron.

Dominic checks to make sure that the redheaded woman hadn't gotten lost in the crowd. The feeling in his gut was now guiding him and he had learned to listen to those hunches. He casually looks around for the wicked looking woman and she is nowhere to be seen. He almost panics, but tries to keep his cool. Dominic curses under his breath and begins to head for the nearest bathroom. He has to come up with a plan to lose this admirer. He wishes that he had picked up a multifunctional tracker to deal with her later, but then he would be faced with the task of getting it on her. He would think of something. He always did.

Imogen watches the greasy man make his way from booth to booth. Her facial recognition software made it almost impossible to miss him. She felt her chest flutter and her face grow hot when she saw him. Imogen slowly separated herself from Blake and Kevin so they couldn't be identified as accomplices if she ever got caught. She followed the short, chubby man throughout the convention center, all while contemplating how to kill him.

He is about to exit and leave the Grand Hall but decides against it and that's when he sees her. She thinks about trying to act casual, but it is too late for games. He on the other hand feels like playing, so Imogen obliges him. The first chance she gets, she takes cover behind a large stand that sells steam punk clothing and accessories.

She hears what he says to the booth model and the curse when he realizes that he had lost her. She expects him to immediately leave, but he turns and strolls over in the direction of the restrooms. She watches him through the throng of people enter the bathroom. She waits five minutes for him to exit and when he doesn't she gets a little suspicious. She casually walks up to the entrance of the Men's Room and waits for the coast to clear then she slides through the door. She doesn't know what she would do if someone said something to her, but she was confident that she could wing it.

A couple of teenage boys, no older than sixteen are washing their hands at the sinks when the hot redhead walks in. They instantly freeze, but to their credit, they recover quickly. One grunts with a smile and turns around. The little punk looks her up and down like a piece of meat. Clearly, he was used to the brainless tarts at whatever school he attended.

"Do you need something honey?" the mouth breather asks with false bravado.

Imogen looks both boys in the eyes, smiles and replies, "Unless you want your balls violently ripped out of your ass, I suggest you leave."

The two boys leave without further fuss. She kneels down to check the stalls and feels the cool gentle breeze nipping at her fingers. That's when she notices the open window.

CHAPTER 10

18 Months Earlier

The grey overcast sky is a damper on the warm weather, but not on the spirits of Darioux and Imogen. Today is the day they become parents. Today is the day they get their adopted child. They dance to old twentieth century music as they clean up the apartment. The windows are wide open to allow some fresh air to circulate in the living space. Though, there isn't much sun this morning, being on the forty-second floor allows for plenty of light to enter their humble dwelling. Imogen prances over to Darioux and wraps her arms around his shoulders. She plants a playfully joyful kiss on his lips. He returns the gesture by pulling her close.

"I'm so glad I found you." He whispers into her ear. His firm grip around her narrow waist softens. His hands begin to migrate south, over her smooth rounded hips, toward her toned rear end.

"I don't think so mister," she teasingly slaps his hands. "You don't get any till later." She leans in close enough for him to feel her warm breath on his lips, "Consider it the perfect night cap." Her sultry smile tugs on Darioux's neck, tenderly pulling him toward her. Imogen allows him to move closer to her. Her lips poised for a sensual kiss, then she turns away to clean some more.

Darioux smiles, knowing he had been defeated, while she walks over to the nursery to finish decorating the baby blue room. Darioux couldn't help but go stupid from watching her hips sway from side to side. The blood finally flows back into his brain and he picks up cleaning where he had left off.

Imogen unpacks the many stuffed animals and places them along the shelves and dresser in the room. She then moves to the changing table and places a few more swaddling blankets nearby for easy reach. Her mind runs through different scenarios of changing, dressing and even rocking the baby to sleep. Imogen had known happiness before and she cherishes those memories, but the complete jubilation coursing through her now was almost too much. Her body shakes from all the excitement. She then looks over at the crib and realizes that it is practically bare. She plucks a white floppy bunny from a woven bag then places it in the left corner of the crib. The stuffed animal glows against the earthy tones of the bedding.

◊

Outside the tall apartment building, Desirae nervously fidgets with her dark brown hair and contemplates if she is doing the right thing. She's practically licked off all her ruby red lipstick, leaving her lips covered in a patchy pink mess. She would have never thought that she would be sent out on an assignment her first day on the job. She definitely wouldn't have thought that her boss would have trusted her to practically be the point man of a pacification mission.

"You gonna ring it honey or just stare at it?" Francis says. His gravelly voice was grating to her ears. She found the man to be repulsive. Every chance he thought she wasn't looking he would look at her like she was a thing to be used. It was like he didn't see her as a fellow human being. She already didn't like the job but she and her newborn son, William, needed the money.

Francis sucks his teeth, "We don't got all day ya know." He practically presses himself against the backside of her body. He's so close, he can identify the shampoo she used this morning.

Desirae lifts her finger to the buzzer and pauses. Her stomach is in knots. Out of habit, she uses her thumbnail to pick at the nail of her forefinger. The skin is raw. She had been doing that for the past three hours. Looking down at the floor, Desirae doesn't feel right. She doesn't know if she has the guts to do this.

<What if the synthetic that lives here is psychotic?> she doesn't know if she can risk leaving her son behind. She's all he's got. The worry nibbles viciously at her mind, like a rapidly growing cancer. Her hand sits poised over the call button, ready to ring it for a second time, but she can't. Her finger begins to waver. She turns slightly to walk away, but Francis blocks her path. She doesn't have the nerve to stand up to the ugly man. He pushes the call button.

A little sliding door opens and a camera the size of a ping pong ball inches forward. Desirae freezes for a moment as she stares at the cam. The group of men accompanying her step out of view. Just then, a man's silky voice is heard through the speaker.

"Hello? Can I help you?" the unseen man says. Desirae thought she heard something gentle in the man's voice, which made her feel even worse for what she was doing.

Desirae smiles as natural a smile as she can manage and tries to remember what she was told to say.

"Oh hi. I'm Miriam. I'm with the agency." For a long moment she thought that she was going to blow the entire thing by throwing up right then and there.

The man's voice immediately perks up. Desirae didn't know exactly what that meant to the man, but it had worked.

"Oh yes of course. Here let me buzz you in," he says with barely contained enthusiasm. The connection ends and the door buzzes. Francis pulls open the metal entry door to let Pete Roberts, Dominic Vespucci and Desirae Deponet inside. The tiny woman felt so out of place next to these thuggish men. They pushed her with their bodies over to the lift. For some reason, they weren't letting her go home. She felt like she wanted to cry.

Imogen delicately handles an old fashioned mobile from a box that was marked *Baby D*, which was left to Darioux when his mother had passed. She stares at it reverently, trying to imagine how his mother felt when she watched him in his crib. This was it. She would finally know what it is to be *Mother*. She couldn't say how or why, but she felt the call. She had heard many women talk about the motherly instinct and she knew that this yearning had to be it. It had to be the call she felt in her chest.

The individual plush animals on the mobile were still so pristine and so delicately detailed that she was almost afraid to handle them. The fine thread attaching each piece to the stained oak umbrella was still flawless and glossy after all these years. Imogen runs her finger along the wood, feeling each individual grain. This all still feels like a dream.

She connects the mobile and winds it up to hear the comb rake over the notched cylinder. She loves hearing the beautiful tune. A knock at the door tugs at her attention, but the social worker isn't due to arrive for another two hours, so it could wait.

Darioux jogs to open the door. He can't believe that they are here early.

<Gen is going to be so surprised,> he unlocks the deadbolt and wraps his fingers around the brass sphere of the knob.

The door explodes off of its hinges. The edge of the door crashes into his forehead, splitting him open. Darioux is knocked to the floor. The long gash on his face marks where the door collided with his head. A hulking man steps through the opening, followed by two other men and a distressed woman. Darioux tries to stand, but the big man slams a heavy footed boot on his face.

Imogen jumps at the unexpected sound of the splintering crack. She hollers for her husband, but hears nothing. She waits before hollering again and inches toward the noise. The door opens and two men are standing there. The looks on their faces were gnarled and angry, but their eyes-those cold, dead, eyes threaten to rip Imogen's soul right from her body. For a moment Imogen doesn't know what to do. She recognizes the man with the eye implants from outside the restaurant.

"What do you want?" She says, her quivering voice amuses the men. The thicker of the two steps into the nursery. Imogen steps back away from the menacing man.

"Get away!" She yelps. Fright seizes her body and mind. She tries to side step one of the men with no luck, then she screams for her husband. Nothing. The little frog man laughs. Imogen begins to panic. She doesn't realize that she has just backed into the changing table. The narrow corner digs into her back.

The greasy haired man stops inches away, taking sick pleasure in her fear.

"You got nothing I want," his breath is rancid. It lingers in the air between them, "In fact, you're worth more to me dead than you are alive." He reaches out for her and in her frightened state she jerks a hand out and slaps his face. For a moment, he seems shocked, but then he grabs her dark hair and yanks her from side to side. Hair follicles are torn from her scalp in the man's tight grasp. Imogen screams as he knocks her into furniture and rains heavy fists into the side of her face.

Desirae screams when she hears breaking glass. The sound of flesh on flesh and a woman's shriek in the other room was almost too much to take in. She rushes over to the commotion and is almost clobbered by the body of the woman that is tossed out of the small room. She turns to find Dominic and Francis heading out of what seems to be a baby's room. The mirror, dresser and crib, along with everything else was destroyed. Splintered wood lay scattered everywhere. Desirae rushes into the room in search of the baby she knows must be there but finds no sign of it. She rushes back out to the living room to find the husband trying to remove Pete's massive foot from his throat. The bloody man receives a solid kick to the face for his trouble. Desirae glances back at the woman to find Dominic sitting on her chest, savagely slamming his fist down on her face. The woman tries to move but her arm hangs by a few bloody strands of something.

The skinny reject of a man knocks over shelves of pictures and slashes their couch with a big knife.

"Stop it!" Desirae screams, but they just ignore her. She screams again, "Stop!" Her throat burns from the exertion.

Dominic stops hitting the woman, Frog Stops ransacking this couple's apartment and Pete takes a break from bashing the man's brains out. They all stop long enough to look at her as if she were insane for opening her mouth. Francis stomps up to her and puts a boney finger in her face. "If you got a problem with the way we do our fuckin' job," he shouts, making sure to spit in her face, "you can take your opinion and shove that shit in your fart box."

Desirae's mouth opens as if she wants say something and that's when Frog grabs her hair and yanks her down to his level.

"You got somethin' ta say bitch? Huh? Huh?" he screams. The blood vessels in his face burst, leaving red splotches on his pale skin. Desirae looks up at his lifeless mechanical eyes, her voice frozen in terror. Frog releases her hair and she runs for the door crying. The men can hear her thumping down the hall. At one point she tumbles to the floor and the brutal men just laugh.

"Fuckin' people. No stomach ta do the dirty work," Frog giggles as Desirae runs for her life.

A battered Darioux reaches out for his unrecognizable wife. The tears streaming from her eyes shatters his heart, but makes him want to fight that much harder to try and do something. Anything. Maybe he notices that the huge man wasn't putting as much weight on him anymore or maybe he can't feel it anymore, but that's when Darioux had a burst of strength. He pushes the booted foot off of his chest, shoots up, latches on to Pete's face and sink his teeth into the giant's cheek. Pete roars in pain. The big man snatches the smaller man by his dreads and yanks him off. Darioux falls to the floor. A piece of Pete's flesh comes away with him. Pete's hands fly up to his face. The slightest touch stings and his palms come away covered in blood. Pete's whole body tenses up as his face glows red.

"You stupid fucking bastard!" he bellows and starts to stomp on Darioux's face.

A couple of stomps and a wet crack later, Darioux stops moving. His head is upturned toward his wife. His vision begins to fade around the edges.

He fights to keep his eyes open and after a heartbeat, he realizes that it doesn't even matter anymore.

Dominic pulls a long ice pick from his jacket pocket and waves it in front of Imogen's only open eye. He taunts her. He pretends to jab at her cheek, smiling a cold emotionless smile the whole time.

"How does it feel bitch?" he leans in to whisper in her ear.

Imogen quivers and tries to turn toward her husband. Dominic grabs her by the chin, yanking her face toward his. He squeezes her cheeks so hard that her shattered teeth are exposed.

"I want you to tell me," Dominic continues, still melodically whispering in her ear, "How does it feel to be treated like a real human. Do you feel special? Are you afraid of what's going to happen to your soul when you're dead?" He lifts his head and looks at her expectantly. Imogen can barely see the man inches from her face.

"Of course not. You're just some dudes hi-tech fuck doll." He declares smiling. He jams the ice pick into her eye to shatter her central crystalline processing unit. Imogen lets loose a blood curdling scream. Her body jerks and spasms violently beneath Dominic, nearly throwing him off of her. After ten seconds, she stops moving.

Frog fiddles with a small cube while sitting on what was left of the couples red couch.

"C'mon guys. Let's wrap this up," He stands and walks over to Darioux's limp body, presses a button and places the small cube on his chest. Dominic removes the slender piece of metal from Imogen's skull, wipes it off on her shirt and places it back in his jacket. The men walk toward the shattered door and continue down the hall.

Moments later, Imogen coughs and begins to turn her broken body and crawls over to where she last saw her husband. Every time she throws her broken arm forward it sends jolts of pain through her entire system. Bloody tears of coolant stream down her bruised face. All she cares about is checking to see if her husband is still alive. She feels with her good arm and finds his shoulder. He doesn't move. She feels for his neck. Nothing. Tearless sobs forces her body to shake uncontrollably. She tries to pull him to her, but she lacks the strength. All she can do is lay his swollen head on her lap and scream.

The cube on Darioux's chest tumbles to the floor. Imogen hears the thing hit the hardwood floor, but neither wonders or cares what it could be. The digital counter on the small box counts down.

Imogen forces her swollen eye to open as she looks down at the wrecked face of her husband. She tries to scream. Her vocalizer is stressed beyond its limits. No sound leaves her mouth as she tries to scream. She doesn't understand why or how people could be so vicious. She rocks back and forth while she caressed Darioux's cheek and brushes his dreads away from his face. Her head sinks in shame. Shame for what she is and shame for what terrible things she brought on a good man. She mouths the words, *"I'm so sorry,"* over and over again. She couldn't see the blast coming. A part of her no longer cares to live.

On the streets below, the people move about the sidewalks, carrying on with their daily lives. A black SUV casually pulls into the flow of traffic. Moments later, the forty-second floor, along with the forty-first and forty-third erupt in a ball of super-heated electrical fire. Debris is thrown into buildings across the street, shattering windows and even setting a few structures ablaze. The citizens on the ground shriek in terror as glass, stone, wet red and black chunks of other things rain down on them from above. Half of a bloody charred body smashes into the viewport of a sky car which causes it to veer into oncoming traffic, smashing several cars. The mangled vehicles plummet to the streets below. The sound of the cars crashing to the pavement is deafening.

Imogen's body is violently thrown from Darioux and crashes through the window. Her clothes trails fire, she collides with a stone building, shattering her shoulder before crashing down in a dirty alleyway three blocks away.

The thick dark clouds in the sky finally opens up to let loose its cold deluge upon the earth. It's like the Gods are shedding the first tears for all the innocent lives lost.

CHAPTER 11

18 Months Earlier

The thick cobalt clouds in the sky flashes with bold sparks of purple lightning. The crackling rumbles through the air as the large droplets batter the rooftops and concrete like bullets from an automatic weapon. The distant sirens of emergency vehicles echo through the narrow passages that lie in darkness, like hushed secrets between the tall buildings of the inner city. The dead end alley rests secluded, like an old relic in a forgotten city. The acrid stench of the waste permeates the narrow corridor, seeping into every crack. It saturates the cobblestone pathway with its sour smell.

A large rat cautiously inches its way toward the foreign body that dropped into its home. Its tiny, wet, bead of a nose grazes a bloody fingertip before taking a nibble. The finger jerks to life, sending the dark rodent into a swift retreat to the safety of a dark hole.

Imogen feels the jolting pain through the fibers that make up her nervous system. Her agonizing scream comes out as nothing more than a rasp. She opens her good, but damaged eye to a rainbow of vibrant colors. The world around her appears drastically distorted and grainy. She accesses her diagnostic and emergency protocols. She runs a quick check on her vitals. The internal HUD barely flickers to life. A status bar becomes visible. While she waits for the diagnostic to finish, Imogen looks down at her left hand that is about six inches away from her wrist, held together by threads. Her wedding ring is still on her finger. She tries to reach for it with what's left of her wrist, but the pain stops her. She cries out, but finds, that not only is her voice completely gone, and she can no longer produce tears.

Her body jerks involuntarily as the diagnostic is coming to a finish. A *power level critical* warning flashes in large yellow script nearly blinding her. A list populates once the scan is completed and shows that nearly all her life support systems are completely depleted, which is certain death for any synthetic, no matter how advanced. She starts shutting down all non-essential functions to conserve power.

<*What could I have possibly done to deserve this?*> She thinks to herself. Imogen watches the puddles around her dance in the rain. The way that every drop created a perfect endless loop, only to end up shattered by another, almost

identical drop, troubles her. Watching each ripple become lost in the cacophony of the storm around it is a reflection of life. Every drop was unique, yet they destroy the beauty of the drop that preceded it. The sun will eventually shine, dry up the rain and there will be no trace of it the next day. Was this the way of the universe? It's not just. A just universe wouldn't tolerate the existence of the beings who did this. <*Is this all that life holds?*> Imogen couldn't think of this anymore. She sits in the rain, dejected.

She recalls the last images of Darioux, before those thugs shattered their dreams. She remembers his glowing smile and the way his hazel eyes sparkled when he was being magnanimous. Her head falls forward as it is suddenly too heavy to hold upright. Soon her whole body slumps under its own weight. She knows that she is dying. She shuts down a few more redundant processes and then she accesses her memory core. She searches the data to find the shell that holds the memory of her first encounter with Darioux. Once she finds it, she plays the file. If this is going to be the last moments of her life, she doesn't want to spend it looking at her mangled body.

Imogen was attending a conference in New York that featured several different speakers. The topic of the

evening was atmospheric energy and how the world could benefit from the vast applications. She was standing in the back of the auditorium searching for an empty seat. She noticed a good looking man walking down the aisle with his nose in a personal data pad. She figured that the guy would just pass her by and she would continue her quest for the unoccupied seat. When the tall man bumped into her, he said a few choice words that would have made a sailor blush. That's when Darioux, who was seated nearby, stood and demanded that the rude man apologize to her. After some heated words the rude man muttered what could have passed for a child's reaction to a parents scolding then stomped off to the nearest exit.

Darioux offered an apology of his own and then offered up his own seat for her to sit, but she declined, stating that she actually had dinner plans. She was so nervous. Being a gentleman, he offered to walk her to her car, just in case the man with the PDP (Personal Data Pad) was still lingering around.

Once outside he introduced himself and offered his hand for a shake. She took it. She noticed that his hand had the perfect soft to rough ratio. She didn't notice how handsome he was inside the large and very dim auditorium. She couldn't help but blush. Once they had reached her tiny hatchback, he waited for her to enter it and start the engine. Once she was inside, he began to walk back to the conference and she noticed that he looked back more than once. Realizing that she was missing out on an opportunity, she flipped down the driver side visor and checked her make-up. She knew she had to play it cool. She didn't want to come off as skanky or desperate, but she hadn't been in a relationship for years.

She was re-applying her lipstick when a knock on the passenger side window startled her causing her to paint a red streak across her cheek. She looked up and rolled down the window and saw that her rescuer, Darioux was bent over peering in on her with a smile. She smiled back and tried to casually wipe away the thick red line on her face. She knew it was too late and that he had already got a good look at it, but she thought it would be a great topic of conversation over some chocolate mousse cake at a cozy diner she liked in the heart of downtown.

Imogen sits in the pouring rain for hours, replaying the memories of the love that was stolen from her. She wants to remember something beautiful before the lights wink out.

Detective Ed Mason arrives on the scene of the bombing. The extensive damage done, not only to the initial blast site, but the surrounding properties was astounding. The guys from the morgue have already loaded up the few bodies that were ejected from the building. There were a few large black bags and far too many small bags. He'll have to go over the photos of that mess later. The gaping maw in the blasts origin still smokes, even though the firefighting crew extinguished the blaze. The crashed vehicles in the street look as if they've been put through a meat grinder a few times, before finally being torched with some thermite.

Mason pulls up the public records from his wet-drive and begins to enter the main building where he's met by a young officer. He's lead to the scene by the thin chinned young man, who looks like he's been around the world a few times. The kid says nothing. The distant stare in his eyes tells Mason that what he is going to see is pretty gruesome.

The climb up the many flights of steps makes Eddie's thighs burn, but he doesn't complain. He wouldn't complain. It was a small price to pay to help those who had lost loved ones. Besides, if they burn, that only means that he needed the workout.

The smell of burnt metals and plastics is odd, but it was flavored with the smell of burned meat and Mason knows that it's not the good kind you get at a fancy sit down restaurant. The young cop leads him to the yellow holographic police tape then stops as if he's afraid to go in. Mason looks at the man questioningly.

"That bad?" Mason says. The young cop says nothing. Mason walks through the tape. A chip in his badge allows him to enter without receiving a debilitating shock.

The blackened apartment is barely recognizable as a living space. Most of what filled the living area was either charred or turned to ash instantly. Mason was careful not to get in the way of the crime scene photographers. He logged potential evidence on his wet-drive while he gingerly picks his way through the weakened and partially collapsed floor of the apartment. Mason maintains a professional calm throughout the initial look over, but once he comes across a nursery and the things belonging to a child, his whole mood shifted to seething rage. His thumb rolls over his scarred wedding band. Now was not a time to show nerves. He did well to hide it.

The charred mobile and baby toys makes his eyes water. He had seen too many crime scenes where children were caught in the crossfire.

<What the hell is wrong with people?> He once again brings up the public records on his wet-drive and finds that the couple who lived here had just adopted a child. The good news was that the child had never made it here and was safe within the walls of the adoption agency. Mason made a mental note to check the place out for potential leads. On his way back through the family room, he notices that something extremely dense was thrown by the blast through the window. On closer inspection, his onboard statistics calculated several trajectories based on the estimated weight of the object. He only needs to settle on one. He zeroes in on the point of impact on the façade of a distant building.

"I need a unit at these positions ASAP to collect potential evidence. I'm marking the position on the units HUD." Scanning the exit point, he notices some fibers and produces an evidence collection kit, "Let me know what you find," he added as he places the fibers in a plastic bag.

Mason makes one last visually recorded sweep of the burned out scene, taking note of a victim in the center of the room. The person lying on the floor looks like an ash sculpture. Mason offers a moment of silence, before moving on to the rest of the affected floors. Within the other apartments, the residents weren't as unlucky as what appeared to be targets in the homicide. Mason accesses the buildings internal security system then pulls the data recorded for last seventy-two hours. He'll look over that a little later. Hopefully something good will come of it. He'll grab the city's data once he is back at the precinct.

"Hey Ed!" a female voice from his internal com calls.

"Go ahead," he replies as he makes his way down to the ground floor of the building.

"I got a few things here," the woman says, then adds, "You'll want to see this, but I'm sending you a vid feed now."

The images streaming through the video connection show a drying pool of what appears to be blood in a dark unkempt alley. The female officer on the scene highlights some disembodied wires and scorched cloths. Mason had seen those types of wires before. He knows that they could belong to a syn. He has a sneaking suspicion that this explosion was more than just an act of terror.

"Collect samples and cordon off the area. I'm on my way," Mason says.

"Copy that," says the officer recording the scene.

Mason begins taking the steps two at a time and cursing the maintenance guy for not having the lifts up and running yet.

Once on the scene, Mason is greeted by the officer that sent him the feed.

"We've found several items of interest," she says. "Hair, scraps of clothing, but this isn't blood," she adds.

Mason scans the drying crimson pool for DNA, but the analysis reveals an organic chemical compound of ethylene glycol and other organics.

"Coolant," Mason mutters.

The officer who took charge of maintaining the integrity of the crime scene decides now is a good time to speak, "Synthetic sir."

Mason nods without looking at the speaker and waves his hand in an, *I got it* gesture.

"You got the bag of hair?" Mason asks. The female officer hands him the clear bag containing the chocolate colored threads. He scans the thin dark fibers. The results confirm his and the young upstart officers hypothesis.

The hairs are made of a space age nano-carbon that repairs itself with microscopic spiders when damaged. Only the last generation of syn had hair that actually grew and skeletons that knit themselves back together. They almost healed as well as a normal human would. Mason stuffs the bag containing the hair in his collection kit and stands.

"Where are you now?" Mason's eyes scan the narrow space suspiciously. He turns to look behind him in case he missed anything while coming into this dark hole. It doesn't surprise him that the syn was gone. Somebody probably found it and was going to make big money on the scrap.

"Sir," the female officer huffs, "If you are looking for tracks or debris, there are none." She laces her fingers around the back of her neck. She looks around once more to ensure that she had not missed anything so she would feel comfortable with her statement.

Mason eyes the young woman appreciatively then nods. She has an eye on her. The fact that she was able to distinguish the advanced coolant from blood is impressive. The rookie didn't even have implants. Mason glances at the officer's badge, looking for a name. A smiley face sticker rests over top of her shield.

"I didn't catch your name," Mason says, knowing that she never announced her name.

The woman places her hands on her kit belt with an attitude, "What's it to ya pops?"

CHAPTER 12

Present Day

Jaina Trent tries repeatedly to open her eyes, before realizing that they are indeed open. There just wasn't anything to see. The room she finds herself in is completely devoid of light. The last thing she remembers is screaming in the trunk of a car. Before that, she was asleep in her apartment her father pays the rent on. She had been waiting to hear back from an officer that had contacted her earlier the day before. Her throat is dry and there is a steady, icy current of air blowing from what must be a vent above. She starts to panic. Her heart begins to thump so hard that she can hear its deafening beats in her ears. The constant *thump, thump,* of her heart drowns out everything else, so she didn't realize that the high pitch screaming was coming from her.

She takes a couple of cautious steps backward to find a wall. She bumps into something hard then falls to the floor with a shriek. Her hip is throbbing. She nearly brains herself on the hard floor, but the stinging in her hand reminds her of what it had cost to keep her face pretty. Whatever she knocked her hip on must be bolted down because it did not budge when she tripped over it. She inches forward to feel the thing that she fell over when the lights snap on. The sudden illumination burns her eyes causing her other senses to ache.

Blinded, Jaina raises her hands to shield her eyes. The sound of a latch turning echoes in the small room. The door opens. Jaina squints at the doorway, trying to see who is coming in. She spots a giant of a man in an olive drab military jacket walking in. The blank stare in his eyes makes Jaina's heart stop mid beat. He's holding what looks like a roll of industrial tape. Jaina shuffles back against the wall.

"What do you want?" She screams hoarsely. All she thinks is how this is the end.

The man doesn't say a word, instead he reaches out and grabs a giant handful of her orange hair. Jaina tries to break free, but the man's grip is solid. She beats on his fist, but she might as well be a fly trying to pull away from some sticky tape. He jerks her around to show her that there isn't a thing she could do to get away. Jaina yelps as the man drags her to the metal chair. She can feel some of her hair rip free of the roots in her scalp as she is briefly lifted, then shoved down into the cold seat. The man, who she can now see has a circular scar on his cheek, shoots her an icy, emotionless glare. He begins to wrap the tape around her body and the chair.

"Who are you?" She says, but she might as well be talking to a wall, because the man doesn't even look in her direction. "What do you want?" she asks frantically. The man just tears off the tape from the roll and walks back out of the room. She hears the lock in the windowless door click home.

Jaina tests the sticky bonds only to find that she can't move but a few inches in either direction. Her thick eyeliner trails down her face, following the path that her tears have already set. The cold air from above does nothing but send shivers through her body when it touches the sweat that coats her skin. She cries aloud. She doesn't notice the small bubble camera mounted behind thick glass in the corner of the room. She moves her body in quick jerky motions trying to weaken the grip of the tape binding her in the chair.

David Jennings watches the young woman from a monitor in his home office. He rolls a small, pear shaped, sapphire, apothecary jar no bigger than his thumb in his hands. The jar contains a lock of his mother's hair. Engraved metal caps the tiny bottle. Intricate metallic weaves wrap around the base. The platinum catches the light with every roll of his fingers. He looks away from the monitor and stares through the small bottle with glassy eyes. The bound blonde hair within the tiny flask captivates him and sends him back in time. Visions of his younger brother sitting on his mother's lap deflate him.

He breathes in deeply through his nose and out through his mouth, imagining that he is releasing those negative thoughts in the space around him. He looks back at the monitor, completely disgusted with the crying woman. He knows her father, Mr. Trent who offered to donate to the cause in exchange for favors. David took his money, but had ideas of his own.

David knows that the girl in the room has no idea why she is here. Hell, David would be amazed if the girl knew how to cook her own food.

The lamps on the wall are mainly for decoration and don't offer much light from their tiny bulbs. The fireplace spits and cracks as the wood is consumed. He sips a glass of whiskey, contemplating what he should do with the girl. Now that she has been brought to his private interrogation room she couldn't leave. He didn't need her. He had the video off of Francis's hard drive. He knows that a redheaded *thing* came into the modification shop and killed Francis. David wasn't shocked that Francis had spilled the beans on everyone.

"At least the little fucker had enough presence of mind to leave my name off his lips," he mutters to the bottle. David leans back in his leather chair and sighs to himself. He loses his focus to deep recollections of the past.

The stained glass window offers a pleasant light display on the far wall as the sun sets. David focuses on the splash of color across from him.

A couple of knocks on the thick wood door brings David back to the present. He sets the tiny bulb-like jar in front of an old framed photo on his desk. He hates when others see him nerved out. Control was the key to success. <*People see that you are in control and they respect you. They follow you.*> David composes himself in a matter of seconds.

"Come in," David says. The hulking man strolls into the room. David offers him a drink and a cigar. Pete declines the smoke but takes the whiskey.

"What do you want to do with the girl?" Pete asks before taking a drink. The burn of the aged liquor in his throat makes him exhale heavily.

David turns his attention back to the monitor. "I'm not sure yet, my friend."

Pete takes another swig, "I'll get ahold of Dominic and let him know what's up with this fucking robot." Pete walks over to the bar and pours himself another drink then adds, "It's funny that Frog gave her away by mentioning Desirae," Pete caps the bottle and drinks some more of the golden liquid. He moves to the chair opposite David and takes a seat. "We only used that spineless bitch on that one job," Pete growls.

David glides back and forth in his comfortable chair remembering the interview of the *green* girl, "Do we know where she is nowa days?"

Pete glares at the monitor for a long moment, "Dom may know. He tends to keep up on shit like that," he says, then leans back into the seat. He watches the girl rocking back and forth like she thought moving frantically was going break the concrete adhesive.

Pete was about to bring up the unfortunate girl in the soundproof interrogation room when David takes a long draw from his cigar, points at the screen and chuckles to himself. Pete study's the man. Pete had a gift for taking care of unsavory business and had an idea of what his boss was going to say.

"I thought about letting her go. But that would just be stupid," David infers. "How about you put a bullet in her brain and make it look like this robot is responsible."

Pete huffs in amusement then finishes his drink in one gulp. He stands and turns to finish the girl off, but David calls out, "Give her a few days," he continued, "I want to have a little chat with her first." Roberts chuckles over his shoulder as he leaves the large room.

CHAPTER 13

18 Months Earlier

Blake struggles to get the one hundred-twenty five pound synthetic out of his car. He wasn't worried about being tracked by the city's security system, he made sure to use his jammer when he saw the android fall into the alley. The plastic tarp wrapped around the droid is slick with moisture from the earlier storm. He nearly drops the thing trying to open the door to the apartment building. A couple walking down the street eyes Blake suspiciously. He smiles and nods, knowing that he must look like he's carrying a dead body. Well, he is. Kind of.

By the time he got to her, it seemed that she had shut down all major systems and was in a hibernation mode.

After a frustrating waddle to the elevator and down the hall, he finally gets the droid into his apartment. He gently places the covered synthetic on floor. Blake turns on the overhead light, then he dashes over to his computer to ensure that his rare little find would go unnoticed. He hacks into the close captioned security network and replaces the jammed video with some old looped footage from a previous week.

After covering his tracks, Blake turns his attention to the nearly destroyed synthetic and unwraps it. Gently he rolls the female body over to pull the tarp away. The top of her crusted shirt tears away. Blake winces and covers up the droids nakedness. He doesn't want to damage it further so he moves slowly. After tossing the large scrap of plastic to the side, he begins to probe, searching for its access panel.

He can't believe that he has his little hands on an Advanced Human, Gen X Synthetic. There are only so many left on the planet. It was like having a tiger cub, if they were still around, in his apartment. He had never seen an A.H. Gen X syn before. The manufacturers only produced a couple hundred of these before they were banned.

There is so much damage to the exterior. Burnt flakes of faux skin fall away from the badly damaged face and body. He notices the swelling and bruising on the artificial flesh, astonished that the last synthetic generation were so *evolved*.

Dried clumps of dirt mixed with ruby colored cooling fluid is so thickly caked to her skin that he can't find the exact points he's looking for. He hops to his feet and retrieves a damp rag from the kitchen. Blake uses his sleeve to wipe the sweat from his brow, then clears the fog from his glasses. The super rare marvel lying in a heap before him makes his palms clammy. He uses the damp rag to wash away the now drying coolant from her face and body. He grabs a few moist wipes and uses them to clean up the blackened scorch and scrape marks all over her face. Sufficiently removing the crusted debris from her face, Blake pauses. Despite the extensive damage, Blake admires her. It wasn't the craftsmanship that went in to creating this machine, it was something he couldn't place his finger on.

Moving past his period of admiration he resumes his search of the panel. Not finding the access points on the front side of the syn, he gingerly turns the badly burned droid over on her stomach to continue the search for the access panel. He digs a fine handheld CT scanner tool out of his little rollout tool kit and watches the monitor closely for the pressure points that will unlock the hatch. After a few passes, he spots the points and begins pressing in specific patterns he had read about in articles. A few failed attempts and a grumble later he hits the right combination. The panel cracks with a hiss. He rubs his hands together in excitement then dries his palms on his pants. He slides the damaged cover over.

Many of the flimsy chips are damaged beyond repair, but the syn is still functional. He didn't understand how it could still be operational, but he is sure glad that it is. A cursory inspection tells him that he would need to replace many if not all of the internal hardware, if he wanted to see it up and running. Blake finds the unlock switches for the main processor. He flips the little levers, then jumps, startled, as a small panel pops up on the back of the droid's head. Blake lifts the panel. What he finds completely bewilders him. The processor is completely destroyed. Cracks run through and around the spherical amber quartz crystal. He returns his attention to the larger back panel, thinking that he may have missed another processor, but he finds none.

"What the hell," he mutters in confusion. He digs a little deeper, expecting to find another CPU stashed away in its chest. Again, he finds nothing but some intact memory drives, damaged cooling systems, melted wires and flimsy chips. "How are you still operational?" he asks, not really expecting the syn to respond.

Blake closes the head panel, confused. He turns to his computer and does some research on the Gen X models, hoping to find some answers there.

After reading more than a handful of articles, Blake finds no reason as to why the synthetic on the floor before him should still be functioning. Without its brain it should be a shell. He would have to replace the CPU eventually. There is just no way around that. He'll have to save its essential functions. He was damn good with code, but he didn't think he would be able to replicate the syn's crucial background functions.

Digging in his tool kit, Blake produces some link cables and connects the syn's memory drives to his computer's jack. He runs through a series of encrypted files to find the androids memory core. He downloads all the background processes. Finding actual *life memories* saved, he downloads those as well. He decrypts the files so that his monitor can display the visual data. He searches for the most recent logged file to find out what the hell happened to her. He plays the memory. The file loads and is just about to play when syn starts screaming in an ear splitting mechanical rasp and jerking violently.

"Shit!" Blake yells in surprise. He tumbles out of his chair, grabbing its shoulders in an attempt to steady the spastic robot. The battered body of the droid rolls on the floor, pleading for mercy and help. Blake doesn't understand.

<*Stop what?*> Blake thinks, but he's sure he knows the answer. The syn's thrashing causes shelves on the walls to shake and collectable action figures to tumble off their perches to the carpeted floor.

Blake jumps on his PC and tries to shut down its motor functions. After a few moments he manages to stop the obviously traumatized machine's flailing.

"What the fuck happened to you?" the question gnaws at his mind like an itch he can't reach. The frozen expression of desolation in the poor things face sends chills running up Blake's spine. The haunted face burned itself in his mind. Unable to look and wonder anymore, he turns back to the monitors, making sure that he has successfully locked up its limbs. He presses play. The memory from the syn's perspective, shows it crying in the dirty alley where he picked it up. He scrubs through the memory until he gets to a spot where he finds her fixing a baby's room and resumes watching from there.

Through her eyes and ears he can hear the buzzer ring, muffled voices talking and then the unimaginable horror that followed.

After watching the gruesome murder, Blake leans back in his desk chair, wiping the tears from his cheeks with his shirt. The realization that he made her relive that as he watched, was almost overpowering. He collapses into his chair weeping uncontrollably for what felt like a lifetime. Eyes red and sore, he takes a moment to compose himself. He couldn't let that memory remain. He had to purge that pain from her mind in the hopes that it would give her some peace. It just seems like the human thing to do.

"Don't worry little lady," he says as he moves toward his keyboard, "I'm going to erase your memory and fix you up."

He begins punching in commands into his computer but stops when the machine gasps.

"Please don't erase that, yet," she says in a calm but overly stressed voice.

Blake turns around as fast as his body would allow him. The syn is looking at him with its one good eye. The glassy orb silently pleads. A thick stream of moisture rolls down her face when she blinks. Blake wipes a tear of his own away and sniffs. The syn's mouth opens, but no sound is produced. Her face scrunches in despair. Her chest heaves, obviously heartbroken from her trauma.

"Please, don't erase that memory," she repeats. The determination in her voice is grim, but it's there like a beacon of hope. The hope was weary, but it is there.

Blake is speechless. He blinks repeatedly trying to clear the tears from his eyes but resorts to using his hands to wipe his eyes clear. He unlocks her limbs then kneels down beside her. He reaches around her, unhooks the link cables from her back and closes her back panel.

"You need to conserve power," he says as a mother tending a sick child would. She nods and lets her head drift down to the soft carpet.

The long moment feels like an eternity of silence as she lay there softly crying. Blake sits stunned.

"Will you help me?" she asks, then continues, "Can you fix me?" the hopeful look in her eye begins to quiver. Hopeless tears fill in around her eye.

Blake tries to clear his dry throat before responding and it seems like she took his hesitation as a negative response. With some effort, Imogen turns her head to look at the ceiling as if to gain the courage to weather the answer he might give.

"Can you fix me?" she repeats with shaky resolve.

Blake slowly nods then says, "I know a guy,"

Imogen interrupts him, "No," she says raising her head with deep concern. "No one else should know about me," she continues as she lets her head rest on the carpet again. Imogen feels a profound emptiness. The total rejection of the world had placed something cold deep within her chest. She quickly falls into a state of self-loathing and self-recrimination, "No one needs to be in danger because of me." After a long pause, a flash of anger plays over her face, "If you can just fix me up, I'll be out of your hair. I don't want to be your burden."

Blake sits back, resting on the soft carpet, "I want to help you." He wipes away a stray tear then continues, "I'll help until I can't anymore. What they did to you," he pauses, searching for the words and waiting until his voice is strong again, "It's unspeakable and unforgivable."

Imogen's lip quivers. She pushes the image of Darioux, on his back bloodied and dying away. She nor Blake look at each other, allowing the other the time to mourn. The deep chasm of overflowing sorrow threatens to take hold of Imogen and drag her down to its hopeless depths once more. *No.* She wouldn't let that happen. She couldn't. She would nurture those seeds of sadness until they were a mature creature of unrelenting cold rage. Yes. That's how she would get through this. That was the only way she would survive this.

"How are you still alive?" Blake asks incredulous.

Imogen smiles at the unintended implication of the question. She focuses on it and most particularly on the word, *alive*. "I am, alive," she affirms. "I sleep, feel and hurt just like anyone else. I had dreams and aspirations of a future filled with love," she continued. All she wanted to do was to live her life in peace. Her chin quivers, "Why was that not enough?" she growls in anger. "My differences from biological flesh, bone and blood really isn't that much different, yet I'm considered an abomination! Something less than the human counterparts that created me." She clenches her teeth. "They are not my God," she says as her anger melts into despair. She breathes in deeply and pauses for a moment. In the silence, she begins to hate herself for being what she is.

With a great deal of effort she turns to her side, away from Blake. She didn't know this man, and yet, she was pouring her heart out. She focuses on the fibers of the eggshell colored carpet, contemplating her next words. "Because I am not a true descendent of the human herd, I am misunderstood and viewed with hatred and fear," she says as her grief pours out. The concoction of emotions she feels swirling in her chest are sharp and deeply painful. "I only wanted to fulfill my dreams. They were the same dreams of any other woman," she cries.

Blake wipes more warm tears from his eyes.

"I wanted to have a child with my husband. I wanted to hold *my* child," Imogen wails. "Why was that so wrong?" she screams as a bloody tear leaves her eye to fall on the white carpet.

Blake's head hangs low as he quietly sobs. He feels that he should say something, anything. The words of condolences and apologetic sympathies that race through his mind seem insignificant. He feels completely helpless and as a part of the human race, partially to blame for what has happened to this *woman*. She lies in ruin on his living room floor because of a chauvinistic ideal.

Blake gingerly places his hand on Imogen's shoulder and gently squeezes. He feels that the gesture is lacking the feeling needed that any clever words of meaning could offer. It's all he's got. Words seem to have lost all meaning.

Imogen curls her legs up to her chest and cries harder. The embrace of another individual during this time of great doubt and inner turmoil, no matter how small, allows the arduous healing process to begin. In this moment, Imogen didn't feel so alone.

CHAPTER 14

Present Day

Mason pinches the bridge of his nose between his eyes as he finishes up the last of the report concerning the death of Dr. Westfield. He takes a sip of his tepid coffee and seems to enjoy the flavor now that most of the heat has left it. He looks at his watch. It's not even midday and he's ready to go home, drink, then sleep and forget that the world even exists. He leans back in his chair and watches the other officers in the department. When a case or the world seems to be closing in around him, he likes to play a little mental game. The game consists of trying to guess why each one looks that much closer to completely breaking down. It reminds him that he's not just a cynical bastard. He doesn't pay much attention to the *noobs* anymore. Their optimistic personalities and unrealistic view of the world reeks like ground beef left in a hot car for a week. He focuses on the detectives that have been on the job too long. The cops that have seen too much to ever have a good night's sleep again. He wonders how long it will take before he's like them; tired, hopeless and bitter. For all he knows, he's already lost his marbles and he has already developed a healthy rage for the world.

It wasn't long after the terror bombing that his wife and daughter were killed by a damned teen, high on stim sticks. It's been one shitty spiral after another since then.

"Two out of three. If this was the lottery, I'd be set," he mumbles to himself. Mason looks down at the seemingly unorganized clutter on his desk, wondering if he'd already fallen into that bottomless pit of emotional lethargy. He looks at his hands. Every rough callus and hard line tells a story of so many personal pitfalls and little to no gain.

A beep on his internal *HUD* breaks him free from his deep introspection. He mentally terminates the beeping between his ears that notifies him that the visual data from Francis's hard drive is ready to view. He opens the containing folder and begins to search the files. It doesn't take long to realize that it has been tampered with and much of the information had been erased.

"What the hell," Mason mutters as he flicks through file after file of deleted data. He scrolls down and notices that the deletion is happening as he is viewing the files. Thinking quickly he saves a copy of what remains to his wet-drive, then disconnects from the Police Network to avoid further loss of evidence. Someone in the department was covering up evidence. Someone was dirty.

Mason almost stands and yells out in anger, but he manages to stay seated. He quiets his growing rage. He reaches out for his cooled coffee and takes a sip to cover his inspection of the officers around him. Nothing seems out of place. Everybody has that same hard look. Well, almost everybody. The fucking *noobs* still carried on with their youthful, un-poisoned optimism.

Slowly, Mason takes a final gulp of dark caffeine goodness, then grabs his coat. He heads toward Chief Galarza's office. The Chief was hard, but she was fair. She wouldn't take too kindly of having a dirty cop in her building.

Just as he turns the corner his partner, Vivian almost runs him over. Her face is flush and she has her coat buttoned up. Her face has a thin sheen of sweat as if she were running. Mason didn't miss that and he also didn't miss that she's ready to go.

"We've got a call," she says as she heads for the elevator.

"Okay," Mason replies. He waits for further explanation.

She turns and studies his face. Vivian wasn't sure how to take all the nonverbal cues that were screaming in her face, "We found Frog's employee." Vivian pulls her pony tail out from between her back and her coat.

Mason slides into his coat and heads toward the garage. He hates having to wait to report to the Chief, but he'll let her know that the department has a rat. Maybe this will give him some time to puzzle it out. "Good," He says, "I'd like to ask her a few things."

Vivian huffs in reply.

"What?" Mason says.

Vivian follows him out the office and into the cramped lift, "She's dead," Vivian says dryly. Mason's glare goes cold.

◊

Twenty minutes later, Mason and Vivian arrive at a large inner city park. Eddie takes note of the parents carrying sleds and shuffling their young children away. The police officers on the scene had set up a perimeter around the dead body. The detectives make their way to the uniformed coroners.

"What do ya got?" Mason questions as he and his partner approach the scene.

"Twenty-something female," the coroner says, "Shot in the left temple. She's been dead less than eight hours." The man had no emotion. He could have been giving directions to a yuppie on how to find the nearest coffee shop. Mason had to stop himself from wondering why he was almost emotionless.

What the hell had he fallen into? This girl belonged to a wealthy family and someone was going to answer for this. Mason wondered how long it would take before there was a massive witch hunt. Phillip Trent wasn't a forgiving man.

"Anyone around here know how she got here?" Vivian asks.

The officer shakes his head, "Nah. Unless we missed someone who was here in the wee early hours of the morning."

It looks to Mason, as if she was just dumped in this spot with no regard to how her body fell. Jaina Trent lay in an awkward position in the snow. Her shoes are gone and it looks like she is still in her night clothes. A layer of frost nips at her hardening bruised skin. Her eyes. The poor girl's eyes are just staring blankly into open space. It chills Mason's soul more than the freezing wind ever could.

"What a way to spend the day before Christmas, huh?" The officer chuckles.

"Do we know what kind of gun was used?" Vivian asks, completely ignoring the man's comment.

Mason answers her question before the coroner could speak, "Pulse pistol. The same that was used to off Frog."

The coroner presents a plastic bag containing a single red hair, "It's synthetic." He says. Vivian takes the bag and examines the lone strand.

Mason was about to stand and let the forensics team do their job, but he notices a couple bits of white fibers caught in her teeth. "What do we have here?" He says as he slips on his gloves and cautiously removes the fibers from her mouth. He places them into a plastic bag.

"What'd you get old man?" Vivian asks.

Mason tucks the fibers into his collection kit and replies, "Probably nothin' but you never know."

Vivian squints then pulls out her tablet and begins to write a report. Mason can tell that she didn't like being left out of the loop, but he had to be careful what he shared with anyone.

"It looked like some clothing thread or something," he says to ease her mind. "Hey, Viv." She doesn't look up from her report, "Do you mind taking the wheel on the way back?" Mason asks.

"You okay old man?" Vivian responds peering down over her tablet at him.

"Yeah. I've just got a splitting headache," he says rubbing the side of his head.

Sitting in the passenger seat, Mason leans back, shuts his eyes and pulls up the data files from Frog's hard drive. He knows that he has about a half hour before they get back to the station, so he plays the last recorded video at double the speed.

"You okay geezer?" Vivian mocks. Mason responds with a grunt. He watches through Frog's eyes, as Jaina works around the shop. He skips ahead to the evening data. Mason plays the video when Frog follows Jaina to the bathroom and begins to beat her. Mason didn't bother to hide the disgust on his face. If Vivian asked, he could always say it was because of the headache. Finally he got to the part where Jaina, looks at something behind Francis and then there is a crash and he turns around. There in front of him is a redheaded woman. Mason makes a connection with the red hair to the murdered girl. For a moment he believes he knows who had killed the Trent girl, but he is completely blindsided when the redhead makes Francis release her.

<Why release her to just kill her later? Oh this stinks of conspiracy.>

Vivian periodically sneaks peeks at her partner as he sits with his head back in the seat. She wonders if she should offer him some pain meds, but decides against it. She figures that if he wanted them, he'd ask.

<He probably likes the pain,> she thinks to herself. Usually Mason would use this time to gripe about the state of society and how everything is falling apart, headache or not. She begun to seriously wonder what he was doing.

"Hey boss. Want a cup of java?" she asks. Mason doesn't even offer his typical caffeine junky sounds of pleasure. "Hey! Old man!" she hollers.

Mason pops forward, "Wha...!" he yelps in surprise. He looks at Vivian's scrunched face, wondering what the hell her problem was.

Vivian glares at him, "What the hell was that all about back there?" she asks, throwing all subtlety out the window.

Mason rubs his face in feigned exhaustion, "I'm just tired," he says.

Vivian returns her gaze back to the road before her, unsatisfied with his response. "I know you disconnected from the network back at the station," she asserts, concern lining her tone.

Mason opens his eyes and shrugs, waiting to see how far she'll go.

"I also know that someone deleted the files from Frog's memory bank." Vivian reveals uncertainly. Vivian glances at him, trying to get a read on his thoughts. "I didn't get a chance to view or save any of it."

Mason stares out the window, "I didn't get to see any of it either," The car comes to a stop at a traffic light.

"What's the plan Eddie?" She asks, giving him all her attention.

Mason continues to look at the people outside. "I don't know. Somebody is obviously covering up something," Mason turns to look Vivian in the eyes. He scans them for anything that may be disingenuous, "The question is, if it's worth dying for?" They say nothing for a long moment. A horn honks impatiently from behind and Vivian takes the wheel again and gently eases down on the accelerator.

Eddie Mason continues his people gazing as they drive through the city. He can't get the redheaded synthetic woman out of his head.

<He thought he had killed her> he thinks.
<That explains a lot.> Mason would have to look up
the names Frog had given the redhead, once he
had a secure connection to the net. The name
Desirae Deponet rang some bells in his memory,
but he couldn't place a face to it. *<Find her. Find the
Syn.>* he thought as he peered out the window.

There were still a few data files belonging
to the former Seeker that Mason could sift through
for more clues as to why this droid is out for
blood. Looking down at his hands he can't help
but think that maybe Frog and his accomplices
deserve what is coming their way.

Mason had seen the monstrous tactics these
bounty hunters that The Chosen employed had
used on synthetics when they found them. He
thought that even he'd seek retribution if he had
survived an attack from those bastards. Mason
squashes that thought process, though, he knows
that he'll have to get some answers before he can
make any assumptions. Things were getting hairy
real fast. The pieces of the puzzle were swirling in
his mind and spinning into place, but they were
coming together too slow–too slow. The entire
situation was fouled up and if there was a way to
fix it, he doesn't know what it is.

"When we get back, I want to talk to
Melody about the tampered files. She may be able
to help," Vivian breaks the silence.

"Maybe. We need some more evidence if
we're going to tell her that a rat's nibbling away at

our data," Mason suggests. He knows that he lied. Vivian probably knows that he's blowing smoke as well. The fact that evidence is being deleted is enough to launch a full scale investigation and everyone would have a microscope on their ass.

<Maybe that would be a good thing?> Mason rubs his eyes, "Never mind. Tell Galarza. She needs to know," Mason reconsiders. He steals a glance at Vivian, trying to catch some hint of worry, but finds nothing but a dispassionate expression.

CHAPTER 15

Present Day

Imogen surges through the dense crowd of the technology convention trying to get back to the booth, where she had left Blake. She hopes he is still talking with his old friend, Kevin. Her cheeks are flush with overwhelming emotion, but she tries to remain calm and focused, despite having lost her target.

<What were you really going to do? Drown him in a bathroom stall.> She thinks to herself. Though, the thought of a piece of shit like Dominic face down and dead in dirty toilet water did put a smile on her face. The thought calmed her down a bit and none too soon, because she found Blake and Kevin looking around aimlessly, searching for her.

"Where'd you go?" Blake asks quizzically.

She playfully tilts her head to the side and says, "None of your business." Before Blake or Kevin could respond, Imogen asks, "Hey! Do you happen to have that little *charm* you showed me the other day?" Imogen dances around like a child waiting to receive some candy. Her boots squeak on the polished tile floor. The odd smile on her face was also a big change from impassive mood she had been in ten minutes before.

Blake squints slightly not understanding her question, "What *charm?*" he questions.

Imogen smiles at Kevin trying to hide her impatience, then turns back to Blake and calmly says, "You know. The one that shows me *things?*"

For a moment Blake had no idea what she was talking about and Imogen was about to scream, *"Tracker!"* when his eyes popped open wide. "Oh!" he blurts. "I left it at the house," he says, regret painfully visible in his expression. Imogen takes a deep breath. She was only mildly upset. After all, she had left her *hand cannon* at the apartment as well.

"Well, damn," she says, "I'll have to go and get it. I want to show a friend of mine what it can do."

Kevin looks at the *"siblings"* as they exchange odd looks to one another, "I can give you a ride," he chimes.

Blake was about to answer his friend and probably look like an ass doing it.

"Oh! That's so sweet. It would help get me there faster, but you've got your booth to run," Imogen defuses him. She turns to Blake then continues with a smile, "Plus you two boys need to catch up. I'll be okay, but thanks anyway."

Imogen begins to turn and walk away with such haste that Blake can't help but worry for her safety. He knows she's not thinking things through.

Imogen exits the large convention center and stops on the busy sidewalk. She begins searching for any indication of the direction Dominic had gone. She thinks of using infrared vision, but with so many people going about their daily lives, it would be impossible to single out any one set of footprints in the thin layer of frost that coated the sidewalk. She relaxes herself with the knowledge that there is a nice tracking monitor at Blake's apartment, so she calmly, but quickly, walks home.

Imogen tunes out the racket from the busy traffic in the streets and the people walking every which way. She feels she can't move fast enough to find Dominic. She thought about hailing a cab, but if things went south she didn't want anyone knowing where she rested her head at night. She brushes her hair away from her eyes and notices that the large television screen mounted on one of the large skyscrapers is broadcasting a news segment. The images on the screen depict the last war between man and machine. It shows forty year old stock war footage of soldiers with big guns scrambling through an old building, killing unarmed synthetics. Some were artificial children.

The next clip was of a woman shielding what must have been her young son from a wave of tracer bullets fired from synthetic soldiers. At the bottom of the large surface, text scrolls across that reads, *"Did we do the right thing?"* referring to the mass destruction of synthetic beings everywhere. On a side panel of the giant screen, a roster of countries that have or are going to lift the ban on synthetics are shown. On the other side, a scrolling list created by the humanist group, Chosen, displays reasons why the robotic beings are dangerous. In big bold letters, Imogen reads, *"They weren't created by God."* She laughs and shakes her head.

<*Religion is not a weapon.*> she thinks to herself with dark humor, then continues walking.

Once his feet hit the ground, Dominic takes off running. He moves as fast as his stocky body will allow him toward the busy street. He circles around the large building, making sure to keep an eye out for the redhead that was following him. Once in the relative safety of his car, he thumbs the little fleshy button behind his ear, "Call David!" He presses the ignition and the vehicle hums to life. Frantically Dominic searches all that he can see for any sign of the redheaded woman. Not seeing her, he pulls out into traffic.

"Hello Dominic," David answers in a cheerful voice on the other end.

Before Jennings can utter another word he is cut off by the angry and panic stricken voice of Dominic, "Cut the shit Dave! I think I've stumbled on to something." His voice is labored from the little running he did to get to his car.

David snickers at the remark, "I think I have as well ol' friend."

Dominic drives frantically through traffic, periodically checking his rear view cam for signs of a possible tail, "Some creepy fucking bitch was scoping me out," Dominic says.

"She wouldn't happen to be a petite sultry redhead would she?" David asks with renewed interest.

The sense of urgency leaves Dominic and is replaced by a niggling curiosity, "How'd you know? Did you get Frog's hard drive?"

David laughs, much to the dismay of Dominic. "Oh I got it. Just head *home*. I'm sending you some back up," Jennings says in a phlegmatic tone. Dominic Smiles and nods, relieved that he won't go the same way as his now deceased co-worker.

◊

Once Imogen gets to the apartment door and unlocks it. She sprints toward a polished metal case under the coffee table and opens it. She pulls out her unregistered *Mk6* pulse pistol and tucks it in her belt. The cold metal causes goose flesh to rise once it touches the small of her back. She moves to Blake's desk and grabs the tiny monitor. She powers it on to ensure that it is working properly. Once the home screen and background satellite link-ups are complete, a digital layout of the city populates and marks her position with a tiny purple arrow. A few short moments later, she is rewarded with a *Ping* noise that marks Dominic all the way across town as a green dot.

"Got you. You son of a bitch," she says smiling an impish grin. She shoves the small device in her coat pocket and heads for the door. As she makes her way down the hall to the lift, she runs through a series of commands that will allow her to link up with the device and populate a mini map on her HUD.

Back out on the cold winter streets, Imogen feels her artificial *heart*, pumping hard to force coolant throughout her body. She can't help but take notice of the rush. It hits her in an unexpected way. She feels a sense of excitement for the hunt. She feels like an apex predator skulking after her prey. She knows that she had spooked him back at the convention center. He should be scared. There was going to be no clemency for him or any of the other iniquitous monsters that stole her and Darioux's life.

The small dot, that marked Dominic for death came to a rest at a building on *Plymouth ave* in a rundown part of town. The estimated time of arrival says that she'd reach her destination within forty minutes. Imogen wanted desperately to hail one of the many cabs on the street, so she could wipe the stain that is Dominic Vespucci from this earth, but her brisk pace would have to do. Besides, he is the one living on borrowed time and she has all the time in the world.

As Imogen walks through the street, she can't help but be bombarded by all the advertising for the New Year's celebration. Flashing lights with the words *"Happy New Year"* or *"What's your resolution?"* adorn the windows of the various shops. Banners hanging from street lamps, further promoting the coming festivities, just in case the pedestrians missed all the flashing lights.

Imogen thinks about her little resolution. The memory of the start of this quest for justice aches in her chest but, then she thinks about what she was going to do to the monsters that killed her husband. It brought a devilish smile to her lips.

CHAPTER 16

Present Day

Imogen arrives at the six story high brick and mortar building just as the sun is beginning to sink into the horizon. To her right, just beyond the steps is a fence topped with eight inch spikes. The iron fence separates a pit leading to the basement of the building and perhaps more living spaces. Graffiti covers just about every surface here. She can't imagine that someone who hunted syn could live in such a place. It was a dump. Most of the buildings here look abandoned and something tells her that this could be a set up.

<Could he have found the tracker?> she thinks nervously, but remembers that the thing practically microscopic. She concludes that he must be extremely paranoid and this place must be some sort of safe house. Slowly, she makes her way up the concrete steps and cautiously pushes

the door open. The rusty hinges squeal eerily in protest as she pushes the rotted slab of wood. The noise echoes into the blackened building. If he doesn't know she is coming, he knows now. With her element of surprise gone, Imogen steps into the dilapidated foyer. Something crunches under her feet. She might as well have stomped and yelled, *"I'm here. Look at me!"* She curses herself and proceeds as inaudibly as she can.

The entrance opens up into a small corridor with steps leading up to the next floor on the left. A narrow dark hall on the right seems to stretch the entire length of the building. Imogen couldn't tell how far back the hall went because, it was swallowed by shadow. There are two doors about fifteen feet from each other, marking old apartments. The nearest is missing its door, revealing complete darkness on the other side. The once white plaster walls are now brown from years of water damage and exposure to the elements. Random piles of trash lay pressed against the walls is if someone had cleared a path decades ago.

The mini map shifts to a detailed, three dimensional view of the building. The green dot, also known as the screwed, Dominic Vespucci, is on the fifth floor, near the far corner of the building. He is most likely waiting for her. Imogen warily gazes upward in the direction of Dominic's position. Her body feels rigid and tense at the possibility that he could have known that she'd be coming for him. The pump in her chest beats harder as her thoughts race at the possibilities of her foray failing because she was too careless at the convention center.

Slowly and going through great pains to make as little noise as possible, Imogen moves toward the rotted wood steps. She places a hand on the grimy banister and peers upward into the blackness of the windowless upper floors. She looks down and places her foot at the very point where the steps meet the wall, then sets her hand against the opposite wall to lessen the amount the old wood would creak.

Slowly, she makes her way up the first and second flights of stairs without a hitch. The light that reaches these halls is barely enough to make out the shapes that make up all the trash on the floor. Imogen switches on her night vision to keep the total darkness from swallowing her whole. Her breaths become shallow but more labored as she makes her way up the third flight of steps. The excitement is almost like adrenaline for her. She physically has to keep herself from shaking.

Reaching the top of the third floor, she turns to start down the hall and to the next flight of steps. Halfway down the narrow chamber, the floor squeaks and echoes throughout the building. Imogen slowly closes her eyes, bites down on her lower lip and mouths the word a four letter word. The sound of a tin can rattling against the tile two floors below startles her out of her self-recrimination. She tip toes her way to the next flight of steps then peers over the banister to where she thinks the sound came from. The main door is open and for the life of her she can't remember if she had closed it. She reaches around to her back, slowly wraps her fingers around the gun resting against her back. With the firearm pointed down at the levels below and leading her sight, she scans for movement. She silently counts to thirty. After watching the floors below like a hawk, she counts to thirty again. Nothing.

Thumping from above knocks dust from the ceiling as Dominic gracelessly moves toward the hall. Imogen pushes herself back from the narrow opening. With a shrill scream, Dominic unloads his gun. The tile floor and wooden fixtures explode into tiny chunks as the hot cerulean bolts from Dominic's plasma cutter slams into them. The rounds from the sub-machine gun, rain down to smash into the old surfaces, leaving them scorched and smoking. A few long moments later, the gun quits, overheated and out of the condensed gas that fuels its ammo.

"God damned piece of shit!" Dominic screams as he drops the gun due to the heat. He stomps around like an overindulged child.

Imogen takes that moment to run up the steps, no longer caring what noise she makes. She turns to head down the hall to the final set of steps. She looks up to find that no one is there. Dominic must have pussyfooted away when he heard her coming. She takes the steps two at a time, then comes to a grinding halt when she spots six heavily armed men in tactical gear pointing their automatic weapons in her direction. She can hear that fish guy from that classic space film, Blake is always talking about, scream, *"It's a trap!"* and finally she understands the wide fish-eyed beings terror.

She hears another tin can clang against the floor, but this time it's heading toward her. She leaps back down to the fourth floor just as the flash grenade explodes. The men open fire as Imogen tumbles down the steps. She crashes to the floor with such force that her shoulder breaks through the tile, shattering it. The boots of half a dozen, well trained mercenaries begin to pound in her direction.

Imogen picks herself up and runs down the hall to the steps, intending to leave when she spots Pete Roberts stomping up them. She lifts her gun and takes a wild shot at him. The big man drops to the floor. The shot passes over him. Imogen jumps into one of the apartments to keep from being caught in the middle of her foes. Her leap carries her well inside the old dwelling. Just as her boot clears the door frame, the men from above open fire on the point she had been a second ago. She leaps again with so much force that she nearly breaks through the rotted wall.

She mentally brings up a live diagnostic checker to reassure herself that she hasn't been hit, and continues to search for cover. On her side, she looks up and down the main narrow hall of the apartment then down toward the other. She spots a window in the latter direction and moves with all speed toward the dim light outside.

Another Flash bang discharges within the narrow apartment. Imogen instinctively dives right into an open door, knowing that a barrage of bullets are headed her way. A second later, the multi-thunderclaps shred through the door frames and walls, showering Imogen with moldy plaster. The eruption of debris covers her with dust.

Dominic hoots and hollers from behind the men, like the brave soul he is. She can't wait to shove her gun down his throat.

"You ain't so bad now are ya bitch!" Dominic calls from the safety behind the armed mercenaries, which really irritates Imogen. She lifts her gun, presses herself to the wall, leans around the corner and opens fire. *Pop! Pop! Pop!* Two of the three shots hit some fleshy parts. She can hear two men scream out in pain.

"When I'm through taking out your body guards, I'll show you how bad I can be when I kick you in your vagina!" she taunts out from cover. She can hear one of the mercs chuckle at her remark. Taking advantage of the time her comment has seemingly bought her, Imogen darts out of the dark room firing another three rounds in the direction of the armed men. No screams of agony this time. Misses.

"Damn," Imogen says to herself as she presses her back against a wall.

She slowly shuffles toward the doorway to get a peek down the hall. Two shots ring out, shattering the rotted doorframe and sending debris scattering across her vision. The hard rhythmic thumping of their boots against the wood floor, tells her that the remaining men are entering the apartment. She follows their movement, by watching the IR light their goggles give off. She crouches down and patiently waits for the nearest man to get a little closer and block the light from his comrades.

"Come out, come out. Where ever you are," one of the mercs says in a menacing sing song voice as he inches his way closer to her position. She watches as the light from his IR turns to shine in the room she was just in. The bastards didn't see her switch rooms.

The cocky merc reaches the bedroom only a foot from where Imogen sits, waiting to pounce. She reaches out, grabs the collar of the man's tactical vest, yanking him toward her and back into the demolished kitchen. Pulling the man down to the floor, she places the muzzle of her pistol to the side of his head and pulls the trigger. His friends in the hall lose their shit and open fire. Imogen crouches down to avoid the flow of bullets tearing through the cheap walls above her head. While the bullets blaze through the wall, she notices tiny metal canisters and orbs attached to his vest and belt. "Jackpot," Imogen says as she rips off a couple of canisters and pulls the pins. She tosses the flash grenades down the hall. The mixture of magnesium and ammonium explodes with a brilliant blinding flash.

Imogen leans out from behind the nearly disintegrated wall and blasts three more men, hitting them in the head and chest. It upset her that one of the men isn't Dominic or Pete. The last hired gun along with that walking turd, Dominic, retreats back into the hall. She had a plan that would leave her free to take out Dominic, if the raging steroid that was Pete Roberts didn't get in her way. She pulls a field knife from the dead soldier's tactical vest and holds it in a reverse grip under her pistol for easy slashing. She creeps toward the apartment entrance and switches her vision to a full light spectrum view, which enables her to see residual heat left by her attackers in stunning clarity.

She can hear the remaining gunman on the step leading downward, most likely waiting for her to poke her head out so he could get what he thinks will be an easy kill.

Dominic cowers behind the last remaining member of his *backup* and searches for Pete, who is nowhere to be found.

"Do you see her?" Dominic asks the man.

"Negative," he responds. Just then, two canisters roll out of the doorway followed by another, *Boom! Boom!* The detonations are deafening. Dominic along with the soldier grab their ears in response and shut their eyes to protect their vision.

The ringing in Dominic's ears begins to fade. He slowly blinks away the white blobs floating in front of his eyes. Once his vision clears, he spots a blur of motion ducking back into the apartment and that's when he notices the small metallic object rolling his way. He grabs the last remaining soldier and pulls the man against him just as the tiny ball erupts. Still holding the man close, Dominic is forced down the hard marble steps. Dazed and trying desperately to suck in air, Dominic rolls the bloody mess that was once a human being off his chest. With a great effort, the stocky man rolls to his side and tries to crawl down the hall to the next set of steps.

Imogen turns the corner, gun and knife at the ready. She inches her way toward the crumbling steps and peers down them to see Dominic sliding on the floor like the worm he is. The debris from the ruined banister crunches under her feet as she painstakingly walks down the steps. The coughs and moans emanating from Dominic's throat remind her of the noises she heard coming from Darioux's lips that fateful day almost two years ago.

Imogen tucks the gun back into her belt at the small of her back and switches her grip on the knife.

"How does it feel?" she says in an icy voice. Repeating the very same words he spoke to her when he and his band of thugs stole her life. She continues to slowly walk toward Dominic's injured body, "How does it feel to be treated like a human, Dominic?" she growls, drawing even closer to him. The tips of Dominic's fingers reach the lip of the first step and he flexes them in an attempt to pull himself closer to the edge.

Imogen reaches down, taking ahold of his right ankle in a crushing grip and pulls him away from the false safety of the floor below. She drops all her weight on his stomach, pushing the hot air from his lungs as she straddles him. Her knees rest on his shoulders, rendering the thrashing of his arms useless. She pulls the knife up to his face and uses the razor sharp tip to trace a bloody path from the corner of his lip to the edge of his eye, "Are you scared of what's going to happen to your soul when you die?" Imogen says behind clenched teeth.

Dominic's breathing becomes more erratic as he has finally realizes that all of his sins had not been forgotten and were yielding their rotten fruit on this very night. He slams his eyes shut and turns his head in a poor attempt to save himself from what he knows must be coming next. Imogen wraps her delicate fingers around his chin.

"You can dish it out, but when it's your turn, your sorry ass can't take it?" she says as she forces his head in her direction. Imogen positions the point of the knife over Dominic's closed eyes ready to return the favor.

A burst of sizzling white hot electricity streaks down the hall to catch Imogen in the side of her torso. The jolting current flows through both

Imogen and Dominic, sending their bodies into fits of uncontrollable movement. Imogen's harsh shrill fills the narrow corridor and is echoed by Dominic's deeper cries of pain.

The current ceases. Imogen falls to the floor still twitching. Every circuit in her body screams in protest of the pain. Dominic coughs and rolls out of the line of fire. Imogen tries to do the same, but she gets blasted with another burst of crippling volts that last longer. She can feel the metal of the gun in her back slowly heat up. She knows that it's only a matter of time before the insulated hardware within her body does the same.

Imogen uses every ounce of will power she can muster to crawl to the nearest open doorway. The bolts come in short but painful bursts. Each time the dancing, hot, tendrils of weaponized lightning lick her body, it sends her into bouts of agonizing spasms. The jerky painful movement impedes her crawl to safety. The assault ceases just long enough for Pete to walk into view holding a massive Tesla Cannon.

"Got ya now, you slippery bitch!" he says with a sadistic chuckle. He squeezes the trigger again. Imogen's screams echo throughout the entire city block.

CHAPTER 17

9 Months Earlier

The warm glow of the morning sun shines through the large windows to kiss the sheets. Darioux and Imogen, lie spooning on the large bed, in cozy comfortable heat. Imogen holds his strong hands between her breasts to rest against her chest. The warmth of the sun gently stirs them both from their slumber. Darioux nudges closer to her and plants a soft kiss on her exposed shoulder. Imogen smiles and pushes her body against his. His hold around her tightens as his head sinks into the crook of her neck. He breathes in her scent.

"I love weekends," Imogen says with a soft sigh. She uses her free hand to brush her long dark hair away from Darioux's face. She wants to feel more of his skin against hers. Darioux moans his approval.

"Let's just be lazy today." He says still half asleep.

Imogen giggles, loving the idea of basking in each other's presence and ignoring the rest of the world. Regrettably, they had made dinner plans earlier in the week. They could always cancel them, but then they'd have to hear more playful quips about how they were anti-social hermits.

Imogen rolls over to face Darioux and slides her hand under his to caress his thin micro-braids.

"You're going to have to come up with an excuse as to why we can't make it to dinner tonight," she gently reminds him.

He smiles mischievously and replies, "I don't have to do anything. We can always say it slipped our minds."

Imogen chuckles and nuzzles closer. A weird sensation irritates her shoulder, "Scratch," she demands.

Darioux begins scratching her back. The odd feeling becomes more intense and she moves her shoulder closer to his oscillating hand, "My shoulder. Up. Left. No my left," she verbally guides him to the spot that seems to be on fire. The feeling becomes increasingly painful and uncomfortable.

Imogen opens her eyes and lifts her head only to find that she is alone. The beautiful earthy tones of the room are replaced with smoldering walls and exposed charred support beams. Imogen panics and tries to pick herself up from the bed, but her limbs are broken. "Darioux!" she screams in alarm. She looks around, frantic and afraid. The ruin around her collapses, sending her falling into darkness. She falls for what seems like an eternity. The skin on her face cracks then crumbles away, exposing the lightweight, carbon fiber skull underneath. The black void swallows her cries for help.

Beads of sweat roll down Blake's forehead as he tightens the remaining bolt to the nano-carbon bone in Imogen's shoulder. Once the tiny bolt reaches a point where it can no longer twist, Blake rolls the new, self-repairing skin over the upgraded skeleton. He uses a modified laser to stitch up the incision. He checks the monitors to his left, to ensure that the new replacement systems are indeed working.

The cybernetic woman rests on her stomach in an old dentist's chair in a deep hibernation mode. The tank top and tight white shorts she wears are stained with dark blood-colored coolant. Only systems important to maintaining her memory were left running, with a bit of juice to ensure that they were kept intact. Blake relaxes in his chair and rubs the bleariness from his eyes. He looks around at the mess of open boxes on the floor around him. Over the past five months, he had spent a small fortune on replacement parts for his new friend in need. He was quite pleased with what he was able to accomplish, given the complicated procedures required to not only rebuild, but upgrade Imogen's body and systems. Blake reaches over to a physical keyboard and punches in a few keys. A soft whine indicating that main functions are starting up dissipates and Imogen stirs. She opens her new eyes and blinks slowly.

"How long have I been asleep? She asks, wincing at the pain in her jaw.

"A little over six months," Blake replies. Imogen exhales and tries to move, but her limbs are clumsy. She's accustomed to a little more weight and has a hard time getting her hands underneath her body. "How do you feel?" Blake asks.

Imogen manages to shift her body, so that she is laying on her back, "My body feels like it's on fire," she grumbles.

Blake double checks the monitoring system now that she's awake, "You're running a little hot, but that's probably from the flushing of your fluids," he says. He leans forward and places the back of his hand to her cheek and forehead, "It's almost like you're running a high fever. It'll pass in a few days," he adds and offers her a glass of water. Imogen takes a drink and rubs her forehead. When she pulls her hands away, she notices the bright red curls.

"What the hell did you do to my hair?" she tiredly inquires. The annoyance in her tone tells him that maybe he made a bad fashion choice and that he needs to choose his next words wisely. One thing one should never do, is mess with a woman's hair.

Blake scratches his nose, "I figured that if they thought you were dead, maybe you should look a bit different," he answers like a child who had just been caught playing with matches.

Imogen extends her arm and holds out her hand in a silent demand. Blake grabs a small mirror and places it handle first in her palm. She raises the small mirror to her face and is almost shocked at the almost familiar person staring back at her. The thinned, lightly freckled face with full pink lips, framed by a thick and curly mane of lustrous red hair was a shock, but amazing.

"You could have been a mod surgeon judging by this inspired look. I love it," she says with a tired smile. "So, what all did you do to me?" Imogen asks in a more solid voice.

Blake picks up a metal clipboard that holds the little check list he had made prior to beginning repairs, "Well, I over hauled your skeleton. The original polymers were too weak. I replaced them with nano-carbon that repairs itself if splintered or broken."

Imogen raises a pleased eyebrow.

"Over time of course," he adds, making sure she understands the implications. She now had microscopic bugs in her body that acted as an artificial immune system. If her skin was damaged, it would heal. If a bone broke, it would have to be set or it would heal malformed.

Imogen flexes her fingers and toes while Blake rattles off the long list of repairs and software upgrades he installed over the months.

"I also gave you a basic self-defense app that'll come in handy if you decide to go through with what you plan to do," he says with a twinge of worry in his voice. "Also you now have a working knowledge of firearms and marksmanship," Blake adds with a smile.

"I see that you've been busy," Imogen says as she yawns and closes her eyes.

Blake stands next to Imogen and runs his hands underneath her legs and shoulders, "C'mon. The couch is way more comfortable," he says while lifting her up.

"I've been asleep for months," Imogen yawns in protest as he gently sets her down on the thick cushioned couch and covers her with an old blanket.

"Yeah, but you obviously need to rest," Blake presses like a parental figure as he tucks the warm blanket around her body.

He looks around the room, realizing that he has neglected to clean his house the entire time she's been down for repairs. He thinks about cleaning, but doesn't want to wake her up. He turns back to check on Imogen who is now fast asleep.

In another life, under different circumstances, he would have made a move on the beautiful woman sleeping on his couch. He felt a bond that was so much more than his primal urges to find a mate. He felt the long forgotten bond of family. Blake wipes a stray tear from his cheek and sniffles. "Sleep with the angels," he whispers and walks away.

An hour and a shower later, Blake lies back in his bed for a well-deserved rest. "Bedroom T.V. power on," He commands. He doesn't even have time to register what show is being aired before he passes out. Meanwhile, in the next room, Imogen rests curled up on the couch, staring at one of the legs to the coffee table. She used her feet to push the blanket off to the edge of the couch. She tries hard to stay tough, but her memories and emotions overwhelm her. She yearns for her former life. The hot tears stream down her face. She holds herself. It takes another hour for her to cry herself to sleep.

The next morning Blake wakes to the smell of bacon that permeates the entire one bedroom apartment. He had never been a morning person. Hell, if he woke up before noon, he still considered that to be way too early. He checks the clock by his bed and can't believe he's actually awake before eight in the morning. He lumbers out of bed and stumbles out of his room wearing a vintage, Detective Comics, Batman, fleece robe.

"Morning," Imogen says, never taking her eyes off of the skillet on the stove.

"Yeah," Blake replies, still half asleep. He grasps a mug from the counter dryer and places under the coffee dispenser, "What are you doing up at this ungodly hour?" he asks.

Imogen continues to shuffle the strips of marbled meat in the pan, "I'm pretty sure that my accounts have been liquidated by the government and I have no way to repay you for what you've done for me," she says, still refusing to look him in the eye. "You had this awesome cookware still in the packaging so, I'm cooking you breakfast."

Blake looks around the counter and is astounded to see scrambled eggs, pancakes, sausage, biscuits and gravy. He didn't even realize he had the proper ingredients to make such things. He had always eaten out. Then he looks around his modest dwelling. She had also cleaned. Not only did she clean the mess he had spent months making while repairing her, she dusted everything.

Imogen slides the crispy bacon onto plates sitting on warmers next to the stove. She uses oven mitts he had received as a Christmas gift from his mother years ago to handle the heated plates and sets them on the round table.

Blake takes a sip of his *Crème brûlée* flavored coffee and sits in one of the chairs across from Imogen. She pulls out the other chair and sits. The pained expression on her face catches Blake's attention. He knows that this seemingly small gesture is an attempt to feel some sort of normalcy in a life that had been so carelessly ripped apart. He doesn't really know what to say or if there is anything he can say to help her find herself again.

After a long moment of watching her, watch the food, Blake finally says, "This looks great. Thank you."

Imogen smiles halfheartedly. A thin sheen sparkles in her eyes and he can tell that she's struggling to keep herself together.

He would have never thought that the *machines,* that everyone thought to be nothing more than complicated automatons, were capable of such complex human emotions.

Imogen smiles more broadly and gestures to the food, "Eat. It'd be a shame for all this to go to waste," she says with a cracked voice.

She takes the fork between her thumb and forefinger and jabs at the fluffy yellow eggs on her plate. Her eyes well up and overflow with tears. Blake grabs his utensil but does nothing. He watches the edifice of hopeful supposition she had spent all night and morning building, crumble under the gargantuan weight of bleak antithesis before his eyes.

Finally she drops the fork and cups her head in her hands and breaks down, dragged away in a torrent of tears and emotions. Blake watches not really knowing what to do to comfort her.

"Why!" she shouts in anger, then swipes her hand across the table, knocking the majority of the food to the floor. Imogen grabs at her hair as if to pull it all out, but she just cries harder. She says something that Blake can't understand through all the tears.

Some nurturing instinct must have taken over, because Blake slowly walks over to the distraught woman and embraces her in fierce a hug. Blake searches for the words that could help alleviate her pain, but nothing seems right. Nothing seems fair. He quickly realizes that there isn't a damn thing that can be said to take away her suffering so, he just holds her as tight as he can. Her body trembles with every bout of intense emotion. Imogen slowly descends to the floor with Blake still holding her. He begins to rock back and forth as she cries into his chest. Each time he rocks, his back gently touches the cold metal door of the refrigerator.

Long moments pass and silence fills the small living space. Blake rests against the fridge with Imogen still curled up in his arms. Her sporadic whimpering has given way to soft steady breathing. Blake peers down and confirms that she is asleep. He allows his head to drift to the side. He examines a stain on the wood floor. It's been there long before he had moved in to the shabby apartment and it'll be there long after he moves out. He ponders how seemingly random events always lead us toward a path that is known and yet, remains mysterious. To say that it is the will of some all-knowing god, implies a sense of entitlement that is neither earned nor deserved. How can one truly justify the acts of animalistic brutality and words that teach hate by claiming that it is the will of God? And here, all his life, he thought that mankind was maturing.

Blake doesn't know if it's his mind playing tricks and making him see what he wants, but the stain looks like the classic image of a broken heart. He rests his head on Imogen's soft hair.

They sit on the floor of the tiny nook, Blake considers to be his kitchen, for what seems like hours. The sounds of the world carrying on outside are muffled as the rumble of old engines flow in the air and through the walls.

Blake doesn't fall asleep. He can't. He thinks about the promise he made nine months ago to the woman sleeping in his arms. He knows that they are now bound together. He didn't know it at the time he spoke those consequential words, but the promise he made to help her, means that he must remain by her side until the very end. He doesn't know what or how things will play out, but he knows that it is the human thing to do.

CHAPTER 18

Present Day

Pete Roberts grins sadistically as he squeezes the six inch long lever that serves as the trigger of his Tesla Cannon. Each burst of electrical energy illuminates the dark hall as it strikes the crawling woman in the back. Every spastic, ultramarine tendril rocks her body while she tries desperately to crawl away.

"Get up!" Pete barks at Dominic, who sits hunched on his hands and knees. Pete pulls on the trigger again and again, each time taking twisted delight in watching Imogen collapse to the floor in an agonizing shriek of debilitating pain.

The searing heat on Imogen's back is enough to blister and blacken normal skin. She knows that if he continues shocking her, blistered skin will be the least of her worries. Any other syn would have been down for the count and fried by now, but she wasn't going to start counting her lucky stars yet. Alarms and warning statuses blink before her eyes, telling her that the heat and electrical levels of her system are reaching a critical point. She knows that she has to do something and do it quickly, if she doesn't want to end up dead. The only thing she can think of, is making a break for the apartment door the next time he lets off the trigger. Imogen plants her left hand on the floor. Biting through the pain, she waits for Pete to release the lever. Every second that passes causes her body to shake even more violently than before. She focuses on trying to keep her hand in place. Imogen clenches her jaw to keep from screaming out right, but the pain is just too great. She cries out.

Dominic watches and wonders how she could still be conscious. He staggers to his feet and looks around for something he could use as a weapon. The automatic rifle the young soldier had is completely mangled, but his side arm looks to be in working order. Dominic crouches down and pulls the handgun from its holster, ejects the clip to ensure there are bullets, and then slaps it back in place. He wobbles back to an upright position and points the gun down the hall at the redheaded woman. He pulls the trigger. The shot goes wide and embeds itself in a wall just above Imogen's head.

"Are you fucking crazy?" Pete yells as he eases off the trigger. Imogen pops up and bolts for the door. Caught off guard, Pete clamps down on the trigger and manages to clip Imogen on the side. The impact knocks her off her feet. The momentum carries her far enough to crash into the inner wall of the abandoned apartment. Imogen's booted feet scramble for purchase on the grimy tile as soon as she hits the floor and she heads for cover.

Pete lashes out with a vicious backhand that almost takes Dominic's head clean off of his shoulders. "What the fuck, Dom? You stupid wop!" Pete hollers as Dominic tumbles to the filthy floor. The heavily muscled man turns his attention to the opening his target escaped through. He inches closer, "Come on out Harper!" he yells, ready to completely let loose on her the moment she shows her face. Once he's a few feet from the door, Pete risks a glance back at Dominic who's still trying to pick himself up off the floor. "I see that we didn't do a good enough job last time we met," Pete taunts, while taking cautious steps toward the frame of the door. He pokes his head around the corner to sneak a peek into the rundown apartment.

The floorboards creak under Pete's heavy boots. He slowly makes his way into the main hall of the small dwelling. Imogen sits crouched in a tiny dark room, which could have been a child's resting place when the building was in use. The mention of her name from the lips of Pete's mouth chills her to the bone. She'll have to worry about the implications later, once she has the time.

The alarms die down and she watches the bars of her system statuses move from being in the red to a more tolerable yellow and then finally a normal green. She can hear Pete on the other side of the wall, moving around in the hall. If he gets any closer, he will be able to smell the burnt wool of her coat. She didn't know what damage had been done to her body by the surprise attack and at the moment she didn't care. All she can think is how big of a blunder this whole thing is. Not only did she not get Dominic or Pete, they knew who she was.

<How could I have let this happen?>

She spots a small window high on the wall, but she doesn't know if she can make it out of the apartment without being hit by that damn cannon again. She hears Pete kick in a door down the hall and let off a burst from his electric rifle. She moves as quietly as she can toward the window and that's when she hears the sirens of distant emergency vehicles. No doubt they are headed to this impromptu battleground.

Pete obviously hears the sirens as well, because he moves quickly toward the exit of the apartment and back out in the hall of the building to collect Dominic.

"Come on asshole," he says scornfully and grabs the dazed man by the upper arm.

Imogen can hear the men stomping down the steps. Instead of squeezing her body through a narrow window, she searches for a fire escape that is common in old buildings like this one. She can hear tires come to a screeching halt in the street in front of the old apartment building. The distant voices of the officers screaming for Pete to drop his weapon puts a smile on Imogen's face.

"I hope they shoot the bastard," she says dryly. She hopes that Pete will get a wild hair up his ass and go postal. It happens all the time, but she isn't that lucky. Maybe it was too much to ask.

Imogen lifts her leg through the broken window and on to the shaky, rusted, iron platform mounted to the outside walls. She climbs down the crumbling rungs of the ladder, trying hard not to make a sound and alert the officers to her escape, though she is sure that Pete and Dominic are telling them all about the psychotic robot they were trying to take down.

Her booted feet finally touch solid ground and she immediately takes off running.

<How the hell did he know my name?> Imogen thinks to herself. She pounds pavement. Her thoughts run wild with all kinds of bad scenarios. She wonders if her face would end up plastered all over the vid screens in the city. Imogen mentally kicks herself in the ass for going into that damned building. She knew it was a trap, but she let her foolish thirst for vengeance get the better of her. "Stupid! Stupid!" she says to herself in between long strides. She wished the fibrous muscles in her thighs would burn so it would give her something to focus on other than her debacle with Dominic and Pete.

After about ten minutes of berating herself, Imogen finally thinks about Blake and the shit storm she has unleashed on his world.

"How could I have been so dumb?" she says as her eyes water. "I've killed him," she mutters as tears fall from her eyes. She's done it again. Someone who cared enough about her is now going to be killed because she made the wrong decision.

"Not this time. Things are different now. I'm different," she wipes the streaming tears from her face. The heavy wool of her sleeve feels abrasive on her skin. Odd thing to notice at such a time.

Within the city streets, Imogen can feel the eyes on her, wondering why she's running. She turns the corner on Ash and Oak Street then, she comes to a jog. From a jog to a hasty walk. Imogen feels the gravity of the situation barreling down on her like a Maglev bullet train. She wipes the cooling tears from her face and racks her brain on possible solutions. She doesn't carry a white wash jammer around like the one Blake keeps on his person, so going home now isn't an option. She needs to get ahold of Blake and give him a heads up and let him know about her royal screw up.

Imogen continues to power walk through the city, but she has no idea where she's going or what she's going to do next. She passes a few stores still catering to customers buying odds and ends for their dwindling groceries. She walks for what feels like hours and eventually finds herself in the heart of downtown. Night clubs and adult novelty stores light up the frosty night with their neon signs.

<A stiff drink sounds nice right about now.> Imogen thinks to herself. She can't get drunk, but the burn of the liquor will feel good. She looks around at the wide selection of bars that specialize in separating the young and stupid from their money. Imogen bypasses all the sparkly, thumping spots and settles for a little hole in the wall. She starts for the door. A commotion down the street catches her attention. She turns her head. A massive lumpy bouncer is taking a little too much pleasure in tossing a drunk patron out on his face. Imogen almost ignores the scene, but the yellow neon lights set against a black backdrop catches her eye.

Imogen forgets the little cut and stab hole in the wall and makes her way through the young party goers with a renewed vigor. The young meatheads congregating just outside the front leather-padded double doors, smile perversely and make cat calls. As if these gelled up Neanderthals had a chance with a woman who wasn't drugged into submission. A crudely scribbled sign next to the door reads, "Help Wanted."

Young party goers stand outside of the building, blasted on mushrooms and stim-sticks. They grumble when they see the figurative and literal, smoking redhead step in front of them. The bouncer at the door examines a three dimensional holographic list. He peers up at her, looks her up then down and raises an eyebrow. He follows her gaze to the sign and assumes that she must be just another tart hard up for cash. He nods and smiles knowingly, then gestures for her to enter the establishment.

"Maybe tonight isn't a complete wash," Imogen mumbles.

Ignoring all the lame attempts the potential rapists were making at mating calls, Imogen blows in her hands like it'll actually stave off the chill. She reaches out and wraps her almost numb fingers around the decorative brass door handle.

<*What else can go wrong tonight?*> she casually pulls the big black door open and walks into *The Cave*.

CHAPTER 19

Present Day

Mason arrives at the station with Vivian following close behind. They got the call that two men had been detained for being involved in a gun fight. The detectives were told that these men may have some information on their homicide case. Vivian flips through her tablet and confirms that the men were in pursuit of a redheaded synthetic and in the process they had lost six of their operatives.

"That thing really did a number on them, old man," Vivian says.

Mason doesn't like that she referred to the syn as a *"thing."* He ignores her comment and stops just outside the room where Dominic is being held.

"You ready?" he asks Vivian flatly. She nods. Mason punches a code into the digital lock and they step inside.

Dominic sits in a hard metal chair in front of a metal table. The heavy furniture is bolted to the concrete floor. He eyes the detectives when they enter the room. Dominic notices the young female detective and eyes her hips, then chuckles lightly. He thinks he recognizes the woman from somewhere, but can't place her.

Mason notices the gesture, but he pushes the assumptions from his thoughts. "Mr. Vespucci. Mind telling us what happened tonight?" Mason says disinterested in the chunky man's reply.

Dominic sighs, obviously annoyed. His annoyance was probably due to all the dried blood covering most of his body. Thank god somebody gave him a wet nap to wipe off his face.

Vivian stands near the opposite wall, facing Dominic tapping away at her tablet. She pulls up an electronic voice stress analyzer.

"I told the last guys what happened," Dominic says, frustration flavoring his tone.

Mason leans on the table in front of the frumpy man and says, "Yeah, but you didn't tell me. I want to know what happened."

Dominic leans forward, paints his best, *you're barking up the wrong tree* face and says, "I was followed by a synthetic. I called for backup and it killed my team. End of Story."

Mason smiles, then he pulls the other chair out and takes a seat, "That wasn't so hard. Now, why do you think the synthetic was following you?" Mason leans back, not really caring what

Dominic has to say next. Mason wants him to think that their on his side, though the sarcasm comes naturally.

Vivian focuses on the readings displayed on her tablet and can already tell that Dominic is about to lie.

"I don't know," he says. He leans back and sniffs, "Maybe the thing went crazy. It's probably one of those so called '*freedom fighters*', which are still illegal by the way!" Dominic says as his frustration grows. Mason barely nods as Dominic continues, "I don't know why you're wasting your time on me, when you should be helping us get that thing off the streets!"

Mason curls one side of his mouth into a grin, "We've got some people on it."

Vivian relaxes against the wall, completely unsure of what her partner's intentions are. "Can you describe the robot you and your team were attempting to capture?" Vivian asks, trying to get some tangible information out of Dominic.

Looking down at the table and noticing all the little imperfections, Dominic answers, "Curly red hair. Dark grey coat. Tight black cargo pants. If she were human, she'd be a hot little piece of ass."

Vivian rolls her eyes. The analysis shows that he's telling the truth, which makes her sigh audibly.

"I apologize for any inconvenience the officers doing their job may have caused you," Mason says as he stands from his seat. "The officer outside will take care of the procedures to let you go."

Dominic stands upright and heads for the door. Vivian cocks her head in surprise. There is no way that they've got enough information to find the synthetic. Let alone continue the investigation. When Dominic exits the room, Vivian confronts Mason, "What the hell was that?" she stage whispers, in a not so pleasant voice that, Mason just seems to shrug off.

"I'm just wanting to talk to his friend," Mason replies. In truth, he wanted Dominic to feel like he was in the clear, so they can catch him slipping up later.

"We didn't get shit from him," Vivian points at the door. The agitation grows in her voice.

Mason walks to the door smiling, "You and I both know, that's not true."

Mason and Vivian watch Pete through a one way mirror in the next room. The big man isn't so uptight or agitated as his buddy. He relaxes in his chair with his feet up and head back. His eyes are closed, like he's enjoying a warm breeze on a European beach. Mason debates whether or not he should go back on what he said in the other room and just send Vivian to talk to the big guy. He quickly squashes that train of thought. "You mind hanging out here for a minute?" Mason asks.

Vivian gestures toward the door. He takes one last look at the genetic mishap that was Pete Roberts, before heading out of the room.

Mason takes a moment to plan a strategy for dealing with Pete. Come off too strong and then he'll end up in a pissing match with the man rather than getting actual information.

Vivian once again activates the voice stress application on her glass tablet and prepares it for Pete's data. While she waits, she examines the data obtained from Dominic's interview, "Not a damn thing worth keeping." Vivian mumbles and she toys with the thought of deleting the data. She pauses with her finger hovering over the digitized button. She decides against it. She closes the file and raises her eyes when she hears the beep of the keypad to the door inside the interrogation room. She intently watches both men as Mason walks to the metal chair and sits.

"I heard you had a hard time this evening. Want to tell me about it?" Mason says in a calm voice. The Microphones in the room distort his voice.

Pete opens his eyes but continues to look up at the ceiling. "I almost had it," Pete says unemotionally.

"What happened?" Mason asks.

Pete lowers his head and smiles, "It got away." The savage look in his eyes is somewhat disturbing. He may have had an appreciation for the syn that bested him and the others. He may also be thinking about dismantling the machine. It was probably both.

Vivian adjusts the camera on her tablet and zooms in on Pete. She's surprised to see that he is as cool as the snow outside. It troubles her that he is reacting so differently than Dominic. She peers down at the iridescent monitor to see if there is anything going on underneath surface of Pete's nonchalant attitude. She finds nothing and returns her gaze to the interview being conducted.

"You had a Tesla Cannon in your possession. The charge in the ammo clip shows that you fired it. Did you miss?" Mason continues with his line of questioning.

Pete scratches at his nose. He finds the question amusing, "I didn't miss. The thing must've been well insulated. Any other bucket of bolts would have been burned out in seconds. This thing took it like a champ," Pete says admiringly.

"So, it's been modified?" Mason says. Mason pretends to write something on a digipad and says, "Have you or anyone in your organization encountered this particular synthetic before?"

Pete says nothing for a moment and that didn't go unnoticed by Mason. "Nah. This is a new one that wandered into our scopes. We'll get it, though," Pete says with a grim determination. The toothy grin on his face doesn't reach his eyes.

"I don't doubt that you will," Mason says with a slight smile, though he believes that things may not turn out as Pete thinks.

The scans on Vivian's monitor picks up a slight reading of agitation from Pete and his body language confirms it.

Pete sets his feet on the floor and leans forward, "You think this is joke?" he says angrily. "A couple of my boys died in that roach motel and you got me sitting in here." Pete notices that Mason is still scribbling on the pad. "I'm talking to you, buddy," Pete says. His annoyance is obviously growing.

"Oh, I don't have to look at you to listen. I can multitask," Mason says, though he probably should have left that last bit out, because it infuriated Pete.

"Fuck you oinker! That thing killed *seven* of my people! Where's the fucking justice there?"

Mason raises his eyes at Pete's statement. He sets the stylus down and purses his lips. "Seven you say?" Mason slightly cocks his head. His little gamble with the sarcasm paid off. Pete leans back in his chair, knowing that he had let something crucial slip. "The body count last time we checked was six," Mason probes, "Who's the seventh?"

Vivian watches the readings spike and raises an eyebrow, "Not as cool as you thought you were, huh big boy." She sighs and wraps one of her arms around her stomach to rest under her elbow. She knows that the old man is on to something. "What are you getting at Pops?" she whispers to herself.

Pete snorts before speaking again, "Maybe my count was off."

Mason smiles and tucks the stylus in his inner breast pocket, "Well, we have a group of geeky analysts combing through the data that was stored in your groups recorded logs," Mason informs the big man. "It's amazing, those things. They record even after the user has died. Maybe there were seven," Mason says as he rises from his seat and heads toward the door. The truth was that he was already in possession of the visual and audio data from the mercs. He had the analyst give him a copy of the data personally rather than trusting it to stay in the archive. Mason knows that Pete and his buddies know the identity of the redhead. Mason opens the door then gestures for Pete, "After you."

Pete slowly stands, suspicious of what Ed Mason thinks he knows and walks toward the door.

Vivian tucks away the data she had collected during the interviews into an encrypted file and stows her tablet into its carry case. She impatiently waits for her partner to come back into the dark observation room. She uses the little time she has to hide her frustration and think of constructive ways to approach Mason about his methods. After five minutes, she heads out of the room and into the main offices of the precinct. She spots Mason at his desk flipping through some old paperwork.

"What the hell was that about?" she asks in a hushed voice once she reached the corner of his desk.

Mason holds up a finger while he gathers up all the old files and photos and tucks them away in an old and grungy messenger bag. "I have a feeling," he says, as if his mind is racing with complex mathematical formulas.

"You mind letting me in on the big secret?" Vivian says trying to hide her annoyance. "You've been acting weird ever since that old guy at the morgue was killed," she says. "What's going on with you? You barely asked those guys anything. What feeling could you possibly have?" she probes, failing to hide the fact that she's annoyed. Vivian leans her body on his desk, causing it to move slightly as it takes her weight. Mason glances up slightly and notices that she has that *all business* look.

"Just trust me on this," he says tucking another old file into his bag.

"I've been meaning to ask you; have you been able to get anything out of that file?" she says while glancing about the random papers and notes on his desk. Mason stands and pulls the old leather bag up to rest on his shoulder. She is referring to Frog's data file that had been deleted from the evidence archive by someone on the inside trying to hide something. He's actually surprised at her inquiry, but doesn't let that show on his face.

"No. I haven't had a chance to check it out yet. You?" He says, making sure to maintain the proper inflection in his tone.

"I didn't find anything worth checking out, but the redhead that killed him," Vivian starts, "Think it's the same redhead that killed Frog's employee and the mercenaries tonight?" she whispers.

Mason sweeps his eyes across the wide office, taking in all the officers at their desks then back to lock onto Vivian, "Can I trust you?" he asks in a serious tone.

"Of course. Ed, what's going on?"

Mason motions her on with a nod of his head and they move to exit the station.

Snow drifts down from the sky like tiny feathers from a torn pillow. The fresh powder glows as it reflects the light from the street lamps and surrounding buildings. Mason unlocks the dark four door sedan.

"You drive," he says as he opens the passenger side door and climbs inside.

Vivian walks around to the driver's side and gets behind the wheel, "Okay, Mr. Paranoid. What do you got?"

Mason takes a moment to compose his thoughts before answering. He's unsure if he should even tell Vivian his suspicions. He had only known her for about a year, but he needed a fresh opinion. He decides that it would be best to show some of his cards. "Okay. The reason I haven't checked out the files, is because someone deleted them from the archive," he starts. Vivian was about to speak but Mason continues with his theory, "I'm pretty sure that there was something on that data file that someone didn't want us to find and that is why Dr. Westfield died. I think the same person killed Jaina Trent and is trying to make it look as if the synthetic had done it. I also think that our friends Dominic and Pete have met this synthetic before."

Mason didn't add that he thought he knew who the synthetic was and why she was after them. Also, he wasn't going to let slip that he could possibly tie seekers and Chosen to the bombing that took out three floors of an apartment building, nearly two years ago. It killed over a hundred people. Now wasn't the time to play those cards.

Vivian listened to her partner's speculations with an almost unenthusiastic ear. She pushed the ignition and began to drive. She doesn't know how he could have guessed all that being the washed up kook, he's supposed to be, but she doesn't like where this is going. "Okay. I hear ya. But what evidence do you have to support all this? And don't give me that, 'I have a feeling' shit," she says, holding up a pointed finger.

Mason watches her micro expressions closely as she listens to his claims. He's searching for any hidden feelings tied to what they are doing. "Pete said that she had killed seven of his guys. There were only six. I think he's referring to Frog."

Vivian chuckles sarcastically, "That's not proof. That's a jarhead who's numerically challenged."

Mason notices a little twitch in Vivian's eye then scratches his chin and chuckles to himself.

"Did you get anything from the interviews?" Mason asks. Vivian's eye twitches again and she shakes her head. "You're right. I must be tired," Mason says jokingly. "I think it's best if I went home and got some rest. It's been a long day," he adds.

Vivian turns a corner and begins heading for Mason's apartment near the outskirts of the city. "I'll say. You're connecting things that aren't there. You need a fresh perspective on things," she says and offers him a cigarette. Mason declines and starts chewing on the inside corner of his lip. They don't speak for the rest of the ride.

Vivian pulls the car to a stop in front of the metal and glass building. She turns the car off then turns her body to face her slightly older partner, "Listen. This is Vivian talking, not your partner. You need a serious stress release if you're going to be any use to anyone."

Mason nods and pinches the space between his eyes, "Yeah. I got it," he says. He reaches for the door latch.

"Do you want me to come up? Maybe talk a bit? Have a few beers?"

He couldn't help but noticed how intense her brown eyes were at that moment, but for her to shift gears so quickly raised red flags, "Nah. I'm fine," Mason says, even though he felt his face go flush.

Vivian smiles as if she's embarrassed and tucks a few loose strands of hair behind her ear, "Not like that old man."

Mason smiles back as best he can and declines again. He opens the door to the car and steps out. He waves and walks to the front doors of his building. Vivian waves back, starts the car and drives off. He steps inside and wonders if he really just dodged a bullet.

CHAPTER 20

Present Day

The air reeked of stale cigarettes and broken dreams. The music thumping through the second set of leather padded doors had a lame techno beat. It was as if the composer left the first five notes he created on a loop for ten minutes. The bouncer with the comb over, sat suspended by a complex mechanical swing behind a host's podium. From the way it looked he could move in any direction with ease. Where his legs should have been, Imogen saw only nubs that had as many folds as his neck. A small metal case sits next to the podium has a disabled sign engraved on it. She knows that it contained his mechanical legs.

He's sporting shiny, *pleather* clothes that are two sizes too small for his *fluffy* frame. Blobs of skin threaten to rip through the poorly knitted seams. He looks Imogen up and down, tasting her with his eyes, "What can we do for you lil missy," he says with a gapped toothed smile.

Imogen finds the man completely vile. <*The man salivates like a Saint Bernard.*> Imogen thinks. She notices that his baby like teeth look too small for his wide mouth when he licks his lips. His almost nonexistent jaw is practically lost in the folds of his chin. "I saw the sign out front," Imogen replies.

The marshmallow man sloppily licks his lips and looks her over again, only this time more appraisingly. "You look like you've crawled out of a salvage dump hun," he chuckles. The look on Imogen's face silences his attempt at tickling her ribs.

Her usual stoicism was next to nonexistent, "Anything else?" she asks. She waits for him to make another attempt at being witty, but she can tell that he's rethinking his approach.

He wipes some spittle from his neck-chin and continues, "But I bet you clean up *real nice.*" He presses his thumb onto a digital reader and an audible clicking indicates that the doors are now unlocked, "You'll want to speak to Marv. He's the guy in charge," the fat man says.

The Heavily padded doors part, revealing a laser light show streaming on the walls, which included just about every color known to man. Imogen was buffeted by the waves of thumping music coming from the ridiculously large speakers placed all around the club. The suspended, obese, host raises a jiggly arm and gestures for her to step inside. Imogen slowly steps through the doors, feeling the host's eyes mentally stripping off her clothes with every step. "See you later, sugar tits," the fat bastard says as the doors slowly close behind her.

Imogen finds herself in a vast circular room. The chamber contains three stages, all with different shows taking place on them. An elevated walkway connects the three platforms, allowing the *talent* to safely move from stage to stage or back beyond the curtains as they wished. The seating is arranged around all three interconnected showcases.

The center stage, which is located near the front of the room, showcases a live and very nude female rock band. Well almost nude. The lead singer is sporting a pair of thigh high leather boots and the lead guitarist has a pair of stripped stockings that reach her upper thigh.

To the right of the large room a woman performs delicate acrobatics from two large silk ribbons that stretch to the vaulted ceiling. If it weren't for the smell of booze and sweat, one would think that the woman belonged in some high class circus act. On the left, two women grope each other under a rain styled shower. The pale blue light that illuminates them adds an almost dreamlike effect to their show of debauchery.

Imogen ignores all of it. She makes her way to a dark corner at the end of the bar, which looks to be made of ice and stone. She takes in the scene and scans every face. Every person sitting at a table and every female server in costume is closely examined.

A few moments later, a very attractive and very buxom woman makes her way to the bar, "Whatcha need hun?" she hollers to be heard over the music.

Without looking in the woman's direction, Imogen leans toward her, "I'm looking for Desirae Deponet. She here tonight?" Imogen responds in kind. The slightly older woman leans on the granite counter and smiles. Imogen glances her way for the first time and practically gasps.

"Do I know you?" Desirae answers, confusion with a touch of intrigue shows in her expression.

For a long moment, Imogen says nothing, which further adds to Desirae's interest, "Look sweet heart, I have a lot of custies to tend to," she presses.

Imogen, has to physically shake her head to knock herself free of her stupor, "Sorry. You just look a lot different from the last time we met. It threw me off."

Desirae nods and smiles. A drunk patron signals that he's ready for some more drink. "I'm sorry, I'm horrible with faces. I get off in an hour. It'll be quieter and we can talk then. Okay?" She shouts. Imogen nods, sits back and watches

Desirae jog to the other end of the bar to take care of the well-oiled man.

The cavernous room goes still. Lights, along with all sound stops. Not a single person shouted in protest due to the disruption. A single spot light shines down from above to illuminate the center stage. A single woman with long black lustrous hair stands at the very tip of the circular platform. The olive skinned woman is wrapped in a form fitting, yet elegant dark evening gown. The sheer material of the dress reveals strategic parts of her body, but not enough for anyone to see her flesh, only the silhouette of her elegantly soft curves.

The single, hot beam isolates her from the rest of the world, like a shield of light that battles against the darkness. A vintage Shure microphone hangs suspended in front of her like an exclamation point for the crowd, letting them know that they must pay attention.

The men and women in the club silently wait as if the parting of this woman's lips is the permission they need to move a muscle. No one, not even the servers moved. All eyes are fixed on this delicate featured woman on the stage. Soft string music plays from unseen speakers to fill the room and the woman in the diaphanous dress parts her full lips and begins to sing.

Imogen is shocked to hear that the dark haired woman is singing an opera, of all things. The woman is singing a piece by the English composer Henry Purcell, entitled, "*When I am Laid in Earth"* also known as *"Dido's Lament."* The woman on stage commands the audience and they don't even try to challenge her or disrupt her performance. Every soul in the room was entranced by her voice.

The last thing Imogen expected to hear in a place steeped with smut, was a seventeenth century opera about a tragic love story. Imogen pivots on her stool to glance at Desirae, who seems to be completely captivated by this woman's haunting and yet, incredibly beautiful voice. She notices that Desirae is softly crying midway through the song. This troubles Imogen. She doesn't want to know that her prey is capable of feelings. That just complicates things.

When the artist completes her set, the room goes black again, giving the woman enough time to sneak back behind the curtain and let the perky metal band take their positions. Once the lights turn back on, dirty business in the club continues as if it hadn't been interrupted by true talent. Imogen doesn't know what just happened, but if she and Blake survives, she would have to introduce him to that magnificent gem hidden a pile of manure.

Imogen turns back to the bar to focus her attention on Desirae, though she did her best to act like she was enjoying the view. It didn't take long for that little plan to backfire though. Not five minutes into the lights being turned back on, an idiot looking to get his beak wet, sat well within Imogen's personal bubble space. The twenty something male, wearing the latest in fashion faux pas, sits an extra drink near her right hand.

<*Yeah. As if I'd take anything from you. This kid must be dumber than he looks.*> Imogen silently muses. She and anyone else who looked at this kid could tell that there were fried nerves in his head fighting over a single dead brain cell.

The guy leans close enough to lick the side of her face, if he wanted, "Hey baby," he says with the stink of cheap alcohol lingering on his breath, "I'm a talented linguist. I'm very talented in the language of pussy."

Imogen slowly turns her head to face the inebriated man. She grabs the drink he had placed next to her, then in a blur of motion, she smashes the thick bottle into his face. The man's head bounces off the wall and he crumbles to the floor like a wet dish rag. The shattering glass didn't make much noise over the music, but it did grab the attention of a couple of bouncers. The two large men use their most intimidating stride as they make their way to what's left of the confrontation.

Imogen is in no mood tonight. She's ready to drop anyone who so much as looks at her awkwardly.

"We got a problem?" The taller man says in his best scary voice.

"We did. It's over now. Don't worry. Go about your business," Imogen smiles. The two men move to grab the small redhead in a firm hold, but stop when, Desirae, of all people jumps over the bar to intervene.

"Hey she's cool. It was the jerk who started it." Desirae marches over to where the unconscious man lie and points, "This asshole isn't supposed to be in here. He was banned months ago for harassing the help." She shouts, standing between Imogen and the bouncers.

The two men exchange a look, shrug then grab the youth and drag him outside to be tossed on his ass.

Desirae eases down on the seat the drunkard had occupied and chuckles nervously, "That asshole had it coming."

Imogen smiles and nods. *<So do you,>* she thinks.

"You look so familiar, but I can't place you," Desirae leans in and says.

"It's been a while since the last time we met, but I see that you too have changed," Imogen says, taking note of her rainbow dyed hair, piercings and augmented breasts.

Desirae smiles with a bashful nod and toys with her hair, "Yeah. I had to change a lot of things recently, but it's for the better." Desirae turns her head to lock eyes with the mysterious redhead, who asked for her by name. There was a flicker of recognition there, but Desirae couldn't put her finger on it, "So what's your name again?"

Imogen looks down at the bar at a loss, but decides to use Blake's semi-fictitious name for her, "I'm Gen. We met almost two years ago," Desirae squints and was about to say something, but stops to answer a call on her nano-phone. She smiles apologetically and holds up her index finger. Imogen waits patiently while she completes her call.

"Oh no, it's fine. Don't worry about it." Desirae says to the person on the other line. Imogen watches her intently and wonders if the person on the other line is Pete or Dominic, warning her of the retribution that's headed her way.

A moment later Desirae disconnects the call and hollers for one of the bouncers that had tossed out the trash earlier, "Hey!" she yells. The man walks over, making sure to maintain that cocky stride. "I've got to go. Can you cover for me?" She asks the man. He nods and takes up a position behind the bar. "I'm sorry, but I've got to go. I'd love to stay and chat, but I guess we can do that another time," Desirae says as she stands.

Imogen nods, "No problem. We'll catch up later."

Desirae smiles warmly. She pulls out an ink pen, jots down her private phone number on a napkin and hands it to Imogen. "I'm free tomorrow. Give me a call and we'll catch up," Desirae says with a smile and heads toward the back to gather her things. Imogen takes the stained napkin, wondering why or how can this woman who had helped ruin her life and now serves drinks in a strip club, could be so obliviously kind. She looks down at the number, "Could this be another trap or is she really that bubbly?" Imogen says to herself. She orders a shot of some blue drink, knocks it back and exits the club.

CHAPTER 21

Present Day

The white walls of the large office seem to glow with the morning light that casts an almost milky fog on the faces of everyone present. Two of the men gathered in the room hide their anxiety of the spiraling situation. Snow drifts down passed the window to the streets below. Very few sky cars travel in this kind of weather. David stands near the bar. He pours himself a glass of brandy.

"Do we involve the cops with this one?" Pete asks. He's completely unsure of how to read the expression on David's face, which seems serene despite the events of last night.

Dominic stands by the large office windows, staring down at the frosted traffic below, "We could really fuck up her whole day if we leaked this to the media," he says without taking his attention from the ants below.

David runs his thumb along the silver cap of the tiny urn he holds in his hands, "No. If we get more people in the mix, it will only make our objective that much harder to complete," David says calmly. He turns to Pete and continues, "If that falls through, then you have my permission to level a whole city block if you have to."

Dominic runs his fingers through his disheveled hair then takes a deep breath, "So we wait to see if your little scout comes through. What the hell are we supposed to do in the meantime? Play cards?" Dominic turns to face the other men. He can't stand the idea of waiting around, "We need to be out there. We need to find this bitch," he yells.

David slides the small urn containing his mother's hair into his pocket and sits back in his chair.

"She can't be too far. She's obviously still in the city and all we need to do is find her." Dominic continues. He paces back and forth like a caged dog.

David's serving synthetic, Silvia, steps into the room and heads for the bar. She begins to mix one of her master's favorite drinks. Dominic's mood goes from angry to full out pissed off when he lays eyes on the machine. David notices the shift and points a finger at the chubby man, "Don't go damaging my property, boy." Dominic glares at the droid then down at David who is still sitting in his seat. David gestures to Dominic, indicating that he should have a seat and relax a little, "Let me tell you a story," David says.

Silvia shuffles toward the men with a tray of drinks. She serves David first, who gladly takes the screw driver, then Pete and lastly Dominic, who hesitates before taking the beverage. The droid shuffles away and waits in a corner of the office. David motions toward the empty seat again and this time, Dominic sits.

"Back when this country went to shit," David starts, "My family didn't have a whole lot of money, so we were used to roughing it." Dominic takes a drink of the cool liquor.

"My pop had kicked the bucket a few years earlier, so my ma had to raise my brother and I, all on her own with practically nothing." David pauses to take a sip of his drink. He sets the glass on a coaster, Silvia had placed on the table next to his chair. "She did good to feed us on a daily basis. Now keep in mind that there were many other folks who were used to having it all and they did some terrible things to scrape by. My ma had to put a few of them down to protect what little we did have."

Dominic leans forward. The look on his face tells the others that he is growing agitated by a story that seemingly meant nothing to the current situation.

David digs in the pocket of his navy blue slacks and pulls out the tiny jar and examines it. "Even when it seemed like she was spinning her wheels in the mud and I got flustered, she always told me, 'Son, even God took some time to make the world.' And I knew what she meant." David reaches over, grabs his cup of orange juice mixed with vodka and takes another drink then sets it back down. He then stands and begins to walk around to Dominic. "She was telling me that I needed patience and a clear head if, I was ever going to do anything worth doing," David says pointedly.

Dominic turns his body halfway around to face David, "Why the fu," he manages to get out before the southerner slams a fist into the side of his head. Dominic falls to the floor, spilling his drink on the expensive marble.

"Now, I was trying to be sensible with you just now and bestow some of my mother's wisdom on your sorry ass," David growls as he shakes the pain from his hand. "Now, I don't mind foul language. Just ask Pete, but the next time you use such language in an unwarranted situation in my presence, you won't have to worry about that redhead, Harper," David says in a much cooler tone. He walks over to the table next to his chair and takes his drink. He snaps his fingers and the despairing serving droid moves from the corner to clean the spilled drink.

Dominic looks up at Pete completely dumbfounded. Pete shrugs, "He doesn't like anyone talking like that while he's talking about his mom."

The look on Dominic's face tells Pete that he's even more confused. Pete just shakes his head, signifying that it's just one of those things you've got to live with. The droid strolls past

Dominic, who is still lying on the floor holding his jaw, and begins to clean up the broken glass and liquor. "I sincerely apologize Dom, but I just felt disrespected by your careless choice of words," David says after polishing off his drink.

Pete motions for Dominic to pick himself up off the floor, "So, is your contact on a time limit?" Pete asks.

David smiles, "No, but if things don't go as I want them to, I got you to tidy things up," David sits and smiles at the men, "In the meantime fellas, I want you to hang out here. Take a load off."

A chime indicates a message received on David's private computer, "Excuse me," David makes for a private room on the far end of the large office.

Dominic rubs his jaw and looks over at Pete, "Take a load off? Right."

Pete shrugs his massive shoulders again and finishes his drink. He sets the fine glass on a central table in front of him and leans into the thick cushioned couch, "That Harper droid has had a ton of modifications," he says while staring at the dark table. A long moment passes without either of them saying a word, then Pete ventures further with his line of thought, "You said you were at a tech convention, right?"

Dominic nods his head.

"Were there any synthetic mod booths there?" Pete questions.

"There could have been. I was mainly on the lookout for security stuff," Dominic says unconcerned.

Pete rubs the stubble on his chin, "Is it still going on today?" he asks.

Dominic finally catches up to Pete's line of thinking and chuckles, "You think she made a stop?"

Pete nods, "I do," he says with a smile.

David sits in the dark room of his private office. The message on his data tablet reads: *Too close*. He sits back and exhales. He runs a hand down his face, annoyed that something as insignificant as a synthetic woman would be causing him this much trouble. The media has been all over him and the corporation he's built. They've been questioning the legality of the nano-machines he's been lobbying to get approved and this mechanical female was one headache he doesn't need.

Detective Eddie Mason wouldn't be the first police officer he's had to eliminate and he's sure he won't be last. David was hoping he could get rid of this problem before it came to that. "What to do? What to do?" David says in a sing song voice. He reaches for the tablet and starts to type a message of his own. He hesitates before pushing the send button. Part of him doesn't really want to be pushed to kill the detective. On the other hand, if this cop doesn't lay off, it could be detrimental to him and all that he has accomplished. He sends the message.

David checks that the message has been received over an encrypted channel then presses a call button on his desk. Moments later, Silvia eases her way through the door. "How may I serve you, sir?" she says with only minimal inflection in her voice.

David cradles his head in his hands and closes his eyes, "Tell me again the history of the pacification of the deciv populations."

The synthetic inclines her head, "Certainly sir. Would you like me to start where we left off last night?"

David takes a deep breath and leans back in his chair. He holds the blue urn of hair in his hands. He ponders the request for a long moment. He rolls the pear shaped glass in his fingers. His cold eyes catches the unblinking gaze of the synthetic woman standing in the doorway, "Start from the beginning."

CHAPTER 22

Present Day

Blake sits on his once comfortable office chair in what served as his make shift body shop in the middle of his kitchen. The coffee mug near the end of the cluttered table, holds the last of the third pot he brewed to stay awake. He had been up all night, guiding Imogen home and practically erasing her presence from the city's security surveillance systems. Now she lay in a hibernation mode while he installs combat software and new upgrades. Empty boxes labeled: *UMDF HARDWARE,* lie scattered all over the floor.

Blake's eyes begin to droop and his body freezes as he drifts into a waking sleep. A few seconds pass and he doesn't move a nanometer. His eyes snap open with a jolt. He snatches the cup of coffee from the table and chugs it. About a half hour later he double checks the little list of upgrades he had made before starting, to ensure that he hadn't forgotten anything. "Finally," he mutters. He closes the maintenance hatch and disconnects his PC hardwires.

Imogen stirs and lifts herself from the old dentist's chair. "How long did it take?" she grumbles, still half asleep. She turns over to face her partner in crime.

"About four hours," Blake yawns, "I would have been done sooner, but I had to basically unlock your processors so you'd accept the military software." Blake rubs the sweat from his eyes and yawns, "Congratulations. You're now a certified bad ass."

Imogen sits up in the chair and pulls a t-shirt over her head, "I need a shower. Do you mind?"

Blake shakes his head, "I'm going to fix another pot,"

Twenty minutes later, Imogen returns to the main room in fresh clothes and tousling her hair with a towel, "You okay, Sparx? You seem a little out of it."

Blake sits at the table resting his head in his hand. He cracks an eye, "Oh yeah. I'm just peachy," he says with a hint of annoyance. Imogen eyes him suspiciously. She pulls the towel around her shoulders and takes a seat across from him at the table.

"What's going on, man?" she asks sincerely.

Blake takes a long pull of his coffee and exhales, "I'm not sure where to start," he swivels back and forth in his seat, "I broke up with Amiya." He looks up to meet Imogen's eyes.

"Why?" Imogen asks suspiciously. Blake focuses on the creamy brown liquid in his mug. He cracks a halfhearted smile as he searches for the right words, "I guess I couldn't pretend anymore."

The concerned expression on Imogen's face shifts to one of apprehension as she waits for Blake to finish saying what's on his mind.

"Look," he starts with a determined fervor, "I know that you have to do what you think is necessary and I don't want to hinder your progress in any way." Blake looks up at her and then back down at his cooling coffee, still trying to pick out key words and phrases from the emotional hurricane that is his thoughts. He shakes his head and smiles. He stands, walks to the counter and begins to fix another cup of coffee, "I'm sorry, Gen. Forget I said anything."

A heavy realization begins to creep into Imogen's chest and she sinks into her chair. She doesn't want to jump to conclusions but, she had begun to notice stolen glances from time to time. She didn't really think anything would have ever come of it. Or maybe she was just lying to herself, "Blake, I," Imogen stammers on her words. She wasn't ready for something like this. She hadn't even given any thought to anything but vengeance. It consumes her and even blinds her from things that should have been so obvious. She is living in the past, oblivious to anything concerning the here and now. Her eyes burn with hot tears. She wipes them away with the towel around her neck, "I don't know what to say."

Blake sets his cup on the counter. Still facing the cabinets, he smiles halfheartedly, "You don't have to say anything." He turns his body, still wearing a weary smile, but she's not looking at him. Her gaze is fixed on the white light coming in through the window. He can see that her eyes are glassy. "Hey," he says, catching her attention. "It's okay," he smiles a smile that is much stronger than the shielded one he wore just a few seconds earlier.

Blake's bare feet softly smack back over to the table and he sets a fresh cup of Joe in front of Imogen. She looks up at him and smiles apologetically. He smiles back. Realizing that he needs to change the subject, Blake brings up the matter of Desirae, "Are you still going to meet up with her?" he asks.

Imogen looks back at the bright morning light, pouring through the window with wet, blurry eyes, "I have to," she answers.

"No you don't," Blake replies solemnly.

"Yes, I do." The determination in her voice cracks.

"No. You know how she reacted to what happened to you. You know that she didn't want any part of it." His tone is almost sympathetic and it annoys Imogen.

<How could he be defending her? Desirae is just as guilty as the others for what happened. Wasn't she?>

"She didn't do much to try and stop them," Imogen counters.

"What could she have done?" Blake probes. His opinion on the current subject matter aggravates Imogen to a point of speechlessness. She rises from her seat, tosses the damp towel on the couch and begins to shove her feet into her boots. "You don't have to do it," he says as she wraps a large scarf around her damp hair and neck.

"I don't have time for this," she says and whips her coat out of the closet.

When she reaches the door she pauses. Her mouth a gape. She says nothing and just shakes her head. The door slams and Blake can hear her marching down the hall to the elevator. He rests his head in his hands and sighs heavily.

He sits upright, "T.V. on," he commands. The holographic television flickers to life on a far wall next to the window.

The projection displays a live news broadcast. A photo of the billionaire, David Jennings sits to the far right corner of the projection. On the other side, plain white text in a list format, displays some random talking points. The photo of Jennings fades and the view is taken up by the bullet points. Blake was about to change the channel but stops when the last two phrases on the list catch his eye. *Nano med bots* and *Presidency*. "Raise volume ten points," he says aloud in a monotone voice. The male voice over on the news cast rambles on about meaningless public opinions that mean nothing to the average person. It didn't take long for one of the other news casters to bring the motor mouth back on track.

"But what about these nano-bots that are supposed to be a great benefit to mankind?" the woman asks.

Motor mouth leans forward on the desk, "These *med bots* were designed by medical synthetics a little over a six decades ago to help regenerate the cells of the human body. What Pharma Corp did was augment these machines to also target the nervous system in order to treat patients suffering from seizures, Parkinson's, Muscular Dystrophy, and so many other diseases," he says with a stern conviction.

The women at the desk nods to acknowledge his point, but that's as far as it goes. "When these nano-machines were first created, the synthetic engineers that developed them stated that these machines could be dangerous if they were programed to target the nervous system. They placed heavy restrictions on their programming to keep these machines from being used this way," A female panelist chimes in. "They warned that if the technology ever got into the wrong hands, everyone, syn and human alike would be at the mercy of whoever held the keys," She raises concerns, not only in the panelists, but in Blake as well.

That was about as much as Blake could hear, before he was wide awake and extremely suspicious. Another male on the show spoke up and vehemently denied the previous woman's claims. Blake knows bullshit when he hears it and he believes that these guys who are in support of these machines are swimming in it. He glances over at an unopened box that his buddy, Kevin had thrown in for free. Well not free. Kevin wanted to come over some time so he could try and get a date with Imogen. <*Yeah. That wasn't going to happen.*>

The box contained two dozen syringes that contained an anti-body of sorts. The government had feared that the synthetics would use nano-machines as a weapon. To keep from falling to their robot overlords, they took steps. Mostly everything Blake got from Kevin, was older military tech that was deemed useless. Now it would seem that this old tech might save some lives.

CHAPTER 23

Present Day

Desirae said that she couldn't meet outside of her home, which was fine for Imogen. She doesn't need to lure Ms. Deponet to a dark place to put a bullet in her head. Her home would do just fine. Imogen finally arrives at the tall apartment building, Desirae had specified earlier. *"Key in Bonnet and ring the buzzer,"* she had said. Imogen punches the keys to spell the name in the buildings digital directory. Once found, she presses a button on the monitor. A short buzzing sound rings out from a tiny speaker. A moment later, the digitized list is replace by a video feed. Desirae's face is on the other end. Imogen forces a smile. "Hey! Come on up. Apartment 697," Desirae says with a warm smile.

In the elevator, Imogen checks her gun to ensure that the power clip is fully charged. She's disappointed to see that the charge is only half full, "Well, all I need is one," she says coldly. She slips the gun back into her belt and waits for the doors to open. A pleasant *bong,* sound indicates that the lift has finally reached the desired floor and the shiny aluminum doors glide open. A tiny plaque on the wall indicates the direction she should take to reach apartment 697. There are only about twenty or twenty six units to a floor so, it wouldn't take long for her to reach her destination.

Imogen is surprised at the cleanliness of this complex. The doorframes are all hand carved. Each knob was either brass, silver or gold, which was a sign that these were owned. The cherry wood floor was buffed to a high shine and it all infuriated Imogen. For someone who worked as a bartender at a seedy strip joint, Desirae must be doing well.

<Bitch probably paid for it by killing people like myself!> Imogen screams in her mind. When she reaches the door, she freezes. The fibers that serve as her muscles bunch. She takes a deep breath to keep her legs from shaking, presses her ear to the door and listens. Nothing. She knocks on the door.

Seconds later Desirae opens door, a broad smile stretches large across her face. To Imogen's dismay, she found that she was smiling as well.

"Come in," Desirae says softly. Imogen steps inside the sparse apartment and is guided to a stylish couch. "Have a seat. You want something to drink?" her host asks.

"No thanks," Imogen replies. Desirae shrugs and heads toward the kitchen to fix herself a cup of hot cocoa. Imogen takes in her surroundings. Aside from the couch she was sitting on, there is a rocking chair with an ottoman, a small coffee table, and a small plastic tub off in the corner.

"I feel like a complete idiot for not being able to remember you," Desirae says from within the nook that was her kitchen.

Imogen rolls her eyes, "Really, I would think that you couldn't forget. Given the circumstances."

Desirae steps softly back into the room and eases herself down on the couch next to Imogen. "Circumstances?" she says. Her voice had hint of anxiety.

Imogen looks down at the mug piled high with marshmallows cradled in Desirae's hands. Without looking up at her perplexed host, Imogen sighs with disappointment that Desirae couldn't remember her part in the murder, "Eighteen months ago we met." The frigid tone in Imogen's voice and the time frame sends icy goose bumps running down Desirae's spine. "You were with three other men. You came into my home."

Desirae begins to shake her head from side to side. Terror fills her expression. Tears well up in her big eyes. An uncontrollable fear grips Desirae and her body goes stiff. Imogen meets her host's tear soaked face, "You helped murder my husband."

Desirae bolts upright. The mug of hot chocolate falls from her hands to spill on the white plush carpet. "I... I..." Desirae stutters frantically, still shaking her head as if it would block out the horrific memories. Imogen slowly stands and pulls the shiny metal gun from her belt. She points the muzzle at Desirae's face. The frightened woman's knees give way to fright and she falls to the floor with a pathetic yelp. She instinctively throws up her hands as if that would stop the superheated slug from ripping through her skull.

"I had no idea they were going to do that. I swear. I... I..."

Imogen marches forward and levels the heavy pistol directly between Desirae's eyes, "I'm not interested in your excuses! You people took everything from me!" Desirae closes her eyes and pleads for her life. Imogen can't hear any of it.

"As soon as I left, I called the police. I'm in a witness protection program now. Please, I have a son," she cries. Desirae's body trembles. She worries at what would happen to her little boy if she wasn't around.

Imogen clamps her eyes shut at her words. Blake's sympathetic predictions were spot on and she couldn't believe it. She didn't want to believe it.

"I'm so sorry. I'm so sorry," Desirae sobs. The steady flow of tears soak the neck and chest of Desirae's white shirt.

Unable to look at her intended prey, Imogen turns away and wills herself to pull the trigger.

Imogen's grip tightens around the handle of the gun. The trigger hits that sweet spot. Any more pressure and the gun will discharge. A soft click to Imogen's left steals her focus. She whips her head around and almost points her weapon to meet the potential threat.

"Mama," a small voice calls from beyond the corner. Imogen drops to her knees and hides the silver gun. Both women turn in the direction of the child's voice.

"Yes, lil bits," Desirae answers, while trying to dry her eyes.

A little dark haired boy steps out from the hall, rubbing his eyes. His diaper bulges from under his footie pajamas. "I pee," his tiny voice says.

Shakily, Desirae turns toward Imogen as if to ask permission to change her son.

The shame deep within Imogen's chest pulls her head down. The heat of her tears are made even hotter by the burning of her cheeks. She knows that if she lets Desirae out of her sight she could call the police and Imogen would certainly be killed, but she knows that she is no monster. Imogen nods her head to answer the silent question. Desirae pops to her feet and darts toward her son. "Okay honey. Let's get you changed and back to bed." She takes the child back to his room. Imogen crawls back to her original seat on the couch. The large gun hangs loosely in her limp hand. Suddenly too heavy for her to hold, she places the hunk of metal on the table. Strands of curly scarlet hair hang in Imogen's view as she stares down at the brown cooling liquid that is soaking into the colorless carpet. Questioning thoughts race through her mind so fast that she is unable to focus nor rationalize them. Completely overwhelmed with emotion, she cups her face in her hands and weeps.

"That was the first and last job, I had ever done with Chosen," Desirae says faintly.

Imogen lifts her head to see the woman standing partially behind the wall. "I had never believed the brutal stories on the news. I thought they were just the media blowing things out of proportion," she continues and slowly inches her way out from behind the wall. A stray tear glistens in the light and rolls its way down Desirae's face, "I tried getting justice for you and your husband, but there were a lot of threats made toward me and my son."

Slowly, Desirae sits on the couch. Her eye's glaring at the shiny metal gun resting on her table. She looks back at Imogen, noticing that her eyes haven't left the wall. Desirae leans forward and finds that her would be killer is crying freely. Desirae slowly leans toward Imogen and in one quick motion she wraps her arms around her, embracing her in a crushing hug.

At first, the move surprises Imogen, but strangely enough, she finds herself hugging back. "I'm so sorry," Imogen's muffled voice moans. Desirae closes her eyes in relief and forgets about the weapon on the table.

"There is nothing I can say that will change what happened," Desirae says while trying to keep her own quivering lips under control. For a long moment the two women hold each other. Each of them feel a little less cumbersome from the temporary release of their burdens.

Imogen lifts her head from Desirae's soggy shoulder and wipes her eyes, "I'm sorry for coming into your home and..." Imogen searches for the illusive words, "I still have to find Pete Roberts and Dominic Vespucci and put an end to this."

Desirae nods her head. Her eyes are red rimmed and misty, "There is a lot more I have to tell you," Desirae utters.

Imogen dries her face with her sleeve, "What do you mean?" she asks.

Desirae picks at her finger nails, takes a deep breath and says, "There's a lot more you need to know."

Imogen knits her eyebrows, not fully understanding what Desirae means. "Those assholes get off on murder. What more do I need to know?" Imogen says. Desirae scrapes black nail polish from her thumb and places it in the palm of her hand. She wipes another bead of moisture from her cheek.

"You need to know about the man who's given them free reign to do the things they do." Imogen sits up ready to listen to what she has to say. Desirae tucks strands of hair behind her ear, "Those men, Pete, Frog, and Dominic take their orders directly from the man himself."

For a moment, Imogen doesn't understand what she has just been told. Desirae sees this and clarifies, "They listen and answer to David Jennings."

Imogen remembers the man from the media vids and news casts, but knows little else about the guy. "I'm listening," She says.

Desirae sniffs before she continues, "I didn't find this out until the investigation of what happened but, he's the one who told them to kill your husband for hiding you. Lack of evidence made it hard to prove, but it did place a magnifying glass on their ass."

Imogen pulls up what little she knows about David Jennings and adds his name to the list of people who have to die.

"He's also the bastard who threatened my son and me. We've been in hiding ever since," Desirae says with a quivering voice.

"How do I find him," Imogen says, resolute in her tone. Desirae looks up at the fiery woman, who is intently glaring at the gun on the table in front of her.

"I'll tell you all you need to know about Chosen H.Q." Desirae says. To their surprise, someone knocks on the door.

CHAPTER 24

Present Day

Mason had been avoiding his partner successfully for the last few days, but he knows that he'd eventually have to face her. She had left more than a few messages on his personal communicator that grew in frustration with each message. Rather than staying at his home, because that would be the first place Vivian would go, he opted to rent a room at a swanky hotel. He needed the solitude to look over evidence and store it in a secure location. He had purchased an external drive and decided that once he had everything stored on it and his wet drive, he could stash a copy somewhere safe. Leaving a copy of the data in the station was not an option because, he was fairly certain that Vivian had been the one who had deleted the data from Francis's ocular drive.

After looking through all the files he had on data discs and old fashioned paper, Mason came across several interesting leads. One pertaining to the arrival and assignment of his partner. She went from a cop on the beat, to his partner almost immediately after the bombing. The name Desirae Deponet appears on one of the reports only once. She is a witness, who had been placed in protective custody following the temporary disbanding of all Seeker cells, after the bombing downtown nearly two years ago. The name rings some bells and is familiar to the detective. Mason can see the strings blowing in the wind, but doesn't have the solid evidence needed to pin them down.

"Red fucking tape. It's always the damned tape that gets in the way," he says before he takes a drink of some iced whiskey.

After stewing on what he knows and what he can't prove, he grabs a stack of papers on the only witness he could possibly get a hold of and hopefully get some answers. After finding her location by sifting through various police archive, Mason grabs his coat off the messy bed and heads for the door.

It doesn't take him long to find the upscale apartment building. He parks a block away, just in case. He sits in his rental car for a time, waiting for something out of the ordinary to happen, but so far so good. The wind from the speeding traffic rocks his car each time a vehicle passes. Mason rubs the weariness from his eyes and looks back at the main door of Desirae's apartment. He finally exits the car and begins to hike the long city block up to the building. After a couple of minutes of walking in the frigid cold, he seriously regrets parking so far away.

He uses an emergency security code known to law enforcement to unlock the door and enter the building. Once inside he blows in his cupped hands to ward off the chill left in his bones. He pushes the call button on the elevator and waits. The lift takes some time to reach ground level, but he couldn't complain. It beats having to use the stairs.

Mason takes his time walking over to Desirae's apartment. He wants to make sure he has the right set of questions for her. He digs in his inner breast pocket and pulls out a little container of *Fresh* tabs. He pops one in his mouth and waits for it to dissolve and erase any trace of the whiskey he was drinking earlier. He breathes in his hand to test the results. Finding no hint of the hard liquor, he knocks on the door.

It takes some time for a woman on the other side to answer, "Who is it?" the voice asks.

"Ma'am, I'm detective Ed Mason. I was wondering if I could ask you a few questions." He can hear some shuffling beyond the door and then some whispering. He raises his hand to knock again, but the door opens just a crack. A small woman with multicolored hair peers up at him.

"Let me see your badge?" she demands.

Mason holds up his I.D. for her to inspect, "I was hoping it would be possible to talk to you about an incident you reported some time ago, about a bombing. May I come in?"

The woman eyes him suspiciously, "I've said all I had to say to the woman that helped get me into the program," she says with a hint of aggravation.

Mason sighs heavily, "Ma'am, I am aware that Chief Galarza got you into this program, but I cannot stress the importance of my inquiry. I believe that you may be in some danger..." Mason stops speaking when he notices her uneasiness.

The shift of her eyes to a person or persons unseen sets off red flags. Mason pushes his way through the woman and the door. Once inside the apartment he finds the infamous redhead pointing a gun at him. He notices that the gun looks huge in her small hands.

Mason draws his gun and levels at the redheaded woman who he knows is a synthetic, "Drop your weapon!" he commands.

The woman holds steady save for the tears in her eyes. Mason didn't want to shoot the armed woman, but she was leaving him no choice. Just as he was about to squeeze the trigger, Desirae steps in his line of fire.

"Stop!" she cries. Mason cringes at having almost shot the only real lead in this fubar case.

"Get out of the way!" he yells.

Desirae throws her hands up as if to keep them from charging each other, "No one is shooting anyone!"

Mason nor Imogen lowers their weapons. Without taking her eyes off of the detective, Desirae says, "Imogen, put your gun away."

Mason's perfect posture sags at the name, "Harper?" he questions. The memory of everything that had happened in that case comes flooding back. The image of the charred mobile is a little too vivid for his liking. "Imogen Harper? I'm Ed Mason. I was assigned to the case that involved your husband, Darioux." Slowly Mason lowers his gun and slides it back into his shoulder holster. He holds his arms out to show that he isn't here to harm her.

With each sob, Imogen's gun falls lower and lower. "They killed us," Imogen spouts. She repeats the words until her shoulders slump and she drops the fire arm. The young toddler screams in the other room. Desirae cautiously moves to tend to her son. Mason watches Desirae exit the other room through his peripheral vision.

"Who killed you?" Mason asks in a gentler voice.

Imogen falls back to lean against the wall, "Francis Ogmayer, Dominic Vespucci, Pete Roberts, David Jennings," Imogen says angrily. Mason's heart flutters, but he doesn't want to get his hopes up.

"Do you have proof?" he asks.

Imogen looks him in the eye. The fire burning in her gaze is enough to melt steel. "I have video," she states.

Mason's heart skips a beat. This was the break he had been waiting for. The link to tie down the loose ends. He can finally put those bastards down for good. "If you get me a copy of the vid data and we find that it is untampered, we can put them behind bars," Mason proclaims.

Imogen furiously shakes her head, "No. You know as well as I do that those monsters will find a way to get off. They need to die," Imogen says harshly.

Mason can tell that there is nothing he can do, short of killing her here and now that will change her mind. She is determined to let them have her extra cold brand of justice. The crazy thing is that, he finds within himself, that he is willing to let her do it. Law be damned.

In all of his years on the force, he watched helpless, unable to do anything while wealthy, guilty, criminals walk free. They had enough money to play the game a little better. He watched young men and women get the book smashed over them for minor offenses, while the *well to do* got off with a slap on the wrist. It was bullshit and it chewed away at him for too long.

"You know I can't openly support that," Mason says in a cool, level tone. His choice of words doesn't go unnoticed by Imogen. He visibly relaxes. He watches some of the tension leave the synthetic's face.

Imogen smiles faintly, "So, you aren't going to arrest me?"

Mason shrugs, "I can't arrest you if I can't find you, but I still need to talk to Ms. Deponet. I wouldn't mind getting some information from you as well."

Imogen nods, smiles weakly and then wipes her face.

Desirae emerges from the room with a two year old on her hip, "I'm thrilled to see that you two have put away your boom booms," she says tiredly. She straps the young child into a small seat facing away from the adults with guns. Desirae plops down in a chair next to her son and shovels mashed produce onto a tiny spoon, "What is it that you want to know officer?" she says, guiding a spoon into her son's mouth.

Mason glances over at Desirae then back at Imogen who had slumped down to sit on the floor. "I need to know what happened that you had to go into witness protection. I also need to know what you know about Chosen and their practices," Mason says.

Desirae runs her free hand over her head, pulling her hair back out of her face and replies, "It should all be on file. The police records should tell you all you need to know."

Mason scratches his forehead and chuckles, "Yeah. Sometimes you can't trust the record."

Imogen pulls her long curly hair out of her face and laughs at the implications of his words.

"You want a detailed record of what happened the day they murdered my husband? I can give you a copy of the video. I stored it on my hard drive," she says. Mason was about to interject and remind her that he needs to be sure that it hadn't been tampered with but, Imogen beat him to the punch, "I can assure you that it is genuine."

"Do you know anything about Chosen and how it's run?" Mason asks. Imogen shakes her head. Mason regards Desirae expectantly, "What about you?" he says. The single mother pilots another spoonful of food into her son's mouth.

"I only worked with them that one day, so I don't know much," Mason nods, disappointed. "But I can tell you about what happened after I contacted the cops about what happened," Desirae adds. That got Mason's attention. He knows that it'll be hearsay, but right now that'll be good enough to build the case.

Imogen listens as Desirae recounts her tale about the death threats from David and his goons. She watches as Mason absorbs all the information as it comes to him. A blinking light on the bottom left corner of her HUD indicates that she had a text and video messages from Blake. Apparently he had be trying to contact her for the past ten minutes. She opens the latest video file.

"I know you're mad at me, but we have a major problem. You need to call or get back here ASAP!" an alarmed Blake says. He spoke fast and frantic,

which only made her that much more anxious about what the *problem* was.

Imogen lumbers to her feet trying to remain calm, as not to cause alarm in either Desirae or the detective.

"Ah, sorry to interrupt," Imogen says, "Where's your bathroom?"
Desirae points to a door just off the hall that leads to the bedrooms. Imogen steadily treads over to the restroom and shuts the door behind her. She pulls up Blake's throwaway line and gives him a ring. She doesn't even hear a ringing on her end before she hears Blake's panic stricken voice answer.

"Gen! We need to find a new place and fast!" he practically yells in her ear. She can hear a ruckus in the background. Her brows furrow as worry intermixed with anger and confusion fill her mind.

"Blake, what's going on?" she says in as calm a voice as she can.
She can still hear clattering and his labored breathing over the line.

"There is no time. Don't come here. I'll call you once I've gotten to the new hideout." Blake says. His words aren't lost on her and she knows that this was the day they had discussed and planned for. She activates the record function on her HUD. If the shit is going to hit the fan, she is at least going to have a record of it. She knows that the only thing that would make him wig out like this is F.B.I. or a similar organization or Chosen, knowing where to find them.

"Blake, turn on your tracker," Imogen instructs, but a loud concussive sound fills her ears, followed by several loud pops. "Blake! Blake!" Imogen screams over and over.

Mason bursts through the bathroom door just as Imogen is about to turn the knob. Desirae isn't far behind him, child in her arms. Imogen tries to access the vid feed tied to the connection. After the third try she finally convinced his firewalls to back down and display full video. Mason silently asks for information on the situation with wide concerned eyes. Imogen holds up a finger.

A grainy image flickers to life, displaying the kitchen and part of the front door that has been blown open. White smoke crawls along the floor as black clouds drift to the ceiling like smog. Flickering movement catches her eye. She can make out a couple of sets of combat boots trampling the debris littered floor. The men seem to be searching the apartment. They don't seem to be in a rush, which could only mean two things. One, they've either killed Blake or he managed to escape. Imogen hopes it is the latter.

A wave of guilty emotions were ready to flood her mind, but she put up a mental dam and prepared for the worst. Mason gestured again for some explanation, but Imogen doesn't know how to answer him.

Just then, Desirae called out from the main room, "I have a link cable!" An insert and moment later, they are watching as men in paramilitary armor storm through the apartment and search for anything that would give them a clue to find Imogen. A voice on the feed yells that they've got eyes on Blake.

Pete Roberts walks into the frame and in a gravelly voice he screams, "Kill that little fucker."

CHAPTER 25

3 Months Earlier

Imogen sits on an old chair she had pulled up to one of the large windows in Blake's apartment. Her eyes are fixed on the many people ambling through the city below. She wants to hate them. They hated her. Why not? It's only fair that they should feel the horror and pain she's had to endure the past year and a half. Months of talking with her impromptu doctor, Blake, helped her get over that sense of prejudice. He had said that not all human beings are as sick as the men who attacked her and Darioux. It took some serious convincing that the world and all the people in it weren't that bad - just somewhat bad. The truly evil beings are the minority. Their acts of predation were just so egregious that they overshadowed the beauty that was abundant in the world.

The terror that mixed with the absolute rage she feels toward human beings had somewhat subsided and she decided to focus that negative energy on those who truly deserve it. Only then would she unleash the twisted thing that had been growing inside her all this time. She needed to know that those people wouldn't exist anymore. Only then could she hope to truly heal from the trauma.

Imogen continues to watch the people outside. She finds herself wondering what each person is thinking and if they even give a thought about the other hapless souls around them. She can't help but feel a certain pessimism toward human beings. She tries breaking herself of her cynical perspective, but looking back on human history all she can see is that they've excelled at creating new and more barbaric ways to kill themselves and each other.

Imogen grows more and more irritated with her line of thinking and almost gets lost in anger. She spies a mother with her child. A little girl or boy? She can't tell from so high up. The child is screaming about something. A toy or the latest Halloween costume perhaps? The mother crouches down and says something to the child that makes it stop crying. Imogen thinks that maybe the lady had threatened the kid, but that thought was squashed when the little one embraces the parent in a fierce hug. The mother then picks the child up and begins to walk again.

Imogen lowers her head. Her anger replaced with shame for expecting a negative outcome. A tear rolls down her cheek then drips on her blue jeans before she even knows she is crying. She stares at the dark blue dot for a long time. She closes her eyes and rests her head on the window pane.

A jingle at the door signals that Blake is finally home. He had been running around like a headless chicken, gathering last minute supplies and random things for his *safeguard* that he'd been working on for years. Blake had been growing increasingly paranoid about the wrong people finding him. He thought that it would only be a matter of time before the authorities caught up with his digital crimes and he wanted to have some kind of escape plan ready. Just in case.

Blake stumbles through the door holding a box that's almost as big as he is. A quartet of reusable bags dangle from his fingers. "Uh, sweetheart, a little help," he says. Imogen slides one arm under the large box and hefts it up off of Blake's strained hands. "Thanks," he smiles and eases the bags onto the floor. He sighs as the blood rushes back into his purple fingers.

"Where do you want it?" Imogen asks. Her monotone voice hints at annoyance and she realizes it once she saw the troubled look Blake shot her. Imogen bites her lip and tries again, "Where do you need this?"

Blake points to a spot near his desk and she sluggishly obliges.

"Sorry, I've got a lot on my mind." She sniffles.

Blake smiles apologetically and kicks the door shut with the tip of his shoe, "That's understandable," he whispers. Imogen sits back in her chair and sifts through the massive box. Most of what she picks up and moves to the side are things that she doesn't even recognize as usable items, "What's all this?" she queries.

Blake is preoccupied with pulling other contraptions out of the bags to answer at first but, after a moment, he replies, "That my dear, is what's going to keep me alive when shit hits the fan."

The gears he was pulling out of the bag are about as greasy as a professional bodybuilder. The oil drips from the cogs and on to whatever surface he places them. "This is all stuff for my secret escape hatch," he continues.

Imogen pulls out a retinal scanner and raises an eyebrow, "Okay, James Bond, how in the blue hell are you going to put a secret hatch in here?" Imogen questions. She chuckles a bit, "I mean you live in an apartment," she muses.

Blake empties the first bag and lifts a finger, "I have bought the apartment directly below us," he exclaims with a giddy smile.

Imogen doesn't know whether to nod approvingly or scoff at the outrageous declaration, so she sits there for a moment wondering where the hell he got the money to buy an entire apartment. She peers back down at the box, then back up at Blake who is practically dancing while digging through the dirty bags. "Should I even ask?" Imogen starts. Blake just shrugs and continues dancing. For a moment she is agitated that he could be in such a great mood while she was in the middle of loathing everything. She wants to slap the taste from his mouth.

After watching him shake and squirm to a rhythm only he could hear, she can't help but smile at his ridiculous moves, "You know if I didn't know you, I'd swear you were having an epileptic fit," she giggles.

Imogen looks back out the window and thinks of the mother and the child again. They were long gone. She can't help but wonder if Blake just did for her what the mother did for the child. She smiles at the idea. The cold icy lump that is stubbornly clinging to the inside of her chest suddenly feel warm. Imogen looks back over at her roommate just in time to see him clap and awkwardly perform a sloppy pirouette. Imogen allows herself to laugh.

As Imogen watches Blake dance, she finally acknowledges the small but intensely warm sentiment that had been growing for this geek all this time. It doesn't feel like a betrayal of her husband, but she squashes those warm emotions immediately and locks them away. Affection was the last thing she needed now. Soft emotions would get her killed. If anything went wrong, those emotions would get Blake killed. She couldn't allow that. She couldn't handle another innocent death on her conscience. She gazes back out the window so he can't see her eyes go misty.

CHAPTER 26

Present Day

Blake was never a star athlete at his high school. Nor is he a guy who enjoys sports, but he expertly dodges all the pedestrians on the crowded sidewalks. The large black duffel bag slung over his back, carrying what he considers essentials, bounces with every stride. A voice from behind yells that they can see him in the streets. A moment later, a car horn beeps frantically. Blake chances a look behind him and spots the big black sports utility vehicles weaving in and out of lanes toward him. He looks down at the tiny watch screen strapped to his wrist and presses a small button on the side. A signal is sent to his apartment which destroys all of his computers with mini explosions. Anyone still in his apartment will be showered with debris moving as fast as bullets. He presses a second button on the watch and immediately the traffic lights begin to randomly change. He hopes the chaos is enough to buy him some time to get off the streets.

A few loud metallic crashes, followed by growling obscenities, indicates that he has the time he needs. Blake turns the corner and hopes he breaks the line of sight. He has an extra set of clothes to change into, but he knows he has to get to a place to change. He begins to move toward a coffee shop at the other end of the block, when a shot rings out from behind him. Brick fragments burst from the wall to his left. People all around scream and duck for cover, leaving Blake to stand out like a giant amongst dwarfs.

Another burst of fire punctuates the screams of the people, huddled on the floor. He narrowly escapes the trajectory of the bullets. Two more bursts echo through the air only this time, Blake feels the nerves in his right arm burning. The hot metal slug that just burrowed its way through the meat of his bicep, shatters the storefront window of the coffee shop. Blake watches as an older man, who didn't get down far enough takes the stray projectile to the head. Blood runs down the cracked glass.

Blake stumbles but quickly regains his balance. He redoubles his efforts to escape the murderous bastards behind him. He leaps over the hood of a car at the intersection in an attempt to put something a bit more solid behind him and his pursuers. More bullets whistle around him, missing his flesh by mere centimeters. Some of the people around him aren't so lucky. Blake is helpless to the cowering bystanders who are being gunned down, because of him. Most people had cleared the streets in fear. Periodically someone would scream in horror from their home. All those stray bullets flew through windows and walls. Most likely they injured or killed some people. He only hopes that no one, especially kids were harmed, but he also knows that hoping and the reality of the situation are two different things.

Blake turns another corner, then quickly jumps into an alley that will eventually spill out into downtown. A busy area is the last place he wants to lead these assholes and he knows that he has to get off the streets quickly.

Sirens echo through the streets. Finally the authorities are responding to the gunfire. Blake wonders how effective they would be in getting the guys in black fatigues off of his ass. He surmises that all they would have to say is that they were after a rogue syn and all would be forgiven. "Fuck," he growls.

Blake knows that he has to make his way across two intersections to reach a secondary entrance to the underground tunnels that would allow him to catch his breath. He punches through the mouth of the alley and narrowly avoids being crushed by a public transport. Blake doesn't even hesitate. He bolts into the next alley. One more street and he's home free. Blake jumps the wood slat fence that divides the narrow passage and makes his way toward the busy street. Again he dashes out without hesitation. He dodges one car, but ends up rolling up the hood of another, cracking the windshield, then he's thrown to the hard pavement when the driver applies the brakes. Pain courses through his body. His vision goes white for a second. It seems like the blindness lasts forever.

"Get up! Get up!" a determined voice shouts in his head. Blake rolls to his side. Stabbing pain brings his vision back into focus and reminds him that he is still alive.

"You lost your mind there, buddy?" the driver of the now damaged car shouts bitterly. Blake doesn't stop to answer the man. Once back on his now unsteady feet, Blake stumbles for the opening of the last alley that will lead him to safety.

He trips over the curb and hits the ground hard. The man who hit Blake with his car changes his tune, "Hey man, you okay?"

Again, Blake doesn't answer. Instead, he grits his teeth and climbs to his feet. He jogs as fast as he can to the adjoining alley that hides a service tunnel.

Blake finally reaches the narrow dead end then trudges over to the iron disk embedded in the ground. The plan was to be in decent health once he reached the manhole, now the damned thing was going to be a bitch to lift. Blake pulls the crowbar from his pack and rams it into one of the outer holes to take advantage of the leverage. At first the thing doesn't budge, "Come on you son of a bitch," Blake groans. After a few stressful seconds, the heavy cover pops up and Blake slides it over enough to accommodate his body. He throws the pack down then turns and enters the dark opening.

Not long after entering the tunnel, Blake hears the sound of many boots pounding the pavement above him. He holds his breath until they pass. He pulls out a set of low light goggles from his bag, checks the wound on his arm. The bullet just grazed him, but it hurts like hell. Blake begins his hasty trek to the safe house, where he can begin to dress his wounds and relax. Paranoia urges him to pull the antique, Mossberg 500 tactical, sawed-off, pump action, shotgun out of the bag. He pulls on the strap to slide the bag back on his back.

Slowly and as quietly as he can, Blake sneaks through the tunnel, following a mental map he has spent months memorizing. After an hour into his trip, Blake hears a strange noise near the spot he plans on using as his exit. He stops moving immediately and listens intently to the noises around him. Blake levels the shotgun in front of him and takes several steady, silent steps forward. He notices a control port sunk into the surrounding wall. The depression is just deep enough for him to flatten his body inside for cover.

The sound of steam valves venting in the distance echo through the tunnel. The normal humming of all the city's underground electrical systems Blake can tune out, it's all the unusual sounds he's having trouble deciphering. Every so often he hears the squeak of a rodent or the drip of some far off leak and that is distracting enough. A soft crunch of a hard soled shoe against stone worries him. Whoever is down here with him is a patient son of a bitch.

Blake wipes the sweat from his forehead with his sleeve and tries to control his breathing. He waits for another fifteen minutes with nothing new, aside from the normal sounds of the millions of volts running through the large wires above and the occasional hiss of a vent somewhere. Blake eases up a bit, chocking up the noises to his mind playing tricks on him. He lowers the heavy weapon and rubs his wounded arm. *Crunch!* The sound of another footstep sends Blake's adrenaline into hyper drive. He double checks his weapon to ensure that the safety is off. Another footstep. Only this time the hard shoe was closer, about twenty to thirty feet away in the same tunnel.

Blake fills his lungs with air then holds his breath. He weighs his options. *<Do I peek out or do I just shoot?>* Blake ponders to himself. His heart pummels his chest with every beat. Blake exhales slowly.

"Look, I know exactly where you're at boy," the skulking man says with an arrogant tone in his voice. The words chill Blake to the bone. He couldn't tell just by the voice who or how many had found him, but he hopes they're not expecting him to have a shotgun. "Something you got on your person is giving off a signal and that's how I found you," the bastard continues. Blake tries for a peek around the corner, but an azure bolt nearly takes his head off before he can see who was at the other end. "I'm going to be straight with you right now, bub," the armed man states, "You're going to die down here today and then I'm going to kill your expensive fuck doll, again."

Blake identifies his pursuer by his choice of words to describe Imogen. He had actually dreamed of killing this man many times before. The fear in Blake was replaced by cold fury that bubbles from deep within him. He could deal with them wanting to kill him. That was fine. What he couldn't handle was threats toward Imogen. Blake steels his nerves and is ready to take out Dominic.

"I remember you from outside the *Palace*," Dominic calls out. "You know, I didn't find the fucking tracker until she was right on top of me. Tenacious bitch," he admitted.

Blake is content to let the loud mouth talk. It gives him a general area to unload in. Judging from the sound of his pacing shoes and his obnoxious voice, Blake feels he has a pretty good fix on the man. "Why are you helping her, brother?" Dominic questions.

"You're no brother of mine asshole," Blake says with a sneer.

"We ain't brothers by blood, but we brothers, son," Dominic asserts. "If I didn't know any better, I'd say you were in love with the lil cunt." Dominic presses. Blake clenches his teeth.

"How-a-bout this? Once we kill her you can keep her head and you can get your jollies that way," Dominic teases. The chubby bastard claps his hands as he hoots and hollers like he's just told some magnificent joke.

Blake uses the little taunt to launch his attack. Spinning out from his cover, Blake levels the shotgun in Dominic's general direction and opens fire. Blake fires one, two, three shots, before dropping down to his belly to avoid another sapphire blast from Dominic's energy weapon. The booming gunfire reverberates through the narrow tunnel and nearly destroys the hearing of both men.

Dominic cries out in pain as the wide spread slams into his gut. Blake jumps to his feet and storms the wounded man knocking him to the ground. Dominic groans in pain, holding his abdomen.

Blake wields the heavy, empty gun like a cudgel and drives it in an arc, down on Dominic's jaw. He repeats the savage process several more times. Dominic coughs and spits out some shattered teeth. Blake drops down to one knee.

"Pleath. Pleath thop," Dominic gurgles.

Blake huffs incredulously, laughs, then slides a single round into the shotgun. He leans in close to the injured man's ear and whispers, "You're going to tell me something." Dominic coughs again. Flecks of blood land on Blake's coat. Disgusted, Blake leans back to look the man in the eyes, "Are you afraid of what's going to happen to your soul when I kill your sorry ass?" Blake raises the shotgun up, then slams it down into Dominic's screaming mouth and pulls the trigger. The slightly muffled discharge sends chunks of skull and waves of blood in every direction. Blake dry heaves then pukes up bile and coffee next to the body.

Blake sits next to the headless corpse, waiting for his hearing to return. He presses a finger to his left ear and feels the warm blood seeping out from his exploded drum. He kicks Dominic's body on basic principle. Still hearing impaired, Blake reaches forward and grabs the dead man's gun and shuffles toward his planned exit. A hatch above flips open and Blake raises both guns at the opening. He's tired, hurt and he can't hear, but he's damn sure he can kill another seeker asshole. He lowers his weapons when, Imogen pokes her head through the hole. Her curly ruby hair hangs over her face but the relief in her eyes meets his.

CHAPTER 27

Present Day

Eddie Mason heard the call over the COMs moments after Imogen had lost the connection with her partner and friend, Blake. Pulling up to the curb, Mason has some qualms about showing up to the call earlier than the rest of his colleagues, but he decides that if anyone asks, he didn't have to tell. Fire crews and other emergency personnel, rush in all directions. The uniforms had the building and a couple of city blocks cordoned off to any and all civilians. Which is fine, but Mason observes a few Chosen agents carrying potential evidence out of the building. He huffs and lets them have their little victory, because in the end, it wouldn't matter.

Any other misgivings he has about showing up early, vanish once he spots his Janus-faced partner Vivian, talking calmly with a man in black fatigues and Pete Roberts. Mason exits his car and paints a cool professional calm over his suspicious face, "I see you confined your assault to the singular unit, this time," Mason quips. Pete shifts his feet as if he anticipates a fight brewing. Maybe he didn't get to relieve all that roid-rage? Either way, Mason can't wait to slap cuffs on him. Vivian rolls her eyes like a jaded teenager.

"Nice of you to finally join us," Vivian says. The look on her face could slay a bull in mid stride.

"Yeah," Mason replies staring a hole in Pete, "I had to follow some intense leads,"

Vivian looks up from her notes to notice that the two men are locked in a silent *mine is bigger* match. She takes a purposeful step in front of Mason, while dismissing Roberts, "Well, I hope they panned out for you. We're just about done here," she says without meeting his eyes. "Some cyber-criminal was harboring our psychotic synthetic. He destroyed most, if not all the evidence and headed north," Vivian points down the street with a black lacquered thumb.

Mason glances in the direction while she continues. "A Chosen Seeker is trailing him as we speak. Roberts agreed to link me up to their tracker here in just a few." She adds.

Mason nods as he surveys the scene. Pete's hateful eyes hasn't gone unnoticed, even though they are about twenty feet away. Mason smiles and inclines his head.

"You done having fun, Mason?" a raspy female voice chimes from behind. Mason turns to find, Chief Galarza walking up, and looking very displeased. Her thick dark hair clings around her face and neck like a natural scarf that's attached to her fleece hat.

"Yes ma'am. Just getting my fill," Mason replies. The Chief smiles slightly and the crow's feet around her eyes deepen.

This is odd and a little awkward but, Mason knows his questions would be answered if he could just ignore the obvious. Vivian hands the digital notes over to Galarza, who downloads the information to her wet-drive without looking it over.

"You know Mason, if you would answer your calls every once in a while, I wouldn't have to take your place in the world," the older woman says with the mildest of attitudes.

Mason and Galarza have always had their differences, but there is a mutual respect between them.

"Sorry about that Chief. I had a few things to take care of."

Vivian shoots Mason a scornful glance, but she leaves the amount of information he'll divulge up to him.

Chief Galarza eyeballs Mason, "Well, just so you know, I'll be accompanying you two on this investigation," she states.

Mason attempts to object, but the hard woman cuts him off, "I think you two are on to something big. Detective Stern filled me in while you were M.I.A."

Mason wants to pull the Chief aside and voice his concerns about his partner Vivian, but rethinks his logic, "If Vivian is good with it," Mason concedes.

Galarza stands with her arms crossed in front of her chest, waiting for the duo to continue their investigation.

Mason turns to Vivian, who looks like she'd rather be anywhere he's not, "What do you got?" Mason asks.

Vivian sighs heavily and looks up at the older man, "Well, some seekers are also after our redhead robot. They tracked her to this apartment building," she points to the burned out windows. "They were attempting to apprehend her and the accomplice, but things didn't go as smooth as they'd wished."

Mason looks up at the singed windows of the apartment, knowing full well that Imogen wasn't here when they attacked, "How'd they know to track them here?" Mason says.

"A tech vender. Unfortunately he can't be reached. Either the suspects have killed him or he's skipped town." Vivian answers.

Mason raises his eyebrows not buying the reasoning behind the vender's convenient absence. Mason glances back over at Pete, who is immersed in a heated conversation with a man holding a small tablet. Pete snatches the device and stomps over to their position. The massive vein in his forehead looks like it's ready to explode.

"Got a problem, cupcake?" Mason quips.

Pete shoots him a dirty look, but ignores the question. "The signal goes dead in a service tunnel about a mile and half from here," Pete grumbles, while he hands the tracker data over to Vivian. She looks the data over, then hands it over to Galarza.

"We'll send a unit over to check it out and we'll meet them there," the older woman says.

The narrow tunnel smells of human waste. The automated lighting system is down, leaving the passage in total darkness. The police in uniform combing the tunnels use their IR goggles to cut through the blanket of darkness and find their way.

"Jesus," a uniformed man gasps. He pulls his gun from its holster then, presses a small button on the side of his neck, opening a channel to available units, "All units be advised, we have a body at my position. The suspects may still be in the area. Proceed with extreme caution." The lone officer takes up position in a nook while he waits for back up.

It doesn't take long for Mason, Vivian and Galarza to find the officer huddled in the shallow crevice. Vivian produces an evidence collection kit, while Mason examines the damage caused by the gunfire.

Galarza touches a point on her neck, "All units, I want three blocks shut down with my position being the center. And can we get some goddamned lights on in these tunnels!"

With gloved hands, Vivian examines the headless body. "Record," she says calmly, activating a record function on her implants. She slowly pans over the body, taking note of the wounds and the vomit nearby. The lights flicker to life and the IR functions of the officer's implants shutdown. "His gun is missing," Vivian remarks for the recording.

Mason uses the time to pull the Chief aside and speak to her in hushed tones, "You got a moment?" he asks.

Galarza squints suspiciously at him, but follows him down the tunnel. "What is it, Ed?"

Mason glances back at Vivian, who is now scraping beneath the dead man's fingernails, "There's been some odd shit going down with this case and I'm not too sure that we've got the full picture on this one," Mason says before looking back at the short woman.

Galarza cocks her head, "What do you mean?" she asks.

"I mean that evidence has been removed or tampered with," Mason remarks, turning back to Vivian.

The body language wasn't completely lost on the Chief's keen perceptive skill, "What are you saying? That one of our own is up to no good?" she whispers with mild annoyance.

Mason looks back at the dark skinned woman, "That's exactly what I'm saying," Mason says flatly.

The Chief looks Mason in the eye studying him, then asks, "What proof do you have?"

Mason runs his hand over his mouth in frustration, "Aside from the evidence being deleted, not a whole lot."

The Chief nods raising one thin eyebrow, "Well, you keep shit like that to yourself until you have something solid. When you've got something you can actually use, then you come see me. Until then, don't waste my time." Galarza grumbles as she pushes her way through Mason and back toward the crime scene.

The coroners finally make their way down to the dead body and begin taking pictures of everything the detectives had deemed noteworthy. One of the men collects blood from a service panel nook and drops it into a bag for later analysis.

Vivian returns from her little assembly with the forensics team and smiles scornfully at Mason, "Well, our headless corpse is our old friend Dominic Vespucci," Vivian says, cutting all joking aside. "He exchanged fire with our perp and didn't do so well."

Galarza smiles tiredly, "Obviously."

Mason notices some displaced dust sprinkled on the ground not far from Dominic's cooling body. He looks up and spots a small access door. He wasn't going to say anything, but Galarza also notices the clumps of dirt and finds the small door, "Looks like we've found the escape route."

Chief Galarza signals for a uniformed officer, who is speaking with a maintenance man. The two men walk over to her. "What's above us?" she asks.

The serviceman thinks for a moment then says, "I think we're underneath an old warehouse." He points up toward the small hatch and continues with his answer, "I'm pretty sure that leads to the basement of an old storage facility."

Vivian nods then orders available units to converge on the building. "Can you open that panel for us?" she says.

The state worker nods, "Sure." He moves over to the door and uses a special code to unlock it and the door swings open. A collapsible aluminum ladder slides down to the hard ground and locks in place.

Mason pulls his sidearm as not to arouse suspicion and makes his way toward the frail looking ladder. The two ladies with a half dozen officers follow close behind. The ladder leads to a dark room containing an old furnace and air conditioning unit. The officers immediately switch to IR and make their way through the cramped space, clearing rooms as they go. Finding nothing in the basement, the officers move to the stairwell and cautiously move to the ground floor.

Worry creeps its way into Mason's thoughts as they move throughout the building. He wonders how he would handle the situation if they were to find Imogen and Blake.

The other policemen register as blue dots on his heads up display, so he's not worried about accidentally gunning down his fellow lawmen, but he doesn't want any of them to find the synthetic woman either. He glances upward and finds large pipes and ductwork snaking along the ceiling. "No second floor. Thank God," he whispers. The men and women in uniform clear one half of the building, while he, Galarza and Vivian clear the other.

Relief fills Mason as he tucks his gun away. The Chief holsters her weapon and turns to a woman in uniform, "I want a thorough sweep of the area. Inside and out." The woman nods and jogs away. The Chief makes her way to the front door and lights a cigarette. She takes a long pull from the narrow stick. She narrows her eyes to keep the drifting grey smoke from burning them. "Vivian send a copy of the evidence to Chosen seekers on the ground."

Mason and Vivian both turn their heads in shock, "What? Why?" Vivian questions.

Mason moves toward the Chief, "Yeah. I don't see a need for them to be in on this. I mean..."

Mason starts, but Galarza cuts him off, "If we help them, they'll help us catch these two murderers." Mason moves closer, intent on continuing his protest, "Chief, I…"
Galarza spins around to face him and jabs a finger in his direction, "I want the public to know that we are doing everything in our power to get that thing off the streets. If that means entering a co-op with Chosen, so be it."

Mason grits his teeth and walks away utterly frustrated with the unexpected turn of events. He turns his attention to Vivian who complies with the Chiefs orders. He kicks a metal storage unit, then walks back toward the basement stairwell. He can hear the rhythmic slapping of hard boots against the concrete floors. A few moments later he hears the female officer report that they've found nothing. He smiles inwardly, taking the news as a small victory. He stoops down and sits on the first step. With a long stretch, he swings his neck from side to side, relieving the tension that has been locked up since he pulled up to the hacker's apartment building.

He looks down at his feet, again taking note of the layer of dust on the floor. It had collected there due to lack of activity. He notices his and the other officers footprints, along with two sets that don't belong. He follows the prints up the stairs. Slowly, he stands and makes his way back down the steps. He places his feet over what must be Blake's and Imogen's footprints, erasing them. He does this until he reaches the top of the steps, where the prints stop. He searches around, but all he can see is prints of everyone who accompanied him and his partner. He turns his head to either side, but finds nothing out of the ordinary.

"Hey!" Vivian calls out from beyond the doorway, catching him off guard. "What are you doing?" she asks quizzically.

Mason continues to look at the walls, smiling slightly, "Nothing. Just losing my mind is all."

Vivian shakes her head, "Well, we're heading back to go over the evidence," she reports.

Mason looks at her in confusion, "So soon?" The young lady drops a hand to her side, letting him know that her patience is running thin, "Yeah. We have the entire investigation on vid. We may have missed something, so we're headed back to the station to go over the recordings."
Mason nods. He doesn't see a need to argue with the lady. Besides, she's probably just relaying orders from the Chief.

The pair finds Galarza in the same spot flicking the butt of her cigarette out the front door. "I received a video response from David Jennings himself. He assured me that his ground team will provide any and all evidence they collect," the small woman says. "He, like us, wants this menace off the streets. I thinks it's time we stop the bickering and start working together. At least on this one case," she councils unenthusiastically. Without another word, she steps out of the door and steps inside a waiting squad car. They drive off leaving the detectives to find their own way back to the station.

Vivian turns to the older man, suspicious of his behavior in the hall, "What the hell were you really doing back there?" she questions harshly. Mason inclines his head and sighs.

"I'm serious! What the fuck is your deal lately?" She steps in front of him, arms crossed and very pissed off.

Mason pinches the space between his eyes, "I really don't want to have this conversation right now," he grunts.

Vivian takes a determined step forward, "Well its happening. Right now! You got a problem with me hoss?" she presses. Her voice echoes through the empty building. "Answer me damn it!"

Mason places his hands on his hips and looks the angry woman in the eye. He spends a moment reading her. He can see confusion along with twinge of, hurt? He presses his lips together, debating if he should tell her everything, but decides to give her a nugget of truth. Her mouth gapes slightly as she prepares to yell at him again.

"I don't have the evidence I need, but I am pretty damn sure that we don't have the whole picture," he says.

Vivian chuckles sarcastically and turning around, "No shit Sherlock," she says laughing.

"That's what we're doing out here, getting the pieces to get the whole picture!"

Vivian turns and looks out the door and huffs, "I know you noticed the footprints coming up the stairs." She turns to Mason, arms folded, "I'm not a fucking idiot. I know you don't think that robot is what the evidence makes her out to be." She takes three steps toward him, "I know that she might be the syn that went missing from the apartment bombing two years ago."

The revelations stun Mason for a moment. Speechless, he waits to hear what else she knows as she paces back and forth like an angry lioness.

"She's not an innocent victim. She killed those people. That makes her a dangerous criminal and it's our job to bring her in," Vivian affirms.

Mason watches the tension visibly leave her shoulders as she calms down. He still doesn't know if he should say anything about Desirae or the information she and Imogen have against Chosen. He holds his tongue on that little bit, "I just want to make sure that we're doing the right thing. There are people living everyday with scars, left by those goddamned seeker and Chosen bastards and there isn't anything they or we can do about that."

Vivian shakes her head and looks at the floor between them. She feels that the empty space between them is a reflection of the wedge that had been driven between them recently. There might as well be a vast fissure between them now. "It doesn't give anyone the right to be a vigilante."

Mason laughs at her rebuttal. "Just today, an innocent man is dead from one of their stray bullets! Where's the justice for his family?" Mason adds angrily.

"He was just sitting in a coffee shop. If that were my father or brother, I'd be looking for some pay back," he adds, trying to drive home his point.

Vivian turns shaking her head. She pushes the door open and steps outside. She pauses for a moment, shakes her head again then begins walking up the sidewalk.

Mason places his hands on his head and takes a deep breath. He doesn't understand how she can't see his point of view. Mason almost went out to follow her, but thought that she needed the space. He had no desire to continue their argument outside. He marches back over to the hall where he found the footprints and searches the surrounding walls again. He turns up nothing. Again. "I'm getting too old for this shit," he mutters to himself. He turns and walks to the front door. He pauses for a brief second, then pushes the door open and makes the long cold walk back to his car.

CHAPTER 28

Present Day

Vivian sifts through the visual data collected during the investigation. Multiple holographic display screens hover over her desk. One shows real time data of the blood samples she sent down to the lab earlier. She focuses on the recording of their ascent up the stairwell. She zooms in on the footprints she and Mason noticed. Once the video reaches the top of the steps, she freezes the frame in the hopes of finding where the suspects could have gone. The prints just stop. Then she recalls Mason standing in the hall and looking at the walls on either side. But he didn't find anything. Then it hits her.

"Up," she mumbles to herself. She rewinds the footage to a point where she had glanced up and freezes it. She leans forward to where her nose is inches from the pale blue hologram. The image is blurry. "Enhance," she commands. The still frame on the screen sharpens to reveal the metal rungs of a ladder. "Son of a bitch," she smiles. The move wasn't genius, they were just too stupid to notice it. She's been so frustrated with Ed that she hasn't been thinking critically. She realizes that she has to focus on work and not her neurotic colleague.

Vivian lifts her eyes to see her Partner, Mason shuffling to his desk. The poor tired bastard sits down. There's still snow caked to his pants which amuses her immensely. She compresses the file and begins to prepare it for storage when Chief Galarza, calls her and Mason into her office.

<She must've been keeping an eye out for him too.> Vivian ponders. She shuts down the monitors, but leaves the software running. She takes note of her older partner grumbling about having to get up again and giggles inwardly.

Once she and Mason are inside the Chief's office, she shuts the door. The short woman stands behind her desk, looking over the many different screens built into its surface and then shuts them down. She looks up at the two detectives before her and collects her thoughts.

"Look, I don't know, nor do I care about what's going on between you two," the older woman starts. As she speaks, she shifts from one set of eyes to the other, "What you do on your own time is your own damn business, but you will put your issues aside while you are on the clock."

Galarza walks around to the front of her desk and leans back against it. She folds her arms then locks eyes with Mason, "Now, Eddie, you voiced some concerns to me earlier and I want you to know that I am looking into the matter." The Chief shifts her attention over to Vivian, who stands there as inscrutable as a stone, "Detective, you have brought me up to speed on everything about this case so far, have you found anything else that might lead us to closing it?"

Vivian nods and pushes the urge to look at Mason away, "During my analysis of the video, we've collected, and I may have found were our suspects have exited." The Chief raises an eyebrow and waits for further explanation. Vivian casts her eyes on Mason for a second, then continues, "Back at the warehouse," Vivian says. Mason takes a deep breath waiting to be thrown under the bus. "Mason pointed out two sets of foot prints that seemed to have lead nowhere." Mason keeps his expressions in check, but turns his head toward his younger partner.

"At the time we didn't find anything, but when I reviewed the footage, I found a pull down ladder near the ceiling," Vivian states.

Vivian's cool professional manner would have irked Mason. In fact it usually did. When she wore the blue uniform, she had often exercised her smart ass wit, which Mason loved. Now she takes the roll of detective way too seriously. Or maybe he had seen too much to care anymore.

Galarza nods in approval of the detectives work then looks over at Mason expectantly. He, in turn has no idea what she's waiting for.

"You said you were following up on some leads. What did you find?" Galarza questions.

Inwardly Mason curses himself for having opened his mouth back at the apartment building. He didn't want his partner knowing what he was doing until he was sure she wasn't the mole. He knows a bullshit lie won't fly, so he went with a half-truth, "I found an eye witness that had been secreted away by witness protection. She was there and saw enough to link Chosen and their founder with the apartment bombing case that may tie in with this case."

Vivian's head spins toward Mason so fast, he expected it to snap off her neck. Mason meets her eyes and is surprised to find the hint of a stunned expression. Vivian was about to speak, but Mason continues with the explanation, "I have also been in contact with," Mason pauses to consider his words, "An individual who may have video evidence that proves Chosen seekers knowingly murdered those people on all three floors." The room is so silent that he can hear their jaws hit the floor. Mason takes a deep breath, then reveals, "I have evidence that the synthetic they are after was the target of the initial bombing two years ago and that all this chaos is because they are trying to tie up loose ends."

Galarza lowers her hands to her sides to stabilize herself on her desk, "So, what you are telling me, is that all this mayhem, is because they failed to shut down an illegal robot?" Galarza surmises. Her tone is almost as unreadable as Vivian's deadpanning.

Mason nods. He feels that he has revealed enough information to get the wheels spinning in the right direction. Galarza leans forward, then paces over to one of the large windows and looks out to the snow covered street. "Your witness, she got a name?" the Chief asks.

Mason clears his throat, uncertain if he should divulge that much info, but if it meant getting this case back he has to, "Desirae Deponet, Ma'am."

Without turning back to the detectives, Galarza nods slightly, "Bring her in and I'll get you a warrant." Mason turns toward his younger partner and finds the stolid expression on her face more than a little discomforting. Vivian turns and opens the office door without speaking a word and exits. Mason follows closely behind. Vivian strides toward her desk to collect her coat and tablet. Mason waits for her by the exit, questioning himself.

He hopes he didn't give away too much information about what he knows. If his suspicions are correct about Vivian, he may have just put his witness in harm's way. All he can do now is get to her and keep her close.

Vivian strolls around the corner. The soft muffled thumping of her shoes against the polished floors is the only indication that she is only steps behind him. Mason turns to meet her, but she walks right past him and into the department's garage. She opens the driver's side door, steps inside and patiently waits for Mason, who arrives only seconds later.

"What the hell is up with the walls?" she says. Her elevated voice fills the interior of the car. Mason says nothing. Vivian furiously shakes her head and starts the car.

The young toddler bounces in a stationary seat and giggles at the floppy puppet bunny on the video screen. Desirae rubs her swollen eyes. She's had too much excitement for one morning. The ache in her bladder screams for relief. She moves from the couch to the bathroom and relieves herself. The events of the morning weighs heavily on her mind. She knew that one day, she would have to face the truth, but she didn't think that it would be today.

She washes her hands all the while looking at her tired eyes in the mirror. She splashes the cool water on her face then pat dries with a towel. She pauses and wonders at the sudden silence in the T.V. room.

"Honey?" she calls. Not getting a response from her son and trying to ignore the horrible feeling in her gut, Desirae flings open the door. She stops in her tracks. Fear throttles her heart. There in the middle of the room, holding her son is none other than David Jennings.

David gently bounces the small boy in his arms while cooing in his ear. The greying man lifts his eyes to shoot Desirae a menacing look.

"Put my son down," she croaks.

Jennings smiles at the terrified woman, "Don't be that way darling," he says with a smug smile. He takes small measured steps toward her, "I only want to talk and catch up a bit."

Jennings whistles lightly, summoning three men in black uniforms. Desirae lunges at the bastard, but one of the large men tackle her, driving her body into a glass table at the arm of her couch. The sound of the shattering glass jerks the young boy into a fit. The toddler begins to scream into David's ear. The businessman hands the child over to one of the armed men, who wraps a blanket around the boy's body.

Desirae coughs as she fights to get air back into her lungs. David kneels down next to the bleeding woman, brushing her hair away from her face, "I didn't come here to hurt you sweetheart." Desirae blinks through the tears and rolls over. Chunks of glass crunch under her palm. "I know you talked to a cop about the brief time you were with us." He stands and pats the wrinkles out of his pants, "That wasn't a nice thing to do." David nods to the burly soldier, who responds by grabbing the bloody woman's arms and hoists her to her shaky feet. David takes a moment to glance around the modest apartment and nods in approval. He likes the clean lines and minimal furniture.

The mid-day sun casts a golden hue within the room, creating a heavenly glow throughout. When his eyes come to the dark stain on the otherwise white rug, he sucks his teeth disapprovingly. He pulls the door shut as he exits the apartment.

Down in the waiting car, Desirae shivers from the cold. They didn't allow her the comfortable warmth of a blanket. She was still in her pajamas. A thin trail of crimson trickles down from her hairline, to run along her nose, down to her lips. She glares at the helmeted man holding her son. She can only hope that they won't hurt him. She tries to keep the shaking down to a minimum, but her heavy breathing gives her fear away.
The fact that she can't see the faces of the men around her make them seem inhuman and that makes her heart thump that much harder.

David steps into the vehicle and sits across from Desirae. He shakes the cold off, smiling like the pompous ass he is. He claps his hands together, "Driver, we're ready to go." The luxury car slowly pulls away from the curb and merges with traffic. David looks over at Desirae's bloody face and pouts. He reaches into a breast pocket and pulls out a silk cloth. He holds the material out, offering it to the soiled woman. She doesn't take her eyes off the man holding her son. "Do clean yourself up darling. It's unbecoming of a lady to look like a sewer rat in the presence of gentlemen," he says mockingly.

Desirae sniffs and holds her head high. David shrugs and tucks the handkerchief back into his pocket. "I do love what you've done with your hair. It's," David rocks his head from side to side then continues, "festive." Desirae ignores his snide remarks and focuses on what she can do to keep her son safe.

"Mama, I scared," the small boy softly cries.

Desirae's chin quivers at the sound of his tiny voice, "Everything is going to be okay baby," she reassures her child.

David smiles. If the conditions were different, one would think that he was on a stroll with his family, but his smile only promises pain. He turns to watch the traffic passing by the window, "You'll be fine as long as you don't cause any trouble and help nab an annoying fly." He sighs audibly as his charitable nature wears thin, "I don't want to hurt you or your boy, but I will, if you make me," he threatens. He leans forward, carefully resting his elbows on his fine pressed pants as not to wrinkle them, "Why is it so hard for people to understand that I am only trying to make a better, safer, world?" he says with concern in his voice.

"Now, I know that things get a little hairy sometimes and innocent people get hurt, but in the end, mankind will be so much better off without those emotionless machines running loose on the street," he presses. The expression on his face is the same mask that he uses for the media cameras. "I'm shaping a better world for children, like your son," he spews, gesturing toward little William. David leans back in his leather seat.

Desirae's eyes shift to take in David's overly tanned, nearly orange face. His words makes her blood run hot and she hopes that Imogen kills the cocky bastard.

CHAPTER 29

Present Day

Blake lie passed out on the rich burgundy sofa. It was probably the only thing in the apartment that was new. The toilet barely works and Imogen could swear that she can see something living under the yellow wallpaper. Blake didn't seem to mind or maybe he was just that tired. He was out within the span of five minutes from his head hitting the plush arm cushion. His bag of electronic equipment rests atop the small and slightly rot damaged kitchen table. An antique refrigerator sputters to life in the corner. The noise stirs the tired hacker but, he quickly drifts back to sleep. His wounds weren't life threatening, so Imogen only cleaned and dressed them.

She carries a plastic chair to the corner of one dirty window, sets it down gently then sits. She can feel the cool air from outside seeping inside through the warped wood. She knows that she should get some kind of rest, but somebody should keep watch, just in case his escape didn't go as smoothly as he had thought.

Imogen never would have imagined that Blake would pick a safe house within the city limits, but to her dismay, he had. "They hardly ever think to look for you in their own back yard," he had told her earlier, "Besides, I have this place set up just like the other one. We'll be fine if shit hits the fan," he said just before drifting to sleep. She knew better than to stay in the city, but she wasn't about to leave the man who had saved her life. Not now and probably not ever, even if his secondary safe place was within an old apartment building located in the rough part of the city.

Imogen felt something stir deep within her. She glances over at the sleeping nerd. His mouth agape, but only slightly. His nearly silent snores make her smile. She thinks he's kind of cute, in a boyish kind of way.

It shocks her that the tremendous guilt she expected to knock her flat on her ass, was a slight discomfort. She can't think about this now. She has a job to finish and these emotions, only serve as a distraction at the moment. If she loses her focus now, there's a chance that it could end them both. She neatly tucks that line of thought away, in case they both survive this, she can examine it thoroughly.

Hours later, the sun sinks in the distance. She couldn't see the bright fiery star, but the radiance of the ambient light bathes the snow and frost covered buildings in a blazing orange glow.

She watches the hues of golden kissed vermillion, fade away to a gently darkening amethyst. The peaceful view is in complete contrast with the insanity that was her life. How could minor differences cause such a tumultuous rift between human beings and synthetics? She just wants this all to end.

<I just need to get through tonight. Tomorrow, I'll figure out something.> Imogen knows that she can stay up for a few days, but if she is going to finish this she needs to be clear headed and rested. She peeks over at Blake. He's out cold. She's sure that he has some goodies in his pack that would alert them of unwanted visitations.

Inside the bag, Imogen finds a portable computer, several notepads with various codes and passwords to various networks. She pulls out a few more things that she can only guess at their purpose, then she pulls out a sphere the size of a marble. She searches the oblong bag and finds six more of the tiny round balls. After much digging, she finally finds the base.

She's seen Blake use these little motion cameras before and she was fairly confident that she could figure out how to set up and use the little buggers. She shoves the orbs into her pocket and sets the base on the unstable table. She slips into her coat and opens the door to the grungy apartment and steps out into the dim hallway. She is thankful that the apartment is only on the fifth floor, because this place doesn't have an elevator.

Imogen jogs to one end of the hall and places a motion cam on the ground. She moves to the opposite end and repeats the process. She then opens the door and places two more spheres at the top and bottom of the stairwell. She drops a cam at the back exit. Imogen reaches the front door then hesitates with her hand on the cold metal handle. She scans the street for activity. The large wire mesh within the glass window on the heavy steel door is clean enough to look through. She can see the concrete courtyard surrounded by the other sections of the building. The open end has a short series of steps that lead to the main door. Seeing that the neighborhood is completely silent and still, Imogen cracks the door. She fishes the last spherical camera out of her pocket and places it above the doorframe.

With some minor safety precautions in place, she heads back to the small rundown apartment to rest for the evening.

Once within the confines of the small living quarters, Imogen leans over the small base and powers it on. Three quick consecutive beeps followed by a small projection displaying the multiple camera views, lets her know the device is working. She glances at each angle and sighs at the relief the minor comfort it offers. She looks over at Blake, who is in a deep sleep. One side of her lip curves up in a slight smile. She moves over to an old tattered love seat and rests her head on the stiff arm. Sleep comes quickly.

◊

A large and very still lake is like a mirror, reflecting the crystal clear sapphire sky. Hints of white clouds drift lazily high above. Rolling hills stretch for miles and lead up to a majestic blue grey mountain. Near the water's edge, a lone and very lush weeping willow dangles its lazy branches over the water. The gentle wind sweeps the emerald tendrils across the surface, causing ripples in an otherwise perfect image.

Imogen slowly walks through the tall grass. The feel of the soft blades against the palm of her hands causes little goose bumps to race up her arms. She closes her eyes and smiles faintly. A soft *plop* in the water grabs her attention, but by the time she investigates the noise all that is left is a gentle ripple that rides the smooth surface in a growing ellipse.

Looking back at the willow, Imogen can see someone sitting under its shade. Curiously, she searches around, but there is no one else here. Only the single person admiring the glasslike surface of the water.

In an instant, Imogen finds herself under the lazy branches of the tree, looking out over the wide lake. She hadn't noticed before, but there was a large heron, resting peacefully on a small island in the middle of the lake. Its long outstretched neck reaches for the heavens, soaking up the warmth of the sun's rays. The large blue feathers on its wings shine like polished metal. Imogen loses herself in the elegant beauty of the creature and takes small steps toward the water's edge to get a closer look.

"Absolutely lovely. Isn't it?" a serene familiar voice says.

Imogen gasps, remembering the person sitting under the tree. She peers down, tears filling her eyes. The old wounds of Darioux's death, she thought were thick scars on her soul tore open again. She falls to her knees before the man leaning against the trunk of the tree and without moving, she is by his side, buried in a warm embrace.

"I miss you so much," her voice cracks as she tries to hold back the sobs.

He caresses her soft hair, turning it back to its original shade of brown, "I miss you too," Darioux whispers softly. For a long while they sit under the willow, savoring the love they once shared.

Imogen can feel Darioux's head shift as he glances down at her. "You've been busy," he says with a smile flavoring his voice.

Imogen isn't sure how to respond to his statement. She looks out to the heron resting on the small patch of land and admires its simplistic existence. She sits up to look her husband in the eyes. She had almost forgotten how his brown eyes sparkled. A twinge of shame pulses through her chest and she looks away.

"I couldn't let them get away with it," she says, still looking at the bird. Her voice wavers slightly as if her proclamation contained some doubt. To reinforce her statement and somewhat defend it she says, "I can't let them do this to anyone else."

Darioux nods solemnly and looks at the sparkling lake. Imogen reads his expression as disapproval and was about to press the need for her to keep on this path of vengeance, but Darioux voices his thoughts, "I know you are doing what you have to do." He looks at her and smiles. He places a soft hand on her cheek, using his thumb to wipe away a tear Imogen had no idea she shed.

"You've let what happened in the past define who you are now and it's consuming you. Don't let it destroy who you are," he says tenderly.

Reflecting back on the choices that had led her to this point, Imogen lowers her eyes to the soft grass. Her quest for justice had brought her to near ruin and almost got Blake killed. Darioux lifts her head to meets her eyes, "I know what you are thinking and don't let the guilt control you either." His supportive tone makes her lips curve in a smile. "I'm gone baby, but I will always be right here for you." He says as he leans against the trunk of the willow. "Should you need me," he adds with a wry smile.

Darioux pulls Imogen in for a hug and she lets him. The ache in her chest is telling her that this was a goodbye and that her mind shouldn't disagree. Their end was so abrupt, and she had been so haunted by those events, it sheared off a part of what she considered her soul.

<Was this his way of saying it was time to move on?> Imogen calms her mind. She didn't want any of these thoughts taking away from this time of peace. She'll have enough time in the waking world to think about all the questions she doesn't want to take the time to answer now. All she wants to do now is focus on the rise and fall of each breath Darioux takes.

It seems like they sat under that tree for days. Not a single thought, beyond the current moment that they were in passed through Imogen's mind. Through all that time she had even forgotten that she was dreaming. The pain of knowing that she will indeed wake from this blissful place and probably never find it again is too heavy to contemplate. Her eyes fill with hot tears at the thought of not being able to stay in this place. She tightens her grip around Darioux's torso and presses her face into his chest.

"What's wrong?" he says calmly. Imogen hesitates when trying to answer his question. She's terrified that if she audibly acknowledges that this is only a dream that she will be violently pulled out of it and left in the torment that had been plaguing her mind for nearly two years. So she doesn't answer him, instead she places her ear over his heart to listen to a heartbeat she knows cannot be real. Darioux smiles and rests his head against the trunk of the tree.

"This is a dream, but I am here of my own will," he says as if he had read her mind.

"Will I ever find you here again?" she sniffles softly.

He chuckles lightly and replies, "Only if you need me to be here." His response gives her minimal comfort, but it was enough and they continue to lay there in the shade, wrapped up in each other's arms. She doesn't know what qualifies as a need and she wasn't sure if it was truly a need that had summoned him here now, but she was happy that he was here.

The heron that had been resting on the small patch of land perks up quickly, looks at the couple under the tree, then spreads its large wings and rides the winds in the opposite direction. The gentle zephyr that had been caressing the bodies of the two lost lovers, suddenly turns into a howling gale towing thick ominous clouds behind. The once lazy vine like branches of the weeping willow, whip through the air like the tentacles of a ferocious creature.

Darioux sits up from the tree in a panic, "I lost track of time," he says in alarm.
Confused, Imogen looks at him, "Lost track? What do you mean?" In an instant he is on his feet, though she never sees him move. He lifts her up.

"Baby, you've got to wake up now!"
Still at a loss of what's going on, Imogen shakes her head, "Why? I don't want to leave. What's going on?"

Darioux pulls her small frame into a fierce hug. She can feel his hurried breath on her earlobe, "You have to wake up now," he says. The once vibrant field turns to an almost black wasteland. Darioux's body and voice begin to fade as the darkness sweeps across the hills, swallowing up the land like a glutton devouring her nirvana. "You have to wake up. Now!"

◊

Imogen wakes and bolts up to an ear-piercing screech. The bright yellow rays of the morning sun shine through the dirty window in sharp beams that run the length of the room.

Blake is up and running over to the motion sensor cams, "Shit! Shit! Shit!" he shrieks rapidly. He turns back to Imogen, his eyes wide, and sweat running down his face, "I got six. No eight armed men coming up the steps."

Imogen runs over to the small table to see the monitor for herself. He wasn't kidding. The men headed their way were armed to the teeth with assault weapons and hardcore tactical armor. She grabs her gun knowing that it would do little good. Blake shoots her a crazy look, "Are you nuts? Get the hell out of here!" he yells. He pulls her over to a trap door in the floor, "This leads down to the apartment below. Go now." He says in a determined voice.

Imogen looks at him as if he had just lost his mind, "Are you fucking nuts?" she growls at him. They locked eyes for only a micro second, but it felt like an eternity. Blake rushes back over to the bag and pulls out a lump of something wrapped in plastic. He rips it open, then scoops out a glob of what looks like putty and begins to gently place it along the edge of the door. He then takes the large lump of what was left of it and presses it in the center of the door.

The muffled thumping of the mercenaries' boots can now be heard down the hall. Blake snatches the bag, the computer by the sofa and then jumps over toward the trap door. He lifts the seamless door, then ushers Imogen through. The boots thunder down the hall and come to a stop right in front of the door. Blake steps inside the entry in the floor just as the men outside use a battering ram to knock the door open, but the putty Blake had liberally slathered on the door is impact sensitive.

The moment the force of the heavy ram shocked the door, the kinetic force ignites the putty. The explosion shakes the entire building and most definitely knocked the hired guns on their asses, killing the men closest to the blast.

Dust falls from the ceiling as the room upstairs rumbles and the floors below tremble.

"What the hell was that?" Imogen asks a smiling Blake.

"That was how I got away last time," he says moving to the old fire escape.

Imogen follows him down to the narrow alley leading to a dead end. "Where the hell are you going? The opening is the other way!" Imogen calls out. Blake doesn't answer, instead, he depresses a button on his watch and what Imogen had thought was a brick wall begins to rise. Blake jogs over to the new opening and stands beside an old fashioned, combustion engine, motorcycle. The white *Victory* decal emblazoned on the tank practically shines against its sleek black design.

"Here's your ride," he says.

Imogen stops by his side, "You're coming, right?"

He shakes his head, "I'd only get in the way," he says. "Besides there is another hidden door in there and I have one more thing I've got to do. You need to go now."

She looks at him, then wraps her arms around his neck. She feels that time is truly running out and it is time to get a move on. As she pulls away, she kisses his lips softly, "Thank you," she whispers before running to the bike, turning it on and speeding to the end of the alley.

CHAPTER 30

One Day Earlier

Chief Galarza rubs her cigarette out in a blue, swirled, antique, glass ashtray. She exhales the silver smoke from her lungs. She's tired from the stress of the day's adventure. She stands gazing out the large window of her office contemplating what Eddie Mason had just told her about the synthetic suspect. The implication of the incredibly wealthy and powerful founder of the humanist organization is a huge concern. If what he has said is true, it could stir up one hell of a shit storm. It could shut down Mr. Jennings and his organization, but it could also bring down many powerful individuals and plunge this healing nation into chaos. On the other hand, she can't have some rogue machine running around and dealing out what she perceives as justice.

Galarza likes Mason. He's a good cop, but she can't wait on his witness, nor can she put all her eggs in one basket.

From her vantage point she can see Vivian and Mason's designated on duty car exit the garage. She purses her lips as she weighs her options. With her decision made, Galarza walks over to her desk and activates her personal computer. She puts out and *All Points Bulletin* containing recent photos and information on Imogen Harper. She attaches photos of her human accomplice, Blake Sparx. Immediately she can see units all over the city acknowledging the order.

Galarza leans on her desk and eyes the drawer containing extra bullets for her side arm. She opens the thin compartment and takes the extra ammo. She grabs her coat from the dark wooden stand then exits the office. She hesitates with her hand on the knob. She turns around and glances around her office, searching for something. Once her eyes land on the tiny box that holds her full flavored cigarettes, she snatches them up, then heads back out the door.

Eddie Mason and Vivian Stern pull up to the curb in front of the tall apartment building that Desirae Deponet and her young son call home. They spent the entire twenty minute car ride in awkward silence. The pair reach the front door and immediately realize that something is not right. Mason notices that the digital call roster is flickering and sports a new crack in the corner of the screen. Vivian examines the rectangular box. She shoots a glance at the front door and points, "The auto lock has been disabled."

Mason draws his gun then uses his hip to nudge the door open. Vivian follows suit. Inside the building everything else seems to be in good working order. "At least the elevator still works," Vivian says with a hint of optimism. Mason grimaces as he pushes the call button. The elevator doors open and the two detectives step inside. Mason pushes the button for Desirae's floor prompting the doors to close.

"I'm going to patch into the building's surveillance system and see what I can get," Vivian says. She kneels down and begins to open the panel on the elevator. She pulls a cable from a pocket on her pants, plugs one end into the input jack on the lower panel and, the other behind her ear. Mason feels a little relieved that she is able to put aside her agitation at their situation and be professional. Though he did wonder what she'd do with the evidence once she got it.

"Get me a copy while you're at it," he says. Vivian sighs heavily and bites her lip. He looks down to confirm that she heard him.

She rolls her eyes, "Yeah. Whatever." She answers after a moment. Vivian tucks away the cable and holsters her gun.

Mason eyes her suspiciously, "What are you doing?" he asks impatiently.

Vivian slowly shakes her head in response. Mason waits for a more detailed response and when he doesn't get it, he repeats the question.

Vivian opens a wireless link to his wet drive and finds that it is still locked. "I'm trying to give you the vids. Unlock your drive. We don't need our guns. We're too late."

The polished metal doors open and Mason runs to the apartment. He finds the shattered table and speckles of blood on the white carpet. In his HUD, he watches the video of David Jennings and his men assaulting Desirae. He watches helplessly as they take her and her son out of the building. Vivian enters the small apartment and takes in the scene.

"Mason," she says softly, but he doesn't respond. She calls to him again. Still nothing. She places a hand on his shoulder, which seems to bring him back to the present. "You didn't tell me that you were here with the synthetic," Vivian says softly. Mason turns to her.

He forgot that his visit would also be on the security video. The intensity in his eyes challenges her to reveal that fact to the officials that mattered. She lowers her eyes, yielding to him.

Vivian peers down at the chunks of jagged glass and the blood that stain the rug, "You don't have to look at me like that," she reassures him. She turns to meet his burning eyes, "I hear you loud and clear. Let's go get us some bad guys," she added.

Mason isn't sure how to take her sudden shift in attitude toward the situation they are in. He could use the back up, but he doesn't feel like having to keep a close eye on her while trying to arrest David Jennings.

In the car, the silence is still there, but the awkwardness has vanished. Mason wants to trust his partner, but the fact that she was in charge of the evidence that had been deleted, left him with a nagging doubt about her loyalties. He shoves his negative thoughts aside, but doesn't forget about them. He knows he's taking a risk by trusting her, but he doesn't see any other way to get this done, that doesn't include a metric ton of red tape.

"We've wasted enough time on this case. Let's finish this tonight," Mason says. The solid and gruff tone in his voice sets the mood of their not so by the books mission. Vivian turns on the sirens and slams the gas pedal to the floorboard. The late evening New Year's Eve traffic parts to either side of the road allowing the two detectives to make good time.

The long stretch of road that leads straight to the front doors of the tall building is clear of pedestrian vehicles. Mason notices the automated window cleaner platform high on the side of the tall building, sitting idle and guesses that the operators must be getting prepared for the festivities.

"Everyone is Downtown for the celebration," Vivian observes.

Mason nods, "That just means that no one will get in our way."

They double park on the street, leaving the blue lights of their car on and make for the front door. A titan of a man greets them in the lobby, "State your business," the man demands. Mason should've have guessed that David Jennings was the type to make employees work on the holidays, but judging by the giant's posture, Mason would bet that he enjoyed the iota of power his post granted him.

The detectives flash their badges. "We're here to speak with the big boss man," Mason answers curtly.

The big man chuffs and smiles, "Sorry, but Mr. Jennings is indisposed for the evening. May I take a message?"

The sarcasm in the man's voice annoys the officers. Mason smiles at the man, gesturing for him to move closer, "Yeah. You can." The man leans in to receive Mason's message and catches the butt of a gun to the side of the face. The man drops like a sack of potatoes.

"What the fuck!" Vivian shrieks in alarm.

Mason glares at her, then moves with haste to the directory.

"I want this over as much as you do, but I'm not trying to lose my badge over it," Vivian cautions.

Mason locates David Jennings's office on the very top floor of the one hundred and ten story building. He moves toward the turbo lift and presses the call button. "He was obstructing," Mason insists.

Vivian shakes her head and smiles. The black metal doors open with a chime and they step inside. Vivian hits the desired button with the muzzle of her gun and the doors glide to a close.

The speed at which the lift accelerates makes their insides sink and compress their internal organs. Mason grips his gun so hard that the balls of his knuckles turn white. He's not sure what to expect once he reaches David's office, but the adrenaline pumping through his body almost ensures that he'll be ready. Mason checks out his partner, Vivian, who has set up a linked vid to record what transpires for evidence. He notices that she's in a similar state of readiness and that makes him a little more comfortable in his decision to allow her to come.

The doors open up to a lavishly decorated room that takes up most of the entire floor. A brunette woman in a black, pinstriped, dress and, top, pauses when she spots the two detectives exit the elevator with their guns drawn. Mason assesses her in a split second.

"Jennings?" he demands and she glances at the glass doors on the other side of the room.

"I think it's time you went home," Vivian tells the woman, who wastes no time in shuffling into the elevator. The duo take measured steps to the office door. Vivian checks the side opposite her and nods. Mason swings the door open and enters the curved room with his gun leveled at the average man's head height. Vivian follows closely behind.

They follow the gentle arc until they see David, calmly discussing business with someone they can't see. Not caring who or what Jennings is discussing, Mason says, "David Jennings, you are under arrest for the crime of conspiracy to commit murder and kidnapping and whatever else I can pin on your ass. You have the right to remain silent. Anything you say can and will be used against you in a court of law."

David turns startled, then smiles. The man's cocky grin begs to be wiped off his face with a bullet. "Ahh! Detective Mason. We were just talking about you," David says.

Mason stops in his tracks. His eyes shift to ensure that Vivian is by his side and not at his back. Ignoring David's words, Mason opens his mouth to continue speaking the Miranda rights. Just then, David's guest steps into full view and stops Mason's heart cold.

"Put down the gun, Ed," commands Chief Galarza.

Mason can't believe what he is seeing. He blinks just to make sure that the person standing in front of him is indeed the Chief of Police.

Vivian's eyes shift from her partner, to David and finally the Chief. She allows her gun to lower a few inches. Galarza repeats her command, but this time she puts a little steel in her voice, "Lower your weapon detective. That's an order."

Mason glances over at her, then back at David who is just smiling at him. "What's going on Chief?" Mason questions without lowering his weapon.

Galarza raises her weapon and points it at Mason. He shifts his weapon and locks his boss in his sights, "What the fuck Chief?" Mason says while staring down the sights of his gun.

Again, Vivian is completely thrown off guard. Her partner and her boss are pointing guns at each other. The young detective waivers for a second as her brain has just stopped in the middle of processing the information it is receiving. With her weapon lowered to the floor, Vivian watches as the standoff drags out.

"I have had a long discussion with Mr. Jennings and we are going to handle this the right way. Lower your weapon. I won't repeat myself," Galarza warns.

Mason can hear Vivian shift on her feet. He chances a glance in her direction and finds that her gun is leveled at his head. Disappointment clenches his heart, making it skip more than a few beats. He knows now, that his chances of survival if things came to a shootout have just dropped down to zero.

"I'm sorry old man, but you are pointing a gun at the Chief," Vivian starts, "I need for you to comply or I will be forced to shoot you," she says coldly. Mason grits his teeth, but it only takes two seconds for him to switch the safety on and hold his gun out to be collected by Vivian. In a second his gun is taken from his hands and Vivian starts to place cuffs on his wrists behind his back.

"Oh that was intense," Jennings says, clapping his hands together. Vivian rolls her eyes. Galarza lowers her firearm and gestures for Vivian, "Bring me his gun, Vivian."

Sluggishly, Vivian complies with the Chief's orders. As she walks past Mason, head down like a whipped dog. Vivian gives him a wilting glance. She walks over to Chief Galarza and places the gun in her hand. Once the cold metal hits the older woman's hands, Vivian knows she has made a major mistake. Galarza wraps her fingers around the handle of the gun and squeezes the trigger. The explosion of the discharging bullet and the frightened yelp that escapes Vivian's throat was all Mason had heard before everything went silent.

The ringing in his ears tunes out everything. The grapefruit sized exit wound in Vivian's back fills his vision. She collapses to the floor dead. Mason only has seconds to react and nowhere to run. Galarza raises her own weapon toward him and begins firing. Mason leaps backward and to the right, hoping that the curve the room would give him some kind of protection. The first shot misses, but the second catches him in the inner thigh, narrowly missing his Femoral artery. The sting of the bullet is replaced by the burning of screaming nerves. Mason inches toward the door, but he's making slow progress.

He can't believe he has allowed himself to be handcuffed, let alone fooled. He can see his chances for survival dropping with each step his traitorous Chief takes toward him. Mason accesses the open network, begins to broadcast his last moments and hopes that someone will find it.

Galarza stops right on top of Mason, who has stopped crawling. "Why Chief?" Mason asks desperately.

Galarza shakes her head, "The answer is simple Ed. The money is too damn good." She levels the barrel of her gun at his face.

Mason rolls to his side exposing the short barreled gun in his hands. Two more explosions fill the room. One hits Mason in the shoulder and the other puts a hole in the Chief's neck. Mason grunts. Galarza stumbles back holding her throat, trying to keep her life's blood in her body. Mason can see a wave of emotions flowing passed her eyes. He thinks he spots some regret, but at this moment, he doesn't care.

Galarza tries for another shot, but it goes wide as she falls to the floor. Mason tries to move the fingers in his arm, but can only manage a faint twitch. He tries to reach for his keys in his pocket to unlock the cuffs, but his right hand can't reach his left side pocket. He knows that he's not out of the woods yet and the pressure increases when he hears the footsteps turning the corner of the large office. Mason stops going for the keys and looks up to find David pointing Vivian's gun at him.

"I truly am sorry Eddie, but this is much bigger than you," David says then he opens fire.

Mason feels the slugs slam into his back. He loses control of the muscles in his neck and his head droops to the cold marble floor. His vision fades to black and all he can hear is David's voice, calling on someone to clean up the mess. A set of soft footsteps follow. Everything goes dark. Mason loses consciousness.

Silvia shuffles over to Mason's still body. She crouches down and places two fingers on his neck to feel for a pulse. Her eyes open wide for a second when she feels his heart beating and spots the flak jacket under his shirt. The serving synthetic's eyes return to their normal emotionless state to cover for her initial shock.

She takes ahold of Mason's upper arm and hoists him up. She carries him out of the office and over to a holding cell disguised as a maintenance closet. She drops him inside, turns to leave, but she pauses. She looks back at the unconscious detective.

David sets the heavy metal gun on the liquor bar and uses a fine cloth to wipe his hands, "Why is it so damn hard to find good help?" he mumbles to himself. He pours himself a drink and knocks it back. Setting the glass down, he turns and looks down at Vivian's expanding pool of blood. He steps back and around the crimson puddle, "Silvia!" he calls. When she doesn't respond immediately, he starts for the glass doors. "God damn machine," he grumbles.

Silvia stands poised at the door with her hands clasped in front her, "You called, sir?" she says. David looks at the inexpressive robot utterly annoyed at her lack of discipline. He storms over to her, yanks her by her hair and drags her over to the enlarging red circle of gore.

"I said to clean this shit up!" he snarls as he shoves her into the slick liquid. She slips and falls into Vivian's lifeless body with a squeal. She grabs the dead woman's arms and begins to drag her to the office exit.

David pinches the bridge of his nose at the trail of blood left in their wake, "Silvia," his menacing voice freezes her limbs. She doesn't look up at him. "Don't track blood everywhere. Pick it up and get rid of it!" his voice grows increasing louder with each word. The synthetic woman lifts the blood drenched body onto her shoulders and carries her out of the office. Silvia returns covered in cooling blood and repeats the process with the Chiefs body.

When she returns, she finds David sliding an expensive rug away from the large elliptical puddle. He stands and looks at her expectantly, "Well! This isn't going to clean itself now is it?" he says utterly annoyed. She shuffles over to the cleaning closet that doubles as her quarters and gets to work soaking up the crimson mess. The weight of the blood covering her makes the thin blouse cling to her body. David watches perversely as he taps into the Police Network. He chuckles then makes a few calls to his security detail.

Once the office is cleaned, David saunters over to the blood doused synthetic and brushes her stiffening hair away from her face. The drying liquid is dark against her pale skin. "You know, I don't like hurting you, but you have to learn to obey," He says and he unzips the back of her ruined shirt.

"I understand, sir," she whimpers. Silvia cringes as he pulls the cold fabric off of her body.

"Let's get you cleaned up, shall we,"

CHAPTER 31

Present Day

Minimal traffic flows through the streets. Much of the population were either at home nursing their hangovers or at work, nursing their hangovers. Few dared to be out and about the day after the *Ball* dropped and that was fine. It makes Imogen's task of driving the antique motorcycle easier. She shifts gears and increases her speed. The cold wind whistles through her hair, numbing her face and she instantly regrets not grabbing the helmet that rested on a hook in the secret garage. Trying to ignore the discomforting cold, Imogen sets her mind to the brawl that's been marinating for two years. This fight has gone on long enough and she felt it was time to put an end to David Jennings and his bigot cronies.

The thought of this violent path coming to an end makes the muscle like fibers in her arms and legs tremble. Maybe she could have gone away with Blake, but what quality of life would she have? A couple more years of security at best? No. This has to end. She has to finish what began so long ago. She has to finish what David started.

Imogen slows to a stop at a red light. The vibration of the engine between her legs helps to calm her mind. She blows in her hands like it's really going to do something.

"I should've brought my gloves," she whispers to herself, rubbing her hands together. She pulls up the quickest route to the *Chosen* tower. The mini map on her HUD outlines a path in purple, while Imogen watches the light opposite of her. It's changing and soon she can be on her way. She leans forward and grips the handlebars. A siren chirps from behind. She looks over her shoulder and spots a white and black police vehicle behind her.

"Turn off the bike, get on the ground and place your hands atop your head," a disembodied voice orders.

Imogen crinkles her nose. <*That lying cop must've had a change in heart,*> she thinks and the thought infuriates her. She trusted the bastard. The traffic light turns green and Imogen cranks the throttle.

The tires of the old bike screech and burn rubber on the asphalt before blazing down the street. Imogen passes three intersections before the cops in uniform finally give chase. She can hear the screaming sirens drawing closer with each passing micro second. Her motorcycle is fast, but compared to the muscle of the car chasing her, she knows it will only be a matter of time before they ran her off the road. She deviates from the highlighted path by turning down a side street into oncoming traffic in the hopes that the cops won't follow her. To her surprise, another squad car is heading in her direction.

<Shit!>

Civilian vehicles veer to the left or right trying not to smash the obviously insane woman on the motorcycle. The mini map displays an alternate path through a nearby alley, to get back on route. The shortcut is wide enough for an individual on foot or someone riding a narrow antique motorbike to get through just fine. She smiles to herself, turns and enters the cluttered backstreet. The police car keeps moving forward through traffic. She knows they won't catch up, but running into more trouble is a real possibility. Imogen almost downs her ride when she swerves to keep from slamming head on into a wide metal trash bin that takes up nearly all the space in the alley.

Imogen blasts out of the alley and clips a parked car when she leans into the left turn, going with the flow of traffic. She checks her mirrors and spots three more patrol cars crossing the intersection behind her. Looking forward she can see that the traffic light suspended on wires above is red. She guns it and narrowly misses getting creamed by crossing traffic. She swerves wildly into the opposite flow of traffic to bypass a stopped car, then turns right to continue toward the tower.

She safely navigates the motorcycle down the street, narrowly missing other vehicles on the road. She doesn't slow down. The odds were never in her favor, but the situation took a turn for the worst. The cold wind beating against her face is no longer a worry nor does it even register in her mind. The only thing she is focusing on now is not becoming a bloody smear on the road. She slows and makes another right, clipping a cop car heading down the same street. Her back tire burns the black paint off of the front fender as she peels away. The cops stomp on the pedal, fishtailing after her. Moving her narrow, two-wheeled, vehicle between cars and even going as far as to drive on the sidewalk, Imogen is able to put some distance between her and the police.

With the distance growing between her and her pursuers, Imogen hits the clutch and shifts to a higher gear. A large black all terrain jeep squeals behind her as she passes an intersection and she knows that it can only be Chosen seekers. Her assumption is confirmed when the passenger leans out of his window and opens fire. The man is a terrible shot, but Imogen isn't about to make it easy on him by traveling in a straight line. She begins to deviate in her trajectory by weaving in and out of traffic. Shots rattle off behind her and she can hear the glass of rear car windows burst from the impacts. <*They really didn't care who they killed in the name of purity.*>

Another black SUV joins the pursuit ahead of her. The large jeep barrels down the street, trying for a head on collision. Imogen hops onto the sidewalk to evade the psychopaths. The driver of the car points his gun and fires. Brick and glass shower Imogen as the superheated plasma rounds zoom past her face. She can hear the man screaming and cursing her, but doesn't care to make out the words. She bounces as her tires meet asphalt once more.

The traffic ahead is heavy with little in the way of gaps to pass through, but Imogen can't afford to slow down. Not with the ruthless seekers on her tail. The first black jeep accelerates to close the distance. Imogen spots the front grill of a freight truck making its way across the junction. She holds her breath as she enters the busy intersection. She ducks under its trailer, leaving the seeker's jeep to smash headlong into the massive tires of the rig.

She chances a look behind when she hears the thundering crash of crumpling metal and spots another set of police cars, alongside seeker jeeps rounding the corner. With the tower in sight, she can't afford to be rundown before she gets there. She pulls her pistol from her belt and aims it behind her. Imogen doesn't want to kill innocent men and women who were just doing their job, so she opens fire on the jeep. A three round burst slams into the tinted windshield of the SUV. Immediately the car swerves hard to the right sending it grinding into a row of parked cars before flipping several times and skidding to a halt.

With the tower only blocks away, Imogen can't help but feel a rush of apprehension. She knows that nearly every person in that building will kill her on sight and yet, she knows that there is no other way to end the egregious ideals they represent in this world. She steels her resolve and grits her teeth as she dodges the flow of traffic leading to her final destination. The distant thrum of the V-52 Osprey rips Imogen from her thoughts. That dull rhythmic sound of blades cutting the air told her that things went from extremely hazardous to dangerously serious very fast. She hopes that the choppers headed her way were operated by the police and not the seekers. The police, though not good, would at least show some restraint and not fire on her while she was on a busy street. The Chosen on the other hand wouldn't care who was in their way. She truly believes that they would kill their own mothers if it meant that they would be able to slaughter a synthetic.

They are the worst of humanity and everyone just seems to turn a blind eye to their savage acts. There is something terribly wrong with the moral compass of society and it seems that there is no fixing it any time soon.

"I'll at least wipe one stain from this earth," Imogen vowed through gritted teeth.

The dampened thumping of air being pushed down is now above and behind. Imogen doesn't even bother to look up. If it were Chosen seekers, there would be nothing she could do to stop them from blasting her into a crater. Ahead police vehicles form a makeshift barricade in front of the gleaming tower. Men and women in uniform stand behind their cars, weapons drawn and ready to shoot. Imogen looks past them to see metal shutters being lowered over the glass entrance. She can feel her chance slipping away. She pushes the old bike to its limits.

The motorcycle's speedometer needle is pegged at one hundred and forty miles per hour. The uniformed police fire low, aiming for the tires. One lucky shot hits the gas tank and sends liquid fuel spirting out the other end and still the bike zips past a gap between their cars. Imogen lifts her right foot onto the seat of the rumbling motorcycle and tilts the bike back in order to clear the steel gate. The three hundred seventy five pound bike streaks across the concrete, sending sparks arcing into the air and igniting the flowing gas. The blazing motorcycle crashes through the lower half of the window. Imogen kicks the doomed bike into one of thirteen waiting guards before it explodes, sending chunks of hot metal in every direction, and killing six men.

The gate rumbles to a close behind Imogen as she rolls to her knees, gun at the ready. She lets rip a three round burst, taking out a helmeted security agent and moves on to the others. She kills another armed man before moving for cover behind a large stone pillar. Chunks of the polished stone explodes into a fine dust all around her. A super-hot bullet passes through the stone to graze her arm. The sting just pisses her off. Just as she is thinking there will be no way for her to find new cover, the men stop shooting. The idiots were reloading at the same time. Imogen smiles inwardly and dashes out from behind the pillar. Every burst from her gun finds a fatal impact point and two more men farthest from her drops dead.

She rushes the nearest man, who is fumbling with a canister of gas, slams her gun into his unprotected throat and crushes his windpipe. With her free hand, Imogen yanks free his side arm before he falls to the floor struggling for air. Without losing momentum, Imogen slips around the gasping man, drops to her knee and squeezes the trigger of both handguns. The azure streak left by the plasma pistol burns straight through the nearest man, while the hot metal slugs slam into the last guard.

Imogen looks around to ensure that there are indeed no more surprises. The motorcycle burns in front of the greeting desk, blackening the wood and the man it smashed. Bodies lay strewn all around the reception area. Blood splatters adorn the walls and dark cooling puddles of blood expand on the floor. The acrid smell of death permeates the air. Finding no immediate threats, Imogen kneels down and collects a tactical belt from the dead man at her feet and all of his spare ammunition. She snatches a rifle from another and after searching the rest, finds that only one was carrying a single grenade. She hadn't noticed before, but she can hear the police beyond the metal security doors pounding and screaming obscenities. Imogen examines the room again and takes in all the carnage that she caused. The burning bike cooked the flesh of the man pinned underneath. Take away the smell of burning chemicals and oddly enough, Imogen thought the man smelled like unseasoned pork chops. If she survived this, she would probably never eat any pork products again.

She searches for the office of her intended target on the directory. She couldn't find his name and is beginning to wonder if she smashed through the wrong building. Then she spots it.

<Of course you'd be on the top floor. Prick.>

She thought that she'd feel something, anything at this point, but she is just numb to it all. She welcomes the emptiness and presses the call button on the elevator. The smoke finally sets off the ear-splitting fire alarm. The elevator freezes in its decent. Strobe lights flash steadily high on the walls. The pulsing white flashes followed by the hiss of special foam on the burning wreckage should have been enough to raise the security gates, but it wasn't.

Usually when the fire alarm systems are set off in any building, all external and internal locks are disengaged, allowing easy escape for anyone inside. The same goes for emergency responders who would need to enter the building to assist in the evacuation or rescue of potential victims. For some reason that is not the case here. Once the fire is extinguished, the alarm is silenced and the elevator continues its way down to ground level.

The sinking feeling in Imogen's chest tells her that they are expecting her. What did she expect? Did she really think that she could just crash through the window and not be noticed? The place is covered in an array of sensors, cameras, and other monitoring systems. David Jennings knows that she is coming and he probably has the mouth breathing, knuckle dragging, lumpy bag of beaver shit, Pete Roberts by his side. The memory of what he did to Darioux makes her burn with unreasoning rage. Imogen is ready to do some damage.

A chime signals the arrival of the elevator. As an afterthought, Imogen steps to the side of the doors with duel pistols at the ready and out of sight of whoever may had been on the ride down. The doors glide open. She waits and counts to five. Her lips silently mouth the numbers. She turns guns drawn at an empty lift. She steps inside, knowing that if they really wanted to be diabolical they could detach the cable while she was on the ninetieth floor, sending her screaming to a crushing death. Imogen is placing her confidence in the fact that they are the kind of monsters who want to be face to face to get their rocks off. That's okay, because she too wants to see the look on their faces as they take their last breath. She depresses the last tiny button on the large panel. The doors come together with another chime.

Imogen rocks back and forth to the old twentieth century pop elevator music. She bites the inside of her lip and watches the numbers ascend. At about the half way mark, Imogen turns, placing her hands against the wall and presses her feet against the opposite wall. She doesn't want to get caught in a hail of bullets, so she walks up the narrow box until she reaches the top and waits for the doors to open. She is glad the effort isn't wasted. When the doors open, a volley of bullets and heated plasma rounds riddle the interior of the elevator.

"Hold your fire!" a gruff man yells and the storm of bullets subside.

Judging by the amount of holes in the elevator, Imogen knows that if she jumps down she will be shredded in an instant. She tenuously reaches to the dangling sphere on her newly acquired vest and pulls it off as noiselessly as she can. She grimaces at the movement. Not because it is strenuous. The sour expression on her face is because she had planned on shoving the tiny explosive ball down Pete Roberts's throat. She'll just have to find another method to end the bastard. Clutching the pin between her teeth, Imogen yanks on the compact ball and chucks it out the door just before they close. The booming detonation and agonizing screams are music to her ears. Imogen releases the tension in her limbs and she drops to the debris littered floor and presses the button for the floor below.

The doors open to an empty hall and Imogen steps out ready to start shooting. Once she is sure that the hall is clear, she reaches back into the elevator and presses the button for the floor above-just for shits and giggles. She bolts for the nearest stairwell and takes the steps two at a time. She can hear the muffled sound of multiple weapons discharging at once, again, only this time they punctuate their ceasefire with a couple of grenades themselves. The *Boom, Boom, Boom,* of erupting explosives shake the building. The railing rattles as if it is a plucked brass string of a guitar.

The loud then distant grinding of metal on stone as the elevator plummets to ground level tells her that it wouldn't be operational again anytime soon. A dull rumble reverberates through the whole of the building, loosening dust from above and possibly some structural support columns. Imogen doesn't mind if the building comes crumbling down. She just prefers that if it is going to collapse, that it do so with her at a safe distance.

<*The media must be having a field day with this,*> Imogen thinks darkly.

She takes another step and continues to the door marked as the final floor. There are some steps that lead out to the roof, but there is no need to go that far. She isn't Charles Bronson and she doesn't have any rope. So, a dramatic entrance is out of the question.

She peeks through the narrow vertical window and finds that she hasn't completely missed with her blind grenade throw. In fact, she has scored a pretty decent hit on her would be ambushers. The gore is everywhere. Men in black masks are dragging away the wounded, while others look to be organizing a plan. The big man with his back to her, barking orders gestures toward the steps. He must've have told them to stand guard - just in case. Two men limp toward the door. Their guns aren't at the ready and that is a huge mistake on their part.

Once the men are less than a foot away from the door, Imogen delivers a running front kick to the push bar. The edge of the door slams into the face of the man to her right. Imogen jumps through the opening, raises the plasma rifle and squeezes the trigger, unleashing a spray of projectiles that cut through the nearest man. Unsuspecting mercenaries behind him have no time to turn around before they feel a hot punch slam into their spines. The soldiers on the far side of the large room raise their weapons and open fire on the exposed woman, who is now running for cover. She crashes through the glass door of an unoccupied office. She can hear the men shouting orders and the loud stomping of their boots. More metal slugs rip through the walls above Imogen's head. Drywall and chunks of metal burst through the exit holes, peppering her with dust.

The men stop shooting and everything goes eerily silent. Imogen chances a glance through one of the holes in the wall. She can see that one of the men is hefting something large onto his shoulder. He crouches and aims. Not wanting to find out what kind of ammo that thing has, Imogen slams the muzzle of her gun against the wall and pulls the trigger. The first four shots miss, but the last six hit home just as the guy with the giant launcher fires. A grapefruit sized metallic ball bursts from the muzzle then slams into the ceiling. The impact is followed by a high pitched whining. Seconds later, hundreds of metallic darts spring in all directions from the sphere lodged above the soldiers, bombarding their bodies with the deadly needles and making them look like human pin cushions. The man in charge manages a yelp just before the darts erupt. Mini explosions rip him and his remaining men apart.

Imogen laughs out loud because she knows that Jennings is probably holed up in some safe room freaking out. Or at least she hopes. She peeks around the destroyed doorframe. Her jaw goes slack. The little needles tore apart the heavy wood desk, leaving it partially in splinters. The walls crumble around her and the once white room is blackened. The blood and guts of the soldiers are completely cooked to a charcoal mess.

Imogen steps out of the small office and pauses. She listens for the reinforcements that she knows must be coming any second, but the deafening silence fills her ears. Not even the emergency systems are active. Something is definitely wrong with this situation and she doesn't like it.

She inches over and past the piles of what used to be human beings. The glass door to the large office that must belong to the big boss is just a metal frame surrounded by shards of glass. The walls on either side are pockmarked with various sized craters. The debris falling from the walls all around her and the utter silence unnerves her to a point where she begins to tremble. She places an unsteady hand on the handle of the door, pulls it open and slowly steps inside.

A determined growl to her left startles her. She turns to find Pete Roberts, head down, charging like a bull. He slams into her midsection and they both crash through the weakened wall. The impact rattles Imogen's skeleton. Pete slams her to the hard uneven, jagged floor. Her vision flutters when the back of her head slams into the shattered marble. The giant of a man wraps one meaty hand around Imogen's throat and raises his massive arm. Imogen grabs his tactical vest and raises one hand in defense of her face. Pete's monstrous fist arcs down. The smile on his face is sadistically insane.

CHAPTER 32

Present Day

Blake sits in the dark five by eight, windowless, stone, room furiously typing away on a spare keyboard. The four walls of the room are damp, but solid. The four inch metal slab that serves as a hatch above him is locked from the inside, just in case someone discovers it. The muffled noises from the outside world is only a slight distraction. There is enough room for him to have his equipment and ports where he needs them and not much else. The only visible light emanates from the glass monitors he had mounted on the walls months earlier. He had been planning and building his escape routes in secret. His reasoning was that if something ever went wrong on Imogen's end, he could continue the fight unobstructed and show the world what their intolerance had birthed.

The blind fear the public had of synthetics, lead to giving terrible individuals practically unlimited power to do almost anything they please. This ignorance of the public strips them of their freedoms and they didn't even know it. Or maybe they don't care? Either way, the world has to have the blinders removed from their eyes so, they can see the horror that the abuse of power can unleash.

Blake accesses the National Emergency Broadcasting System and from there he links the Global Broadcasting Network to the feed he is preparing. He feels daring and even taps into the Police Network and searches for the evidence they have on the bombing and Imogen's recent retaliation. To his dismay, he finds nothing. It was just gone. As Blake prepares to leave the network, he spots a pulsing blip. He taps on it with his index finger.

"What have we here?" he says to no one in particular.

His main screen goes black, flickers then displays a recorded video file ready for view. He taps the play button.

Within the first couple of seconds of the video, Blake knows where it is leading. He copies the vid file to a virtual hard drive while the original file plays on. Tapping some commands, Blake patches into the feed, disrupting regular programming. He allows the feeds to go black, then plays the scrolling message he had prepared a year after he had met Imogen:

In this golden age of technology we have watched our cavitation rise, fall and rebuild. We have created artificial life that nurtured us and picked us up from our nearly cataclysmic failure. How have we given our thanks? We allowed our misunderstanding to give rise to hate and fear. We allowed the Chosen to institutionalize that fear. We have given them unlimited power to rid us of this thing that fuels our irrational fright. The Chosen claim that they have humanity's best interest at heart. This is what that abuse of power has given us.

Blake taps the play button on a compilation video of various assaults and destructions of synthetic beings and their human counterparts. The first montage depicts the slaughter at the Lincoln Memorial, followed by random and very brutal murders of children at parks who just happened to be playing with a synthetic child. Parents on a bridge being tied together with their adopted mechanical child, pleading for their lives before they are pushed into rivers. Individuals being detained without due process or even forced to their knees and executed for trying to hide a syn.

In every clip, Chosen seekers were the aggressors. The compiled video clips play for the next five minutes.

Blake manually types the question:

"Still okay with this?"

Then he plays the gut-wrenching video of Darioux's murder and the mutilation of Imogen in its entirety.

People walking the busy streets look up at the giant digital billboard downtown. People stand frozen, unable to peel their eyes away from the much smaller video advertising screens in store windows and bus stops. All of them stand in rigid horror to what they are witnessing. Families at home shield the eyes of their children from the scenes displayed on every monitor in their house. People all over the world stop in the middle of the menial tasks they are doing and watch. Their eyes are stuck to the nearest screen, unable to look away from the brutality taking place right before their eyes. The People flinch when the bomb goes off.

Blake splices the CCTV footage taken from outside Imogen's apartment to show the full extent of the explosion that nearly leveled the building. Blake clenches his teeth as he fights off the network programmer's attempts to disconnect his feed. He isn't about to let them stop him. He will relinquish control when he feels the message has been received. He wants everyone to know that not only did they mercilessly kill Darioux, they slaughtered families on two separate floors. Debris on the streets consisted of clothes, various pieces of furniture and children's toys. The feed goes black.

The question, *"Is it sinking in yet?"* scrolls across screens all over the world. Blake smiles as he cues up the last and newest video in his arsenal. The silence outside is the sound of millions of people collectively pulling their heads out of their asses. Blake smiles.

◊

Mason jerks awake in a dark cold room. The fetid odor of death fills his nostrils and makes him gag. Sweat drenches his body and the wound in his leg aches with the slightest movement. He tries to stand, but the cuffs holding his hands behind his back restrict his movement. Men shouting and the stomping of boots draw his attention toward the narrow bar of light streaming through the gap at the bottom of the door. He slithers toward it, lays his head as flat as he can and looks out the narrow opening. All he can see is feet. He is about to call out, but remembers what got him here in the first place.

Mason curls up into a ball, straining to pull his arms over his waist. With a great deal of effort, he manages to get one foot then the other over the metal shackles around his wrists. He searches his pockets for his keys, but finds nothing but lint. Disappointed, Mason places his hands under his bulk to lift himself up, but drops back down to the floor when he hears automatic fire rattle off in the chamber beyond the door. He shields his head just in case any stray bullets burst through the door.

The shooting stops and Mason checks to make sure that he doesn't have any extra holes. He peers under the door again glimpses something metal clattering along the floor. Recognizing its shape, he pushes himself back and curls into a ball to protect his vital organs. *Boom!* The shock wave rattles the door so hard that Mason thinks it is going to be blown in off its hinges.

The howls of pain emanating from the throats of the men outside, make the hairs rise on the back of Mason's neck. He quickly squashes any feelings of empathy he feels for the hired guns working for the son of bitch that shot him in the back. A man starts to bark orders to whatever remains of his men, then without warning the staccato bursts of an automatic weapon rings out. Hot projectiles punch huge holes in the door, pelting Mason with splintered wood and dust.

The light pouring through the many holes in the door, reveals Vivian and Galarza's cold and stiff bodies. Vivian's unblinking, lifeless, eyes catch his. The sad and, shocked, expression frozen on her face yanks on his heart. In that moment, he instantly regrets thinking that she was ever capable of betrayal and corruption. He shakes his head slowly. His paranoia got the best of him and clouded his judgment. He couldn't see the truth of what was truly going on and it cost a good, young, cop her life.

"I'm sorry Viv," he said as his lip quivers. He wipes hot guilty tears from his cheeks.

During his self-reprimanding something sparkles on the floor near Galarza's feet. Mason's eyes grow wide and he lunges for the tiny metal set. He shakes with anticipation as he drives home the thin rod and turns it. The click of the lock being released makes his heart skip. Mason positions the key in his fingers over the next lock when many tiny, but powerful, explosions rock the walls and loosen concrete blocks above. Mason is pummeled by heavy stone and is nearly knocked unconscious. His vision blurs and fades, but he fights to stay awake.

Mason distantly hears a wall collapse and what his mind can only describe as a scuffle can be heard on the other side of the door. Grunting and flesh colliding with flesh echo in his mind. He stumbles to all fours and crawls over to a large hole in the door. He can make out two blurred shapes locked in an epic struggle. A red blob on the smaller one marks the place where the head should be, tells Mason that he knows who was here tearing up the place.

"Imogen," he slurs while climbing to his feet.

He forces himself to focus and clear his vision. They weren't going to get away with what they had done. Mason knows that he is in no shape to go out there and assist in the brutal fight that she is engaged in, so he turns to search the corpses sprawled on the floor behind him. He carries an extra firearm and he is pretty sure that Vivian or Galarza has one on their person as well. He just hopes that whoever had brought them here didn't bother to search them.

He gently pats their bodies starting with Vivian's back - searching for anything that can be helpful. Not finding anything but stiff muscle, he moves to her legs. Mason finds a decent sized plasma pistol strapped to Vivian's upper calf. He gently pulls the bloody pant leg up and over her bruised and darkening flesh. Another debilitating wave of guilt sweeps over him and nearly takes every ounce of strength from his muscles. The emotional pain almost robs his will of the fortitude needed to carry on.

He brushes the loose hair away from Vivian's face. He blinks the mist from his eyes and gently closes hers, allowing her to finally rest. Overwhelmed with disbelief and hurt and anger, he presses his forehead to hers. He places her stiffening hands over her chest.

"Thank you Viv. I'll get him for this." He promises. He tries to stand, but his wounded leg can't support his weight. He tumbles back to the floor.

CHAPTER 33

Present Day

Pete has all of his weight on the small woman, trying to pin her wriggling body under his immense bulk. He uses one massive hand to clamp down on Imogen's throat in an attempt to hold her down on the debris littered floor.

"Stay still you bitch!" Pete bellows in frustration.

Dark grey smoke clings to the ceiling, rolling over itself like waves on a turbulent shore. Glass and stone crunch under their bodies, ripping clothes and skin. Pieces of charred bodies crumble like ash when they come into contact with the struggling pair. The big man slams his fist down intending to smash Imogen's face, but she jerks her head to the side. She feels the wind brush her face as his club of a hand crunches against the ruined marble floor.

Imogen realizes that she has to get out from under Pete's giant body if this fight is to end the way she wants it to. If he manages to stun her, she's lost and everything will have been for nothing. She uses his near miss to gain some kind of leverage. She grabs the sleeve of his t-shirt with her left hand, then pushes upward with the left side of her body, causing the big man to push down even harder on that one side. Seeing her chance, Imogen quickly releases the tension on the left side of her body, throwing Pete off balance and allowing her to throw him off with a roll of her right fist. Sitting on top of Pete's massive frame, Imogen rains down a flurry of right hooks and a few elbows. Pete Manages to get his large boot in between their bodies and kicks, knocking Imogen off and back.

Imogen turns to grab her gun just paces away on the floor but, Pete reaches out, hooks her foot and sends her face first into the jagged floor. Pete rises, grabs her by the collar of her shirt and pulls her into his punch. The blow connects with the back of her head, making her see white for a split second as she slams back down to the floor. A piece of jagged stone rips through the skin just above her eye. She tries to push herself back up, when Pete grabs a handful of her hair, lifts her up and slams her head first into a wall.

Imogen turns, fist at the ready and catches the war veteran in the jaw. Her quick strike knocks him back a step, allowing her to turn and grab the gun laying on the floor. She turns, ready to start shooting.

Seeing that she has a gun, Pete reaches out, grabs her wrist and delivers a solid punch to her lower back. He twists her arm, rolls over, making sure to lock his legs around her chest and stomach. He brings her down so that her arm and the gun are locked up. He applies pressure to the joint at her elbow. In her desperation to break free, Imogen tenses her muscles, trying to pull away from his iron grip so her elbow doesn't break. The gun, pointed at the ceiling goes off. *Boom! Boom! Boom!* Seeing no way out, Imogen comes up with a tactically sound plan. She sinks her teeth into his calf. The big man grunts in pain, but has no other choice but to let go or have a chunk of flesh torn from his leg.

Imogen rolls to her feet raising the gun while she turns and sees a flash of white as Pete's fist collides with her face. The impact sends her bouncing off the wall behind her. Pete slaps the gun from her grasp then throws his big foot out in front of him. The hard combat boot connects with her chest and sends her through the wall to land in an empty office.

Imogen coughs and nearly throws up from the impact. Before she can fully get air flowing again, Pete takes ahold of her ankle in his giant hands and drags her back out through the hole. She uses her free leg to kick him in the groin. He doubles over, holding himself, then Imogen, still on her back, kicks him in the face. The flat of her boot shatters his nose. The blood pours from the two small holes in his face. He stumbles back and away from her as he falls to his knees. Imogen jumps on his back, wrapping her arms around his neck and squeezing for all she's worth.

Pete gags as he tries to suck in air. He runs toward a solid looking wall near the ruined desk of David's assistant and rams Imogen into it. Once, twice, three times, Pete slams her into the wall before her grip loosens enough for him to break free. He stumbles forward sucking the precious air into his lungs. Imogen reaches down, takes a large heavy beam from the desk and shatters it over Pete's back. Imogen kicks Pete in the back sending his head into the metal stairway door, denting it. She Grabs his square head, spins and uses her momentum to slam his head through the reinforced metal wire glass in the very same door. Blood trickles from Pete's face like a fondue fountain.

Desperate, Pete throws out an arm to defend himself. The back of his open hand smacks against her face and splits her lips. Imogen spins away, "Fuck!" she hisses in pain.

Pete turns to her laughing. His bloody toothed grin finally matching his sadistic personality.

"Damn. Who would of thought that I'd have this hard of time killing one little fake bitch. If you were real, I'd be turned on right now," he says while spittle mixed with blood dangles from his chin.

Imogen chuckles while holding her face.

"You're putting up more of fight than your nig..." Imogen slams her fist into his mouth before he can finish uttering the racial slur. Chunks of shattered teeth bounce and splatter blood across the floor.

"Shut your fucking mouth!" she demands.

Pete goes for a right hook. Imogen ducks his fist and goes to work on his midsection. She slams her fists into his gut. Just as he arches over from the blows, Imogen swings her leg up to collide his face with a devastating knee lift that knocks out more teeth. She goes for another right hook to the side of his face. Pete ducks under her swing, moves in for a tackle, but instead of driving her to the ground he lifts her up, turns then slams her down and through the once sturdy desk. Imogen bolts upright with another right hook, cracking Pete's jaw and knocking him back several steps. She sprints at him, jumps, pulls her fist back and smashes it into Pete's mangled jaw.

The flying punch rocks Pete's head back. Imogen continues her assault with more strikes to Pete's body. Pete doubles over and fumbles for her. Imogen swings her head up, slamming the back of her head into Pete's already busted nose.

Pete reaches out and grabs Imogen by the neck and pushes her into a wall. He punches her in the stomach, once, twice, before she chops the bend of his elbow and twists his arm. She kicks him in the face, while still holding his arm, then kicks the back of his knee bringing him down to the floor. She frees his arm, spins and drives her knee into his face, knocking him to the floor, where she begins to stomp on him.

Rage completely consumes her. Imogen steps over Pete and starts to punch him in the face. Every blow hurts her hands, but she isn't willing to stop until he is dead. Every time her fist connects with his face, flashes of Darioux bleeding in their living room pass before her eyes.

Pete bellows in fury and kicks her off of him. Imogen's ankle twists in the uneven floor and she goes sprawling. She gets to her knees quickly only to feel Pete's boot on the side of her head. He kicks her again before he palms her face and rams her head through a wall. He yanks her head out of the hole and throws her through the wall leading to David's large office. Imogen slams into the wooden cabinet that serves as a bar. Bottles of various liquors tumble to the floor and shatter on impact.

Pete steps through the hole and picks Imogen up from the floor and body slams her through the fallen bar. Imogen coughs and rolls to her stomach. She tries to crawl away. Every move sends bolts of pain shooting through her body. Pete follows behind, toothlessly grinning.

"You know, the day I came to your place, I seriously hoped you would try to run," he lisps with blood trailing from his lips. "Your fucking man though - he was a surprise," Pete shakes his head. "I didn't expect his black ass to bite my face," he chuckles and rubs the circular scar. "He got what was coming to him though. Didn't he?" he grunts humorlessly.

Imogen's eyes well up with tears at the thought of Darioux on his back dead. The pain gives her much needed strength to continue this fight. She doesn't know how much more she could take. It feels like every bone in her body is made of glass and is grinding against each other. It feels like one more shot would shatter her. Hearing Pete's voice above her, Imogen turns over. The big man wraps his large hands around her head and lifts her to her shaky feet.

"You did good, but you aren't shit," he says looking her in the eyes. The blood streaks down her face to stain her shirt. Pete smiles then lifts his knee into her gut and throws her on to a glass table, shattering it. She rolls her aching body over to catch her breath. She notices a large blade-like piece of the table under her hand. She palms the large shard of glass.

Imogen screams in pain as the big man lifts her to her feet. She swings the glass blade in an arc, aiming for the man's eye, but he catches her hand and smiles.

"Fighting till the very end. I like that," he says, not letting her drop the jagged glass.
Pete chuckles then rams her hand and the long glass blade into her stomach. Imogen gasps unable to scream as the pain lances through her body, severing main cooling tubes and system wiring. She looks up at the unfeeling man, willing herself

not to cry. She tries to pull the impromptu knife from her body, but Pete jerks her fist and drives it deeper. She can feel the corrosive digestive liquids filling her stomach, burning delicate instruments and frying important systems.

When Pete feels her body slacken, he lifts her up on to his shoulder, "You put up one hell of a fight lil miss," Pete says as he walks toward a large cracked window. The big bastard steps heavily, making sure to bounce a bit to hear the synthetic on his shoulder whimper. "I'm truly going to miss you," he continues, "Try not to kill anyone on the way down."

Imogen wraps her numb fingers around the bit of glass in her abdomen, grits her teeth and yanks it out with a blood curdling scream. The large shard breaks leaving a good portion to remain in her body, but a large chunk of it is still intact in her hands. She slams the glass knife into Pete's kidney. He screams and turns, reaching for her hand. She jerks her hand away and stabs him again, twisting and breaking the glass off in his body. They tumble to the marble.

Pete and Imogen both howl in agony. Pete grunts as he tries to turn. After feeling his way up Imogen's body, the big bloody bastard grabs her by the throat and squeezes. He tries to pull her head off her shoulders. Imogen growls and lifts the tiny jagged glass left in her hand and nicks his jugular. Blood spurts from his neck with each beat of his laboring heart.

"You bi, bitch," he slurs as he falls over leaking out his life's blood.

Imogen lies on her back next to a dying Pete Roberts, who is gasping for air. She fights to keep her eyes focused on a dark point on the ceiling. Imogen wonders which gun fired the bullet that ended up in here. Could it have been from her gun when Pete had her locked up in an arm bar? The systems that kept her from overheating are damaged and she's leaking coolant.

She rolls to her side and uses the little strength she has to climb to her knees. She's determined to finish the fight. She lifts her head and curiously enough, spots bare feet. Imogen follows the legs leading up to a battered Desirae. She looks terrified. The look in Desirae's eyes is desperate and full of fading hope.

<What is she even doing here? Where is her son?> Imogen thinks.

Slowly, her tired eyes follows Desirae's to a big black gun and the man holding it. The gun rests at her temple and the man attached to that gun is none other than David Jennings.

CHAPTER 34

Present day

David stands in the dark of his private office, which sits just off his public meeting place. The dark wood glistens with pale blue light as he watches the images that play across the monitor of his personal computer. He is overwhelmed with outrage. His white hot anger consumes him to the point that his face doesn't even register emotion. He heard the gunshots, the explosions and now the hand to hand fighting that is taking place in his office. She ruined everything. Everything that he's worked so hard for all these years is literally crumbling down around him and it is because of this insignificant machine.

<This thing thinks she actually deserves justice? She isn't even alive! Not really? She's running on an operating system and she thinks that she deserves to live her life as a real flesh and blood person would?>

David rolls the tiny blue vile in his fingers. With every tiny motion, he feels the beveled glass glide across his skin. He hears what is going on outside his private chamber and it fuels the rage within him. The white hot anger swells and threatens to overflow inside him. He feels that he is close to losing his composure and then the video of him shooting the detective pops up on the screen. That was it! He has reached his limit! He clenches the small vile of hair so hard that the glass crumbles in his hand. Blood and hair mix in his balled fist.

<*Those things and the people who pity them have already taken everything from me!*> David thinks as he glares at his soiled hand. The blood congeals as the hair soaks up the thick dark liquid. A dark clump of warm blood rolls off of his palm and falls to his pants.

That was it! He snatches the female detective's gun off of his desk and stomps toward the leather lounge chair to collect Desirae. The tired woman flinches as David snatches her up by the back of her neck and drags her toward the door leading to the main meeting chamber. He swings the door open and pulls the frightened woman along behind him. He stops yanking Desirae in front of him. He can feel the woman trembling in his grip.

The bloody redhead struggles just to kneel. David can't help, but smile with delight.

"You, Mrs. Harper, I would have been willing to leave you and any other *real* person out of this, but you couldn't leave well enough alone. Could you?" His voice trembles.

Imogen can't tell if he is frightened or just overly pissed off. Either way she doesn't see a way out of the quandary she finds herself in. She slowly rises to her unsteady feet. Her legs, knees and every limb feels like they are made of gelatin. She finds it extremely difficult to keep from falling over.

"Just who do you think you are? What do you think you are? What gives you the right?" David screams, growing more vexed with every question. Foamy spittle sprays from his mouth. The vein in his forehead was ready to burst.

David jerks Desirae closer to him forestalling her attempt to get away.

"Please, just let my son go. I beg you," Desirae pleads with tear soaked cheeks. David responds by jamming the gun hard against her head. Imogen takes an uncertain step forward.

"I... I'm," Imogen stuttered. Her voice box is loose from the fight. It was like two people speaking at once, "I'm the one you want, David," Imogen says, straining to complete each word. "If anyone has to die here and now, it shouldn't be Desirae. Not another innocent."

David snarls as if to let her know that it is too late for anything less than complete closure of this whole affair. "I want you to know before you die - for real this time that, this woman's blood is on your hands." David pulls the trigger.

Imogen's vision narrows to encompass the muzzle flash. It was as if time was straining to move forward. She tries to move, but her feet might as well be lead weights in an ocean of quicksand. She doesn't see Desirae fall to the floor. She barely hears the shot. It's like her mind is trying to substitute reality.

She realizes the gun is turning to point toward her.

<*The muzzle looks so big*,> she thinks to herself before the flashes consume her vision once more. Her body jerks three times. Each burning shot feels like a dull sting in her stomach. Imogen can feel a rush of wind blow past her to sweep into the office.

<*Was there a large window behind me? It must have shattered.*> Imogen thinks with an odd disconnect. Another flash escapes the dark smoking hole of the gun to punch Imogen in her left shoulder, knocking her out into open air.

David howls in his minor triumph, pumping his fist in the air. He takes several measured steps toward the large window, but stops when he hears shoes crunching glass and debris behind him. He turns expecting to see his occasionally disobedient mechanical servant and he does, but she's not alone. She stands side by side with the obstreperous detective he had shot in the back the day before. Silvia had Mason's arm over her shoulders to support most of his weight. The gun in the injured man's hands doesn't go unnoticed.

David steps forward. His face is caught between anger and disgust, "Silvia, I see that you are helping our detective friend get around. How, generous of you," David says with a sneer.

Mason looks at the multibillionaire and can't help but think that he's a waste of space. A waste of skin breathing air that he did not deserve. A fire burns in Mason's chest. His narrowed eyes take in the blood splattered walls, the blood speckling David's otherwise white clothes and the smoking pistol in his hand.

Mason, with the help of Silvia, steps forward, "David Jennings, you have the right to shut the fuck up. Anything you say will provoke me to empty this fucking clip into your face," Mason says furiously and unblinking. He watches the pampered bastard mentally running through his options as if he had any. Mason smiles and asks a *loaded* question. He wanted to see just how dumb the son of a bitch really is, "Do you understand?"

David opens his mouth, but doesn't speak. Mason thinks he is really going to say something. The fact that the man opens his mouth at all is reason enough. David twitches then raises his gun, but gets two burning bullets to the shoulder. The founder of Chosen disappears out the window. Mason motions for Silvia to move forward. Inch by inch they make their way toward the edge and look down. They see David clinging to the automated window cleaning stage on the side of the building. He managed to catch one of the guard rails designed to keep the maintenance men from falling out of the basket. That's when Mason spots the red hair. The redheaded woman, who looks as if she had been through hell, pull herself up. She reaches down and appears to be helping David into the basket. Mason couldn't understand what she was doing.

<Has she had a change in heart?> Mason wonders curiously.

Imogen climbs to her feet and takes the wrist of David Jennings who looks shocked to see that she is still alive. She leans forward, using strength she didn't know she had left to pull the man up midway. She yanks him close, resting his face against her cheek and whispers, "I am retribution."

Imogen pulls him closer then shoves him out into open space. She collapses to the steel grating of the basket. Silvia watches her enslaver flail wildly as he plummets to the earth.

Mason looks up, noticing for the first time the police and news choppers that fill the sky. Apparently they caught everything for the live vids. Mason knows the world had to be watching as everything unfolded. The sniper leaning out of the police Osprey didn't even have her gun drawn. She just watches in awe. She clicks the radio on her shoulder. Mason connects to the network to hear what the woman is saying. The second he connected, he was bombarded with messages from other officers and it takes him a while to navigate through the chatter. He is able to catch the last bit of her communication with dispatchers and other units.

"The son of a bitch is dead," Mason hears over the coms.

Mason and Silvia step away from the window. He can hear the sliding of rope on metal as teams of highly trained SWAT rappel down the face of the building. A few of the men and women stop at the opening and secure the floor while the others keep going down. Mason drops his gun and raises his hands. He doesn't feel like getting shot again.

"My name is Edward Mason. I'm a," he says loud enough to be heard over the whistling wind and choppers outside.

A helmeted man in black places a calming hand on Mason's shoulder, "We know who you are sir," He clicks his radio and calls for emergency medical teams, then the man moves on to secure the floor.

The SWAT teams were able to get through the security gate on the ground floor and they were systematically moving through the building and arresting any armed personnel. Silvia leans Mason against the wall and heads for David's private office.

Mason looks down at Desirae Deponet. Despair and regret that he feels for his former chief and partner weighs heavy on his heart. Seeing Desirae sprawled on the floor, dead, is a sight he just can't stand to bear. He feels something tickling his cheek and wipes it away. He didn't even know he was crying.

Silvia returns with a chair and places it by Mason. She helps him sit. They watch as Imogen floats in a safety basket and is airlifted away somewhere. A female officer returns to her commanding officer holding a screaming toddler in her arms. Mason knows that the child is - was Desirae's son. The tears flow freely from his eyes.

CHAPTER 35

16 Months Later

Blake walks through the crowded outdoor mall. His hands rests lazily in his pockets. He walks passed a women's clothing store, eyes locked on a redheaded mannequin in a light summer dress and high heels. He sighs and continues walking. Young teenagers gently bump into him. They apologize and keep moving. Blake doesn't hear their words. He is transfixed on the crimson curls of the fiberglass woman. He smiles softly and has to physically tear himself away from the display.

The smells of the food court speak directly with his stomach and he allows himself to be pulled in that direction.

Blake sits at one of the small square tables, chewing on what passes for Asian food. He watches the people in the crowd, mill about without a care in the world. He ponders what it means to be alive.

<What was it that constituted a living being?> He watches a new mother rocking her newborn in a shell seat and smiles. She looks so happy. She's practically glowing as she watches the little one sleep all bundled up with soft blankets.

<Who are we to judge anyone?> He looks down at the plastic chopsticks then stabs a piece of meat and pops it into his mouth. *<Aren't we just biological machines ourselves? Our bodies consume food and digest chemicals to convert to energy. Our brains emit electrical signals to our nervous system. Do we not have microscopic machines within us?>* He comes to the conclusion that human beings and all their differences that make them unique aren't that much different from synthetics.

He pulls out his headphones and gently pushes them into his ears. He scrolls through his glass phone and selects his classical playlist. He listens to the *music of the universe* and watches how the commotion of everyone moving about matches perfectly with the melodies playing in his ears. He doesn't know how or why classical music synced with the world around him, but he enjoys it because it does. It's one of those little things Imogen had showed him in their time together. He loved her for that little nugget of truth.

The music helps to get his mind off of the current events unfolding in the government. They had been reevaluating the laws against synthetics since he and Imogen had purged the world of David Jennings and his psychotic flock. Every seeker cell and affiliated organization of Chosen had been disbanded or detained. Their wet drives and collected data was closely scrutinized. Many of them were facing charges while a good bit of them were already behind bars and serving time for multiple counts of murder.

Prosecutors were using the vid data collected from seeker wet drives as evidence to convict. Sadly the seekers were only facing charges for murdering biological humans and not syn - though all of that may change in few weeks when congress and world governments vote. For the first time ever, synthetics had a voice in the world. Even if it were just for these few months that passed, it is a start.

A beeping brings Blake back from his introspective revelry. He checks his phone and sees that he has received a text message. *"Where are you?"* it reads. He responds by tapping the virtual keys and inputs his location. He smiles as he tucks the phone back into the breast pocket of his button up shirt. He sits back in the wicker chair and waits. Blake watches a man carrying a tray filled with food on disposable plates to a larger table. The man's wife follows closely behind with a tray of drinks. The small children prance to their seats. The smiles on their faces, large and carefree, warms his heart.

Moments later, Blake feels gentle hands on his shoulder. He sighs and closes his eyes, "I was beginning to think you guys wouldn't find this place," he says tilting his head back. The visage of Imogen with her pixie-like, dark brown, hair framing her face makes his heart skip a few beats.

A second later, little William hops on to his lap and starts to climb up.

After the final show down at *Chosen* headquarters, the boy was orphaned. Blake wasn't sure if he and Imogen could adopt him together, but that didn't stop them from trying. The agency originally agreed to a trial basis, to see how things would work out. They saw that the boy, though traumatized, was getting positive and healthy structure. They decided to leave the boy with them.

The small boy was happy today, though not a day passed that he didn't ask about his mother or say that he missed her. Imogen and Blake did everything they could to comfort the child when he woke up screaming from a nightmare or when he just wanted his mother. William took to Imogen quickly and went to her whenever he needed a mothers touch. Blake felt for the boy and truly wished that things had turned out differently, where Desirae was concerned.

Blake smiles and pulls the child up to sit on his lap. Imogen takes a seat opposite of the two men in her life. The jean jacket she wears over her sundress has the sleeves rolled up. She sets a couple of bags down at her feet.

"You didn't order us any?" she says playfully gesturing to her heart as if wounded.

Blake just smiles and turns toward the young woman carrying a tray of food to their table, "Don't be so quick to assume hun," he says with a smile.

Blake gasps, looks down at William and reaches down behind his seat, "I almost forgot. I have something for you."

The boy bounces up and down smiling wide. The tyke claps his hands together, "What? What?" he says excitedly.

Blake pulls his hand up holding a scale model of the world ship currently being developed to carry humans through deep space to colonize other planets and moons. The name on its side reads *Ascendance.* "Wow! For me?" William cheers taking the world ship in his hands. Imogen smiles. Seeing William so happy fills her with a tingling feeling that she can not describe. She probably didn't need to describe it, she was sure that every parent feels this joy.

The teen sets the tray of food down at their table, "Enjoy," she says with a bubbly smile then walks away. Blake watches Imogen intently as she looks down and notices the small box next to the plate of steaming food. For a second, she looks confused and doesn't know what to say. Blake slides William off of his lap and slowly takes the box in his hand. He takes a knee and opens the ring box to reveal a stunning red gem. "Imogen, no matter what the suits in the government decide to do, I love you and want to spend my life with you," Blake says. The people in the food court freeze as if someone had just hit the universal pause button. They watch in anticipation.

Imogen covers her mouth. Tears fall from her eyes. She can't imagine going through what happened to her and Darioux again, but she did fall in love with Blake. A tidal wave full of emotions overwhelm her, "Blake, I," she stammers. He smiles softly and reassuringly.

"I don't know what to say," she says a bit shocked.

Blake shrugs, "Say yes." Imogen nods furiously and wipes tears away. Blake places the ring on her finger and they embrace.

EPILOGUE

Imogen was granted a full pardon for what she had done. The courts ruled that the time she had spent near death, was time served. She and Blake moved to a small house in the country and continued raising young, William Deponet. They kept a beautiful photo of his mother by his bed, so that he would never forget the brave woman who gave him life.

Eddie Mason retired from the force. He became the guardian of Silvia and released the restraining parameters David had placed on her. They lived together in the city.

Mason couldn't bring himself to visit Desirae's young boy. He felt guilty for not being there in time to save her. Once a month he visited the grave of his former partner, Vivian Stern and with every visit he placed a white rose on her tombstone.

After much review and deliberation, the United States government, with the help of the Supreme Court passed an amendment stating that the life of synthetic humans were just as valuable and precious as biological human beings. They deemed that the laws passed after the war were unconstitutional and violated the basic rights of all beings. Three months later nations all around the world adopted similar laws, which allowed synthetics to come out of hiding and live freely among the public. Few instances of human on synthetic hate crimes had been reported, but these crimes were soon becoming a thing of the past. Those perpetrating the crimes were charged with crimes against sentient life and punished to the full extent of the law.

Humanist groups weren't forced to disband, but they were forbidden by law to hunt or destroy the syn. The humanists eventually turned their sights toward interstellar travel and the prospects of spreading human life onto other habitable planets. They raised funding to complete construction of the world ship, Ascendance and allowed synthetics to join as support staff. They recognized that their once sworn enemies had the unique gift of not aging and could serve as pilots and maintenance crews.

A bond had been formed between the human's and synthetics that was still new and fragile but, given the time to grow, that bond would prove invaluable.

Synthetics and humans worked side by side to try and better life on earth. Together they were able to develop new treatments and medicines for illnesses that plagued humanity since the beginning of recorded history. Many didn't know how long the peace between humans and their robotic creations would last, but everyone knew that each species was still in its infancy. They knew that there would be setbacks and what mattered was how they handled and solved their differences together.

ABOUT THE AUTHOR

Enrique Alexander Rodriguez is a Latin American author from Bronx, New York. Enrique started out as a traditional artist and was drawn to comic books and game concept art. He has recently made the transition from traditional mediums to digital media. He now resides in Shelbyville, Kentucky with his daughter. He is also a science fiction nut who enjoys martial arts and all things geek.

ALSO AVAILABLE BY E.A. RODRIGUEZ

Syn also available for Kindle download
Augury in paperback and Kindle formats

http://earodriguez84.wix.com/earodriguez

www.ingramcontent.com/pod-product-compliance
Lightning Source LLC
Chambersburg PA
CBHW022151260626
47155CB00017B/265